CHRISTMAS BAGGAGE

CHRISTMAS BAGGAGE

A CHRISTMAS ESCAPE NOVEL

DEBORAH M. HATHAWAY

DRAFT HORSE
PUBLISHING

BOOKS BY DEBORAH M. HATHAWAY

A Cornish Romance Series
On the Shores of Tregalwen, a Prequel Novella
Behind the Light of Golowduyn, Book One
For the Lady of Lowena, Book Two
Near the Ruins of Penharrow, Book Three
In the Waves of Tristwick, Book Four
From the Fields of Porthlenn, Book Five

Belles of Christmas Multi-Author Series
Nine Ladies Dancing, Book Four
On the Second Day of Christmas, Book Four

Seasons of Change Multi-Author Series
The Cottage by Coniston, Book Five

Sons of Somerset Multi-Author Series
Carving for Miss Coventry, Book One

Timeless Regency Collection
The Inns of Devonshire—The Coachman's Choice

Christmas Escape Multi-Author Series (Contemporary)
Christmas Baggage

For my friend, Ali

Christmas Escape Bingo

Read all seven books in the series to get a Christmas romance blackout!

Broken elevator	Sleigh ride through the mountains	Allergic reaction	Snowstorm Power outage	A walk down main street
Candlelit house tour	Define the boundaries chat (multiple answers)	Ice Skating on a frozen pond	Mint hot Chocolate	"Highway to Hell" ringtone
Boat ride	"Fresh" chocolate milk	FREE SPACE	Reindeer Attack	Miniature Christmas Tree
Hot chocolate at a Christmas market	Trip to Ikea	Burning hot chocolate	Home Alone movie night (multiple answers)	Listening to Bing Crosby
An angry dachshund	Blanket fort	Snowy Beach	Mandalorian pajamas	Snowmobile ride through the mountains

ONE

THE BELL ABOVE THE DOOR OF PEONIES & BURLAP Flower Shop chimed out across the small empty street, piercing the cold Colorado air with its jolly ringing. The sound always greeted newcomers with its happy welcome, but throughout the month of December, the bell seemed to sing out all the louder, embracing each customer with a special "Merry Christmas" as it ushered them into the shop.

As Claire Frost arrived for work that morning, she wanted to respond to the ringing bell with a "Merry Christmas" of her own. After all, no one else ever did. There was probably a reason for that, though. Something about talking to a bell just screamed straight-up crazy. Instead, she smiled up at it in silence, then closed the door behind her.

She entered Peonies & Burlap, the scents of the shop taking residence in her nose—roses, lilies, hydrangeas. Even in December, the flowers filled the area with their sweet, aromatic fragrance.

"Is that you, Claire?" came her boss's voice from the backroom.

"Yeah, it's me," Claire responded. "How are you, Mia?"

"Frazzled."

Claire slipped off her yellow and black scarf—Hufflepuff

1

colors, of course—and moved through the shop, sidestepping open boxes and empty vases that would need to be moved before they opened in less than an hour.

The shop's front room was filled to bursting with flowers propped up in tin containers tied with burlap bows, stumps of wood holding them up at various heights. Pops of bright colors shouted out to Claire as she walked past them. Delicate pink sweet peas. White layered camellias. Deep red hellebores. She couldn't get enough of the sights or the smells, but that was nothing new.

"Did you make it to the market?" Mia asked, still calling out from the backroom.

Claire walked past the shelves of glass vases, potted succulents, and poinsettias before reaching Mia. "Yep. I got a nice selection, too."

She hung her scarf on the nearby rack, tucking her blonde hair behind her ears. The room was undecorated, with white walls and metal shelving holding shears, containers of alum, and stucco pots.

"Perfect. I'll help you bring them in just as soon as I finish this." Mia didn't look up from the bouquet she was arranging on the back table, clipping the white freesia stems at an angle and tucking them into the vase of red berries and pine.

The woman had always reminded Claire of a younger Professor Sprout from *Harry Potter*, what with her earth-colored clothing and somewhat crazed appearance. Her black curls stuck out at odd angles, and her gray eyes were wide and focused.

Claire walked closer to her boss's arrangement. "It looks great. Do you want more holly leaves? I managed to snag some before that guy from Fast Flowers stole the rest."

Mia scoffed with disgust, ducking her head low to eye the flowers from a different angle. "I'm surprised you got any at all. Derek is the worst."

Claire smiled. Derek was actually pretty nice, but she wasn't about to go against her boss's opinion. Claire had been thrilled to be hired to work at Mia's shop right out of high school, and she'd learned more from the woman in the last eight years than she ever could have hoped. Of course, double majoring in Botany and Horticulture at Colorado State had also helped expand her knowledge.

Still, Claire would never say anything that would put her on Mia's bad side. Claire intended to work at Peonies & Burlap until she earned enough to start her own flower shop in New York. Or Paris. Or Sydney. The world was her oyster, really. Or at least so her parents had told her.

Then again, they'd said a lot of things that weren't true.

"Wearing braces doesn't hurt at all."

"You didn't really want us at your graduation anyway."

"We'll be home for Christmas this year."

She pushed aside the rising emotions that accompanied the memories of her parents' words. She knew better than to believe them now. Besides, Christmas would be Christmas even if she was spending it alone this year.

"There. I think that should do it." Mia stood back from her creation. "A few more of the holly branches, and it'll be finished. Let's get those flowers now while we still have the energy."

Mia didn't have to tell Claire twice. The life of a florist was no piece of New York cheesecake, the mornings early, the days long, and the labor extensive. Claire wouldn't change her job for the world, but having a few extra hours of sleep here and there would be nice. Such a perk was impossible, though, when prepping for Florence Bradshaw Design's annual Christmas party.

"Melody will be here soon to sign off on the delivery," Claire said as she and Mia piled flower after flower into their arms from the back of the company van. Their breath lingered around them in thick, white puffs.

"Good. Tonight has to be perfect."

As Claire well knew. Much of their income depended on successfully decorating for corporate parties. The pressure was greater, but she far preferred the lively atmosphere of work parties or weddings to decorating for somber funerals.

Besides, being busy was a nice distraction from the disaster that had been her personal life the last few months.

"Let's just hope Melody is on time today," Mia said, walking with her haul toward the shop. "We both know how hard that is for her to do."

Melody Bancroft was Claire's friend from college who worked as the event coordinator for the design company. Melody had been using Peonies & Burlap to decorate for Florence Bradshaw Design for the last four Christmases. Since Claire was the one to land the gig all those years ago, Mia had bumped her up from sweeping floors and helping with customers to taking charge of designs and parties herself.

Claire loved whenever she got to work with Melody, but sometimes, her friend's lack of organization stressed Claire out of her mind. Somehow, though, Melody always seemed to bring it together by the end, pulling off incredible events for the company she worked for.

Still, if Melody didn't arrive on time, Claire's job would be made that much more difficult.

Shuffling the flowers over to one arm, she pulled out her phone and sent a quick text to her friend, the cold biting at her fingertips.

Claire: You coming?

She tucked the phone into her back pocket, then rearranged the flowers in her arms.

"Yes, I'm coming."

Claire jumped, twirling around as Melody came up behind her. Her friend peered up from her phone with a triumphant look. "And you thought I'd be late."

Claire grinned. "No, I didn't. I just wanted to be sure you were awake."

Melody scoffed. "This is to keep my boss happy, too, you know." She moved forward, helping Claire with the flowers still in the van.

"Are you ready for tonight?" Claire asked.

"Yep. Well, not really. But you know me. I'll pull it together somehow."

With their arms full of calla lilies, holly, peonies, and more, they filed into the shop three more times before finishing their unloading of the van. Once they finished, Claire led Melody to the cold storage room at the back of the shop, showing her the final displays she'd put together for the party—the table centerpieces, main centerpieces, and the selfie archway Melody had added that year to help the company "keep up with the times."

"These look amazing, Claire," Melody said, touching one of the berries on the display. "Really. You've outdone yourself."

"You say that every year," Claire returned.

This year, however, she actually felt like the praise was deserved. She often had images in her mind of what her floral displays would look like—something akin to the gardens Mr. Tumnus would have created in Narnia—but very rarely did they turn out better than she had envisioned. Fortunately, now was one of those occasions.

Each woodland-centered arrangement burgeoned with soft red roses, white hydrangeas, and small hypericum berries, with bare branches and flocked pinecones as accents. The smaller bouquets were set within vases covered in bark and reindeer moss, all with fake English robins dotting the surrounding areas.

"No, really. These are perfect," Melody insisted. "So Christmassy and magical."

Claire beamed. "We'll bring them by just after five, if that works."

"Yep, absolutely."

"Set-up should only take an hour or two, then we'll be back to take it down around midnight. Providing you're not all still partying hard."

Melody raised her eyebrows, her chocolate eyes dancing with excitement. "These office parties do get a little crazy." She leaned in close. "Especially when the event planner hires a cute, young Santa Claus."

"You're the event planner, Melody."

"Ho, ho, ho, don't I know it."

Claire smiled, shaking her head as she led the way out of the cold room. "Just how young of a Santa did you get?"

"Let's just say he's old enough to be legal but too young to be anyone's grandfather. Or father."

"Sounds like just your kind of guy."

Melody grinned. "You should stay for it. The party, I mean. Oh, come as my plus one! It's going to be amazing."

Claire didn't doubt that it was. Melody always knew how to pull the best parties at college. Also the *wildest* parties at college. The girls would often catch up with each other the following morning to find out if Melody had kissed more guys than hours Claire had spent studying for tests. Fortunately, Claire usually won, but Melody always gave her a run for her money.

It was a wonder they'd remained friends over the years. Then again, Melody had always been there for Claire when it counted most.

"I'd love to stay at the party, but I've got a few things I need to do tonight before I have to do take-down," Claire said.

Melody stopped her before she could walk to the front room. "By 'things to do,' do you mean you want to stay at home instead and watch Christmas movies alone?"

Claire didn't bother denying it. The girls had roomed together for four years before getting places of their own. Melody knew Claire as well as Claire knew Melody.

"I'll be alone all Christmas," Claire said. "I may as well start now."

Melody's smile faded.

Claire hadn't meant her words to come off as depressing as they'd sounded. In all honesty, spending Christmas alone was more appealing than going on another cruise with her parents, her mom asking over and over why Claire had broken up with "that nice, wealthy boy" and her dad asking for grandkids every day.

Why they would want grandkids when they couldn't even stay in Colorado long enough to see their only daughter was beyond Claire's comprehension. And what mother would ever want her daughter to be with someone who'd made her so desperately unhappy?

"I'm actually looking forward to some time alone," Claire said, scooting the clippings from Mia's floral display to the garbage can at the end of the table. "It'll be nice to clear my head, you know? Figure some things out."

"Claire. You're always alone. What the heck do you have to figure out? Especially around Christmas?"

Claire hesitated. "A lot of things. What I'm going to wear tomorrow. What I'll have for dinner tonight. What I'm going to buy myself for Christmas this year."

Melody was already shaking her head, pressing a hand over her eyes. "This is bumming me out just hearing you rehearse your life out loud." She fluffed up her dark, shoulder-length hair. "Look, I know I've already made you this offer, but I'm going to say it again. Come to England with me."

Claire sighed with a large roll of her eyes. Nearly every year, Melody and her family traveled to the U.K. to spend the holidays with Melody's aunt, who lived in London. Knowing Claire was going to be alone for Christmas this year, Melody had asked Claire to join her. Three times, actually. And each time, Claire had politely declined. It wasn't that she didn't want to go. It was England, after all, and she'd never traveled outside of the western United States—despite the fact that Claire always kept a current passport in the ridiculous hope of one day seeing the world. But there were just too many things that stood in her way.

"I've already told you, Melody. I really appreciate the offer, but I—"

"Wait," Melody interrupted. "Just hear me out, okay? I've

7

been talking to my Aunt Tasha about it, and she said you'd be more than welcome to stay with her. She has an extra room since my cousin will be gone over Christmas, and with her working almost every day that I'm there, I'll have no one to hang out with. Unless *you* come."

Claire shook her head. "I'd love to, really. But like I said, I don't have the money."

Well, actually Claire *did* have the money. But she was saving it for her future flower shop. It would hardly be wise to dip into her savings just to follow her friend to England on a whim.

A slow smile spread across Melody's lips, and Claire eyed her uneasily. "What?"

"I'm pretty sure I've solved that, too."

"I'm not going to let you pay for my flight."

"No, look." She pulled out her phone, tapping a few times before showing the screen to Claire.

Claire swiped the remaining stray petals and stems from the table, then looked at Melody's phone.

Across the background photo of a rainy Big Ben were the words,

DEN — LHR
London, England
$452

Round Trip Flight
Offer ends December 20th

Claire narrowed her eyes. "Nuh-uh."

"*Yeah*-huh," Melody said. She pulled back her phone and scrolled to the caption, showing it once more to Claire. "It's legit. I confirmed it with my aunt. She uses it all the time when she flies. They price them lower because you might have a few extra layovers, but I mean, for that price, who cares?"

She certainly had a point. Four Hundred and fifty-two dollars.

Round Trip. London. Claire was a sucker for a good deal, but that was a ridiculously cheap price for a flight anywhere out of the country, especially at Christmas. But to London...Could she actually go?

Claire's heart raced. "I just don't know if I can make it work. Mia needs me to—"

"I already know you've taken work off until January."

Claire frowned. Of course Melody would remember that. Claire had asked for time off all the way back in October, when she and Richard had still been together, planning to spend Christmas with his parents skiing.

Of course, that hadn't panned out once she'd discovered that Richard had also invited another girl on a similar trip the weekend before—and that his parents weren't going at all.

Claire had kept her time off, though. As much as she loved her job, she didn't want to become codependent on it. That was being too much like her parents.

"Come on," Melody said, breaking through Claire's thoughts. "When's the last time you treated yourself?"

"Last night. With an ice cream sandwich."

"You were eating ice cream in December? Are you crazy?"

"You don't eat ice cream year-round, and *I'm* the crazy one?"

Melody waved a dismissive hand. "Whatever. You've got no other excuses. You have the time off, the money, a place to stay for free." She paused, pulling on her best sorrowful expression, brows drawn high, dark eyes rounded. "You have a friend in need."

Claire shook her head. "I don't know. I wouldn't want to put your aunt out."

Melody sobered. "Really, Claire, you won't. She's been so lonely since Uncle Will died, and my cousin's hardly around anymore. I think she really misses having a full house for Christmas."

Claire looked away, her heart pinching. She knew what it was like to have a lonely life, and she wouldn't wish it on anyone.

She sighed. "Can I think on it?"

Melody pressed her lips together and pumped her head up and down, clearly trying to quell her excitement. "Yeah, of course. Just not too long. The offer will sell out."

After finishing off the paperwork with Melody, Claire promised to let her friend know before the end of the day what she'd decided, then said goodbye.

The moment Melody left, Claire went straight to work, not only to distract herself from making her decision, but also because she didn't have time to waste another minute.

Work was hectic, as usual, but adding the Christmas party on top of that made her run back and forth like a chicken with its head cut off. Finally, after the shop had closed, the deliveries had been made, and the flowers had been set up at Florence Bradshaw Design, Claire spent a good five hours watching all the cheesy, romantic Hallmark movies she could fit in—choosing the ones set in England first and foremost—before returning for take-down.

She tried to speak with Melody while cleaning up the event—which Mia had called "one of the most successful floral displays she'd ever seen"—but Claire hadn't been able to find her friend anywhere.

Of course, it wasn't entirely unbelievable that Melody was probably hiding in some quiet corner with the "young enough" Santa Claus for some holiday cheer.

Just after one in the morning, and with still no word from Melody, Claire returned home. Yawning, she fiddled with her keys to her apartment, trying to find the keyhole through her blurry eyes before unlocking the door and slipping inside.

Closing the door behind her, she turned on the light, kicked up the thermostat, slipped off her shoes, then hobbled through her quiet apartment with aching legs. Claire had usually decorated her home for Christmas by this point in December, her Hogwarts Express miniature train tooting around her white-lit tree.

But the event at Melody's work had taken way too much of her time and energy. She was sure she'd have time to decorate when she had a moment alone, though.

Alone.

Melody's words from before echoed in her mind for the hundredth time that day. London. Cheap airfare. Time off. Lonely aunt.

The silence of her empty front room pulsed in her ears as her eyes roved over her simple wall décor. Not even the paintings of sunflowers, her favorite flower, hanging on nearly every wall could boost her mood.

And when she caught sight of her Poldark calendar pinned to October—Ross still riding across the cliffside on his black horse—her chest tightened. Had she really forgotten to change the calendar for nearly two months? Or had she just been so busy with her mundane, day-to-day routine that she'd wondered what the point was of changing it at all?

She shook her head, closing her eyes and drawing steadying breaths.

What was she even doing? Was the decision really that difficult to make, the choice between spending Christmas alone or going to England with people who actually wanted to be with her —maybe even *needed* to be with her?

She opened her eyes and pulled out her phone, holding her breath as she tapped out her text to Melody.

Claire: Alright. I'm in.

Her thumb hesitated only a moment before she pressed the send button, and a rush of excitement rippled through her limbs. She was actually doing it. She was going to England for Christmas.

She bit her lip and grinned, tapping the phone against her chin before it buzzed.

Melody's return text blazed across Claire's screen.

Melody: AAAAAHHHHHHHHHHHHHH!!!!! I'm so so so so so excited!!! Okay, I'm coming over right now to book the tickets with you so you can't back out. Oh my gosh oh my gosh oh my gosh. We are going to have the best time ever!!!! I can't even. AAAAAAHHHHHH!!!!!!!!!!!

Claire beamed. She'd definitely made the right choice.

Now all she had to do was hope that this Christmas would beat out her past Christmases—puking on a cruise last year or being cheated on the year before by another jerk boyfriend.

Spending the holiday in London would have to be better than that.

TWO

CLAIRE STARED UP AT THE SEATBELT SIGN ON THE airplane, willing its light to turn off. Most of the passengers had already removed their restraints, standing from their seats and gathering their belongings to dart off the plane as soon as the door opened, but she remained seated.

"Please sit down while the plane is in motion," requested the flight attendant at the front of the cabin, her French accent rising above the loud humming of the slow-moving plane.

No one seemed to heed the attendant's advice apart from Claire. Claire didn't understand why obeying the rule was so difficult. She wanted to get off the flight more than anyone, especially to be rid of her wouldn't-stop-eating-black-licorice, next-seat neighbor.

She'd tried to distract herself for the duration of the flight with her Kindle full of new books, but even the Darcy-like men she'd read about weren't strong enough to withstand the awful smell pluming toward her like the exhaust from a dilapidated, oversized truck.

She glanced to the man next to her again as he wiped his sticky hands on his pants, leaving behind glistening smears of licorice.

the passengers still standing, despite being told not

ter another few moments, the plane finally came to a stop, the seatbelt light turned off. A muted bell sounded above, and the pilot spoke over the intercom in another thick French accent.

"Ladies and gentlemen, welcome to London Heathrow Airport. Local time is 11:35 AM. The temperature is four degrees Celsius. On behalf of Air France and the entire crew, I'd like to thank you for joining us on this flight. We wish you all a pleasant stay and look forward to seeing you on board again."

Claire drew a deep breath of relief, only to have it end prematurely in an involuntary shudder as another whiff of black licorice assaulted her senses. The man must have devoured over three bags from France to Great Britain, slapping his gums next to her as she'd attempted to smell the peppermint Chapstick on her lips instead.

Fortunately, only another moment ticked by before the man shoved his way into the aisle and shuffled down the cabin.

Finally. She drew a deep breath and released it with a satisfied sigh. She'd made it. After a ten-hour flight from Colorado, a four-hour delay in New York, then another in France, she'd finally arrived in the U.K. Now all she needed to do was make it through customs, collect her luggage, and find Melody.

Preferring to wait until the herd had passed down the aisle instead of trying to shoulder her way in, Claire pulled out her phone to text her friend, who had arrived in England a few days before.

Claire: Finally landed!! Sooo excited!!...You're going to be on time, right?

She smiled to herself, sending a devil grin emoji before pulling on her coat, a draft of cold, English air sailing through the plane.

Not a moment passed before Melody responded.

Melody: I was going to welcome you to England until you made that joke. YES, I'M HERE ON TIME.
Melody: Although you have Aunt Tasha to thank for it...

Claire grinned again, zipping up the sides of her boots she'd loosened on the flight. Finally, she straightened to look out of the window.

She hadn't been able to see much of the view on the flight in, what with the gray clouds cloaking the skies and a heavy fog hanging over most of the airport. Even now from the window, only the runway was visible with a few bare trees in the distance.

Claire was just itching to admire the green hills and stone walls she'd only ever seen in period dramas—*North & South*, *Doctor Thorne*, *Poldark*, she'd seen them all—but Melody had promised her plenty of gorgeous sights, so Claire wouldn't allow herself to worry too much.

"Care to leave the plane, luv?"

Claire started, turning as a man with gray hair and a friendly smile motioned her toward the aisle. His English accent—the first she'd heard during her travels—slipped around her shoulders and wrapped her up in a warm embrace.

"Oh, that's alright," she said, taking note of the growing line of passengers frowning behind him. "I'll just wait until everyone else is gone."

"Ah, you're being too polite. Come along, or you'll never get off."

A tight-lipped woman stood directly behind him, staring daggers at Claire.

Having a feeling that the man would wait until Claire finally folded, she swiftly stood, swung her backpack over her shoulder, and skirted past the empty seats in her row.

"Thank you," she said hurriedly.

"Have any luggage I can fetch for you?" the man asked next, motioning to the overhead bins.

Claire glanced again to the scowling woman and nodded. "Yeah, just the black carry-on at the far right."

He reached up and pulled down her carry-on with a swift tug, placing it at her side. She expressed her gratitude again, and the man smiled warmly at her. "Welcome to England, luv. And have a merry Christmas."

Her heart warmed, despite the impatient huffs from the other passengers. If he wasn't the nicest man she'd ever met. Were all Englishmen like this?

She returned his smile and faced forward, awkwardly trundling down the aisle with her backpack and carry-on bouncing against the seats until she finally exited the plane.

Excitement propelled her legs faster, the rolling of her luggage's wheels trilling loudly across the ribbed carpet.

Claire: Heading to Customs now.

Melody: YAAAAAY!!! Aunt Tasha and I are waiting by the pick-up area. The cost for parking is out of control here. See you sooooon!

Claire thumbsed-up the message, hesitating before she pulled up the text thread to her mom. She really ought to message her and Dad. They probably wouldn't respond for a few days, but any parent would want to know his or her daughter was safe, right?

When she'd told them she'd booked a flight to England over Christmas and wouldn't be returning until after New Years, they had been ecstatic. Though she couldn't be sure if it was for her sake or their own, as they could now be on their cruise guilt-free. Not that they'd ever felt guilty for leaving her behind. They'd both traveled enough for work and now as retirees to have given up that remorse a long time ago.

She kept her eyes on her phone, moving with the throngs of people to the line forming at Customs.

Claire: Hey, Mom! Just wanted to let you know I landed safely in England. Hope you and Dad are enjoying yourselves. Love you both. Call me anytime.

She sent the message, then put her phone away, determining to set aside any thoughts of her parents just as readily. She was happy that they were happy, and she would leave it at that.

Inch by inch, she moved through the line until she was free to go to the baggage claim. She smiled to herself as she passed garland hung up across windows and a few twinkle lights twirled round nearby stands. Purple candy bars and shiny, red Christmas crackers were on display at the front of a few shops, and English accents filled the air, a jolly chorus of propriety and perfection.

Everyone around her seemed to be getting into the Christmas spirit with smiles and nods of greeting. Or perhaps that was simply her own attitude extending to what she chose to notice. She'd been traveling for over twenty hours, her makeup was no-doubt smeared, and her hair, a mess. But she was in England, and she wouldn't be alone for Christmas—and that was something to celebrate.

Reaching the baggage claim, she watched the empty, rotating carousel, anxiously awaiting her larger suitcase's arrival. With still no sight of the luggage, she glanced to the large ad propped up beside her, featuring a photo of a red telephone booth and a green-scarfed woman grinning up at it.

Explore London at its best—during the holiday season!

Claire took a quick picture of it, pulling up Instagram to post to her feed for the first time in months, now that she actually had something worthwhile to share.

So crazy to believe I'm actually here. Can't wait to finally see with my own two eyes what this country has to offer!

"Excuse me."

A smooth, deep voice spoke directly beside her, and Claire jumped, looking up from her phone in surprise. Who in the world would be speaking with her here? Had she forgotten her bag? Was she standing in the wrong place? Did she...

Her questions melted away like the first flakes of a snowfall as she finally registered the man standing nearly a head above her. He boasted a thick head of hair as dark as obsidian, with a short, neatly trimmed beard. His sharp cheekbones were clean-shaven, and his strong brow hovered over dark eyes—eyes void of any friendliness as he scowled down at her.

Wait, why was he scowling? She shifted uncomfortably under his inert gaze. "Can I help you?"

"I believe that's mine," he said, his smooth voice slightly breathless, as if he'd been walking too fast before speaking with her.

His English accent surprised her, though she didn't know why. Had she already forgotten she was in England?

His stare intensified. What had he said, something was his? She was way too distracted by his navy blue, wrinkle-free shirt that was spread so nicely across his cut shoulders.

"Sorry, what?" she asked.

He shifted his coat to hang neatly over his other arm. "That is mine," he repeated more slowly, his gaze dropping to the luggage at her side.

She paused again. His? He thought her suitcase was *his*? Perhaps the guy wasn't as sane as he looked. She shifted her body away, holding the handle of her carry-on more tightly. "No, actually, it's mine."

His jaw twitched. "Of course you'd be from the States," he mumbled.

Claire blinked. "What?"

The man carried on as if unaware of her questioning. "It makes perfect sense, given your complete lack of consideration for another person's time and energy."

Her lips parted. What in the world was happening right now? Was he seriously criticizing her for being American? Didn't that only happen in the movies?

His accent was crisp and proper, though his clipped words made him far less approachable than the man on the plane.

"Look," she began, "I don't mean to be rude, but can you please just leave me alone?"

She turned away, looking for a security guard in case this crazy person decided to steal her carry-on.

"I'll leave you alone when you return my luggage," he said, remaining at her side.

She sighed, turning back to face him. Why did all the attractive ones have to be insane? "This isn't yours. See?" She swiveled the baggage toward him. "This is my tag right..." She shifted the carry-on back and forth. Where was her purple tag? And how had it turned...black?

She peered closer, only then noting the slightly thinner build of the luggage that was distinctly *not* hers. The blood drained from her face. What had she done? How could she have been stupid enough to take another person's carry-on?

As if reading her thoughts, the man explained. "I saw you nick it before getting off the plane. I've spent the better part of half an hour trying to find you."

Her stomach churned. In utter humiliation, she thought back to the kind man who'd let her out into the plane aisle. He must have accidentally swapped her luggage with this man's. She could have sworn she'd checked her tag before wheeling it off, but then, she'd been so rushed.

With burning cheeks, she slid the man's suitcase over. "I'm so sorry," she mumbled. "I really thought it was mine."

"Clearly." He snatched the handle from her and secured his fingers around it as if he feared she might take it again. "Perhaps if you used the eyes you were given and looked up at the world instead of dwelling so greatly on posting to social media, this wouldn't have happened."

She frowned, swiftly turning her phone off and putting it away. This guy had some nerve. "It was just a mistake," she defended. "You don't have to be so rude about it."

He put on his coat, his clavicle bone appearing as he leaned forward to straighten his collar. "Mistake or not, you're fortunate I didn't call security."

Her mouth dropped open. "For what, me grabbing the wrong suitcase? You seriously can't believe that I was trying to steal it from you."

He raised his eyebrows, denoting an expression that revealed he thought exactly that. In silence, he brushed past her, his carry-on rumbling behind him.

Claire stared after his back, her insides swirling with humiliation and indignation. Who did he think he was, talking to a stranger like that?

"Hey, wait," she called out. "Where's my suitcase, then?"

The man spoke over his shoulder. "Back where you left it."

She scoffed in disbelief. A few others standing nearby glanced at her with wary expressions, as if they wondered if she actually was a thief. She frowned at each of them until they looked away, then she turned back to the baggage claim.

With her confidence shaken and nerves frazzled, Claire folded her arms and waited until the carousel finally deposited her large suitcase.

After double and triple-checking her tag to ensure she didn't make the same mistake twice, she found her way to the service desk nearby, explaining the situation to the worker, who made a few calls to see if she could help Claire locate her carry-on still on the plane.

As Claire waited, her frustration only grew. What sort of person basically shouted at a woman who made a simple mistake, then proceeded to *criticize* her for being from another country?

Well, at least now she knew what to expect from this trip.

Not *all* Englishmen were created equal.

LIAM EVERHART STORMED through the airport, clutching his carry-on as it rolled behind him. He readjusted his coat over his shoulders and stared straight ahead, avoiding everyone and everything. He couldn't afford another delay. After spending way too long tracking down his suitcase, he'd missed his small window to grab a bite to eat. Now he'd have to head straight to work in order to not be late to yet another meeting.

As if he hadn't worked enough for those soul-sucking leeches already, going to France on a last-minute trip that was supposed to extend over Christmas—not to mention the last eight years of life he'd wasted at Peregrine Productions. And how had they repaid him after all of that? Giving away what was rightfully his.

He shook his head, forcing away any last thought of the ungrateful gits. He had only one more day of work before his week off began, then he wouldn't have to spend a single minute more thinking about the injustice of it all—or about how monumentally disappointed his mum would be if she ever discovered what had occurred at his job.

Of course, Liam didn't have to worry about that, as he had no intention of ever informing her of the fact. Just like he had no intention of telling her what had happened between him and the woman at the baggage claim.

A pair of baby blue eyes and wavy blonde hair flashed across his mind, and regret prodded at his heart. From the minute Liam had started speaking with the woman, her innocence regarding his luggage had cried out like a lamb-eyed child.

It wasn't her fault he was in a terrible mood. He was a train with a bad attitude, and she'd just happened to tread on his tracks. Never mind that she had been from the States, reminding him of the ill-fated phone call from his boss he'd received moments before setting off for London. He never should have told her off.

Doing his best to set aside any residual regret, Liam weaved his way past holiday travelers and large Christmas trees, eventually making his way outside to the shuttle waiting area where he breathed in the brisk, damp air.

He was grateful to be back on English soil, even if it meant spending Christmas with his mum. It wasn't that he didn't enjoy being with her. This time of year was simply too painful a reminder of all they had lost. The holiday was far easier when they were both occupied with their careers.

Of course, with his career now on the line, it seemed as good a time as any to step away from work for a bit. Besides, he'd left his mum alone on Christmas for too long. It was time to make it up to her, to show her that her son wasn't entirely worthless.

Who knew, maybe if he did enough for her, he'd be able to relinquish the still-present regret for how he'd treated the American. He didn't know why he felt such guilt anyway. Heaven knew he'd never see the woman again.

THREE

After being reunited with her *ACTUAL* carry-on, Claire finally met with Melody and her aunt—or Tasha, as she directed Claire to call her immediately upon their meeting.

Once she'd apologized for the delay, avoiding any mention of the jerk who'd accused her of stealing his luggage, Claire left the airport with the others in Tasha's zippy, red BMW, heading to their first stop of the day.

"I hope you're excited to see the set designs, Claire," Tasha said from the driver's seat on the right side as they neared their destination. "Melody tells me you love Harry Potter as much as the both of us."

Having married a Brit and then living in England for over thirty years, the woman's accent was primarily British, though she pronounced the occasional, errant "r."

"Yes, absolutely," Claire said. She had been the one to suggest going to the studio tour when she and Melody had planned out their trip together. "I even had a dream about it on the flight last night."

"You're in the right company, then," Tasha responded. "This will be my third time going to the studios."

Claire smiled. She had been so worried that she'd be

imposing on Melody and her aunt's time together. But in less than an hour, Tasha's warmth and encouragement had mollified all of Claire's concerns, especially as the three of them spent the next six hours walking through the Harry Potter set designs, gaping at all the props and costumes, enjoying multiple tankards of butterbeer, and spending far too much time and money in the gift shop.

What made the whole experience even more magical were the sets decorated in snow and icicles, bringing Christmas front and center to their visit.

Claire was so enthralled with the entire experience and was treated so kindly by everyone throughout the tour, that by the time they'd finished, she'd nearly forgotten all about her encounter at the airport. The guy must have just been an anomaly that was her bad luck to meet in her first moments in England—bad luck that seemed to have finally lifted.

When they left the tour and were greeted once again by the frigid rain, their small group warmed up at a local pub, enjoying hearty plates of sausage and mash before heading to Tasha's home.

Jet lag had been following Claire all day long, but sleep never had the chance to catch up until the moment they settled in the car. She hadn't even realized she'd drifted off until the BMW stopped, finally arriving in Brook Green, London well after dark.

Claire straightened, ignoring her cricked neck and climbing out of the car. "How far away are we from central London?"

"About a quarter of an hour east," Tasha responded, "dependent on traffic."

Tasha and Melody insisted on carrying Claire's luggage for her, so she followed behind them as she peered up at the row of red houses visible even in the cold darkness. White trim framed each window, and a green-leafed archway highlighted the entrance to Tasha's place.

Any time of year, the apartments would no doubt stand out for their crisp coziness, but now, all Claire could think of was how delightfully Christmassy they appeared.

Soon enough, they entered the home, a short hallway to the left and a thin set of stairs to the right.

"Bedrooms and bathroom are upstairs," Tasha explained, closing the door behind her and securing the lock. "Kitchen and sitting room are straight through there. Shall we have a cuppa before bed? Hot chocolate? Warm Vimto? Peppermint tea?"

Claire nodded, unable to make a choice right then as she stifled a yawn and followed the women down the hallway. A few photos lined the walls, but with the only light coming from the kitchen, it was too dim for her to make out any of the pictures.

The apartment was modestly decorated with very few embellishments, but it was clean and tidy with dark, hardwood floors, red, oversized couches, and white curtains that opened at the sides of a large bay window. The only hint of Christmas was a string of twine holding up holiday cards near the fireplace and a potted poinsettia placed on the table. Still, the home was simply charming, just like Tasha. In her mid-fifties, the woman was full of life and warmth, like a brunette Molly Weasley.

"I haven't had much time to decorate for Christmas yet," she said, turning on the kettle and gathering a few mismatched mugs —one with a cottage covered in snow, one with holly berries, and the last with an English bulldog wearing a Christmas sweater.

"Has work been crazy, Aunt Tasha?" Melody asked, motioning for Claire to join her at the small table situated just to the side of the counter.

"No more than usual." The kettle behind Tasha peeped. "But I don't mind it. It keeps my mind occupied."

She smiled, but Claire didn't miss the hint of sorrow behind the woman's dark brown eyes. How she bore the weight of her husband's loss was beyond Claire's ability to comprehend.

In a few minutes, the three of them sat together with their hot drinks, Tasha describing her work as an HR rep for an insurance company as Claire struggled to keep her eyes open.

Finally, Tasha smiled with amusement. "I think we'd better go to bed before Claire falls asleep on the kitchen floor."

Claire nodded in a half-daze, eying the white tile with longing. It looked more appealing than going all the way upstairs to bed, but she heaved herself up from the chair anyway and followed Tasha and Melody to the rooms.

"Feel free to make yourself at home," Tasha said as they climbed the steep steps. "I've stocked the fridge with food, so help yourself to anything you'd like. There's shampoo and conditioner in the shower already. The washer's downstairs. Melody can show you how it works. If I've forgotten something or you need anything at all, don't hesitate to ask."

"Thank you," Claire said, more grateful than ever for the woman's generosity.

"I ought to be thanking the both of you," Tasha responded. "It would have been a lonely Christmas again this year without you here." She cleared her throat and stopped at the first door. "Melody is sleeping here, and Claire..." She crossed the hallway and motioned to the door on the left. "You can sleep here. My room is down there, so if you need anything, just give a shout."

Claire rolled her suitcases into the spare room, taking a quick note of the cleanliness of the space. A large, panoramic shot of a wintry sea graced the back wall above the bed, and a small lamp cast a warm glow across the large, green duvet.

"Right," Tasha said. "We'll leave you to it, then."

After another round of hugs and gratitude, Melody and Tasha left Claire to herself as her eyelids grew heavier and heavier. She stumbled into her favorite pajamas, then took a moment to peer outside of the window, if only to remind herself that she really was in England.

Peeking beyond the heavy curtains and the glass of the diamond-leaded windows, the world outside still turned. Black taxis drove by with their headlamps blazing out on the wet road, and a couple only just visible beyond thick oak trees walked through the small park across the street, a red umbrella shared between them as they meandered through the sopping grass.

It was just like a picture.

With slow movements, she clicked the window open just a crack. The sounds of wet tires rushing against the road and rain clicking against the rooftop with its crisp smell was already lulling her to sleep by the time she slipped beneath the thick duvet and rested her head against the featherdown pillow.

She was more than ready to sleep until morning.

LIAM WASN'T SURPRISED to find his mum's house quiet by the time he finished work at quarter past eleven. He usually worked this late, but it was nice to not have to travel the extra hour back to his own flat.

He'd texted Mum when he'd left work a half hour before, but she'd never responded. In hindsight, he should've messaged her long before now, but he'd really been hoping to surprise her with his arrival without a text. Now he could only hope he didn't give her too much of a scare when she discovered him there the next morning.

After leaving a quick note on the table, he quietly crept through the house, noting the bathroom light glowing behind the half-open door at the top of the stairs. Mum had always left the light on, just as Dad had always complained about it. Liam had heard Mum telling his father once that she'd done it ever since Liam was a young boy when he was afraid of the dark. After that, Dad had kept the light on, too.

Liam reached the top step, ignoring the ache in his heart that never really went away when he thought of how greatly he missed his father. Three years had passed since he'd died, and still, the ache returned, that same debilitating, numbing pain.

He slipped down the hallway toward his bedroom—or rather, the one Mum always kept vacant for him—stepping quietly past the spare room. He was fairly certain his cousin had already arrived to stay there, but he couldn't recall the exact dates he'd been told.

He winced. He hadn't paid close attention to his mother in months. Yes, he'd had a lot on his plate, but that was hardly an excuse. He could only hope now that he could make up for all of this by giving her the Christmas she wished for, the Christmas she deserved.

Slowly, he turned the handle to his room, slinking inside before soundlessly closing the door behind him. Once he was sure he wouldn't disturb his mum or cousin, he flipped on the switch and took a step toward the bed.

A lump beneath the covers stirred. He flinched in surprise, his heart racing. Who in the...Wait, was that Melody?

He cringed, backing away slowly to avoid being discovered. Before he had the chance to turn, though, a head of tousled, blonde hair in a loose bun popped up from beneath the duvet.

Blonde? Melody hadn't been blonde since she was three.

"Who are..." He trailed off, his eyes narrowing as he focused on the oddly familiar features of the stranger in his bed.

No. She couldn't possibly be...And yet, there was no mistaking those blue eyes, as bleary as they were. The girl from the airport—the American. She was there, in his room, in his bed, looking at him like *he* was the one imposing.

Fear filled her eyes, and he winced, knowing what was coming next.

FOUR

Claire's chest constricted, her lungs refusing to work as she sucked in a shallow breath.

"You," she breathed, finally recognizing the man from the airport. She scrambled to sit upright in bed, leaning against the backboard and pulling the covers to her chin. "What are you..." She shook her head, her confusion giving way to terror. "Help! Melody, Tasha!"

The man took a step toward her, holding out his hands as if to quell her worries, but his actions only proved to anger her further. This guy must have followed her to the studio tour, dinner, and home, then waited to pounce on her until she and the others were asleep. What a total lunatic.

"Now, wait," he said. "You've got the wrong—"

"Get out!" she shouted louder, fury firing through her veins. "Get *out!*"

She looked to her right, then to her left, settling on a pile of books on the bedside table.

"Listen," the man continued in a soft voice, "this is my—"

His words ended as Claire hurled one of the books at his head. He shouted, ducking in time for the edge of the hardback cover to just miss him. He looked back at her in disbelief, as if *she* were the crazy one.

"Help!" she shouted toward the door, then faced the guy again. "What kind of sick freak follows a woman home? Get out of my room!"

She chucked another book at him. This time, she caught the top of his head as he tried to duck again. He cursed, turning back at her with a furious gaze. "This isn't your room. This is *my* room!"

His room? First the carry-on, now the room. This guy was unbelievable. Why wouldn't he leave? And where the heck were Tasha and Melody? Had this psycho already done away with them?

She held another book over her head, ready to haul it at him when an ounce of confusion slithered its way into her chest, pressing against her lungs.

The carry-on. It *had* been his. The room couldn't be his, too, though, could it? Her conversation from earlier that evening echoed around in her mind. Tasha had mentioned her son being away on business. Had he returned early?

No, she thought. *No, please don't let this be—*

The door burst open, and Tasha and Melody blazed into the room.

"Claire! What's wrong?" Melody asked at once, followed closely by Tasha.

"Are you alright? We heard..." Tasha's words faded away as her eyes jumped from Claire to the man standing in her house.

Melody's eyes widened as she gasped, and shock flashed across Tasha's features before a smile spread across her lips. She ran forward, her arms flinging around the man's neck. "Liam? What in the world! What are you doing here?"

The man—Liam, apparently—embraced Tasha in return, glancing sidelong at Claire where she still sat in bed. "I wanted to surprise you," he said. "Though I admit, not in this way."

Tasha turned toward Claire with a compassionate smile. "Oh,

Claire. I'm so sorry. You must have been scared to death. You don't have to worry now. This is my son, Liam."

Her son. Tasha's son. Claire's mind spun round, trying to catch up.

She stared in silence as Tasha turned back to Liam, taking his face in her hands. "This is just wonderful. I thought you'd be in France until after New Year's."

He shook his head. "I was able to take a few days off for Christmas after all."

Melody moved forward, embracing who Claire finally deduced was her friend's cousin. "You're finally taller than me," Melody stated.

He smiled, returning her side hug. "I've always been taller than you, Mel."

Claire watched the exchange in silence, her fear and adrenaline slowly melting away, weakening her body and mind. So it was true. The man whose suitcase she'd been accused of stealing, the man who'd criticized her for simply being American, was Tasha's son and Melody's cousin. And she'd chucked books at his face. She'd called him a...a *sick freak*.

Because why not? Fate liked to destroy her life every now and again, especially during Christmas. Parents taking extended cruises. Boyfriends kissing other women on Christmas Eve. Hot men finding her asleep in their beds.

"Claire, you must have been terrified," Tasha said. "I'm so sorry about all this."

Claire blinked, looking up from her daze as all three pairs of eyes settled on her.

"I had no idea Liam was coming home, or I would've never put you in here." Tasha sent her son another warm smile.

"Oh, it's no big deal," Claire lied, slipping another look at Liam as her head pounded.

"Liam," Melody piped in then, "this is my friend, Claire Frost."

Liam's eyes settled on Claire, the weight of his gaze painting heat across her cheeks. Would he admit that they'd run into each other at the airport and that he'd been a total jerk?

"It's a pleasure to meet you," he responded, answering her question. Then he paused, narrowing his eyes just a fraction. "You're from the States, I assume?"

The corner of his lip lifted, and indignation burned in her belly. He was referring to their interaction at the airport. Why else would he be watching her with such pleasure? Clearly, he'd found the upper hand with her, dropping his anger from before and replacing it with arrogant amusement at seeing her discomfort.

She had a mind to tell Tasha and Melody that Liam had been a straight-up piece of work, but she hardly wanted to relive that experience again, especially in front of him. More than that, she wouldn't want to hurt Tasha's feelings by revealing what a jerk he had been.

Anyway, would Tasha and Melody even believe her, what with this clear golden boy standing in front of them?

"Don't you remember me saying that Melody was bringing a friend with her, Liam?" Tasha asked.

"It must have slipped my mind," he responded. He gave Claire one last searching look, then smiled at his mother. "I was planning on staying with you for Christmas, but since you have a full house already..."

He said nothing more as his mother shook her head, her brow furrowed. "Oh, no. No, you have to stay here. We've plenty of room still."

Melody pointed her thumb behind her shoulder. "Claire and I can totally share a room. We don't mind, do we, Claire?"

Again, all eyes settled on Claire. No, she didn't mind sharing a room with Melody. After all, they had for four years in college. But sharing a house with this arrogant Englishman? She'd rather hop out of the window and hitchhike her way back to Heathrow.

But what did it matter? She wouldn't be staying there for much longer anyway. She was pretty sure she'd be dead from humiliation by morning.

"Oh, no," Tasha protested. "I already promised this room to Claire." She turned toward her son. "You can sleep in the sitting room instead. And don't you dare protest. I'm not letting you find a way out of staying here. Not while I finally have the chance to spend Christmas with you."

Liam's amusement vanished, no doubt at the thought of sleeping in the sitting room. Claire had a mind to accept Tasha's offer, but the thought of remaining in this guy's room for the duration of her trip was about as repulsive as the thought of drinking fat.

"No, that's all right. I can stay with Melody," she finally responded.

Tasha hesitated. "I can't ask you to do that."

But Claire insisted. At least she thought she did. Her mind was as hazy as a winter's morn in the city. "I'd prefer staying with Melody anyway."

Melody nodded in agreement, and Liam's eyes flitted to Claire's before he smiled at his mother. "If our guests are happy with the arrangements, of course I'll stay."

"More than happy," Melody piped in.

Finally, Tasha relented. "Well, if you're all sure."

Liam looked to Claire once again. "Done."

Claire swallowed. How she wished to duck under her covers and believe this was all just some horrifying nightmare.

"Claire?"

She blinked at Melody.

"Are you going to come with me, or are you just going to chill in Liam's bed all night?"

Claire glanced at Liam's raised brow, and heat burst out across her face once again. Moving faster than she ever had in her life, she scrambled from the bed and darted toward her suitcase, tossing her clothing and phone charger into the baggage as quickly as she could manage.

"I'll get the extra mattress from the loft," Tasha said, already on her way out of the door. "Melody, would you mind making a bit of space in your room?"

"For sure," Melody said, then she wheeled Claire's carry-on from the room.

Not about to be left alone with the guy she'd only just feared would take her life, Claire heaved her full-sized suitcase up and pulled it forward. To her utter dismay, a rustling sounded, and she glanced back in time to watch the contents of her luggage topple out across the floor.

Cursing under her breath, she knelt down, stuffing the suitcase full once again.

"Would you like some help?" Liam asked, his familiar, smooth voice bringing back more unpleasant memories from the airport.

Get me out of here.

She shifted to hide her red face. "Nope. I got it."

Finally, she zipped the suitcase closed and hoisted it upright, ensuring the contents remained inside before turning around and walking straight past Liam without a glance.

"I'm sorry to have scared you," he said behind her.

She didn't pause as she reached the door, attempting to maintain what shred of dignity she had by leaving as swiftly as possible. "You didn't."

"Your shot with this would say otherwise."

She glanced back to see him wiggling in the air one of the hefty books she'd hurled toward him.

"By the way," he continued, straight-faced. "Love the pajamas."

Her pajamas. Good freaking gravy, she'd forgotten about her pajamas. She glanced down at the face of the Mandalorian on her black top, then at the multiple mini Grogus sipping bone broth across her bottoms.

She looked back up at Liam, staring at the amusement dancing in his eyes. He looked so different from when she'd first seen him, scowls and condemnations abounding. Clearly, his mood had improved after he'd relocated his luggage. If he wasn't making fun of her right now, she might have called him charming.

But he *was* making fun of her.

Instead of reaching up and slapping that handsome smirk straight from his stupidly attractive face, she turned on the heel of her thick, woolen socks and walked away with her chin held high. Of course, her confidence faltered again when her suitcase wheel bounced against the small door frame, jerking the luggage to the side and nearly wrenching her arm from its socket.

She stole a quick glance at Liam's growing grin, then raised her chin higher before leaving the man and his room behind. It was only unfortunate that her pride trailed out behind her like useless needles falling off of an old Christmas tree.

FIVE

CLAIRE WOKE UP THE NEXT MORNING TO AN EMPTY room and a gentle rain plinking against the window. She yawned, stretching her arms overhead before checking her phone to see the time.

Eight o'clock. Still enough time to get ready. Thank heavens she hadn't slept in. She'd forgotten to put her alarm on the night before in her delirious state.

Rolling off of the mattress, she gathered a change of clothes and her toiletries, then tiptoed toward the door, opening it just a crack to peer down the hallway.

Both Liam and Tasha's doors were open. Did that mean they were downstairs with Melody already? With a deep breath, she darted from the room, down the hallway, and into the empty bathroom, not breathing until she locked the door behind her.

Her relief at arriving in the bathroom without anyone—particularly Liam—spotting her was short-lived as she turned around and caught her reflection in the mirror.

Good grief. No wonder Liam had been on the verge of laughter last night. The mascara and eyeliner she'd forgotten to remove cocooned her blue eyes with grey circles, and her hair shone as greasy as Rob Lowe's in *The Outsiders*.

Pulling out her makeup remover, she scrubbed away the mess, then jumped in for a quick shower.

The night before, she had been *that* close to booking a return flight to Colorado, but now, after finally getting a good night's sleep, she was ready to put the whole situation behind her. It was obvious that Liam had no intention of apologizing to her, or of telling his family about the airport, so she would keep the knowledge to herself, as well.

After all, what good would it do to slander his name or to bring up her own mistake? More importantly, she was in *his* home. Bringing up his wrongdoings would just wind up making this Christmas as awkward and horrible as all the others—and that was something she wasn't willing to risk again. The two would just have to learn to peacefully coexist for the next little while because Claire was more than ready to leave her baggage behind and *finally* have a good Christmas.

After showering, dressing, applying her light makeup, and pulling her hair up in a soft ponytail, Claire moved with confident steps down the stairs, refusing to allow her footing to falter when Liam's voice reached her ears.

"No, Garrett was fine with it," he was saying. "As he should be. I haven't asked for time off for months."

Claire didn't want to admit how much she liked his accent. It was thicker than Tasha's, and his deep, smooth tone made his proper wording stand out even more, like he was one of those guys in the Regency novels she obsessed over.

Not that she was obsessed with his accent or anything. She liked Tasha's, too, just as equally. Really.

As Claire reached the bottom step, her arrival was announced by a loud creak that startled her from her thoughts.

"Claire?" Melody's voice called from down the hallway. "Is that you? We're in the kitchen."

"Coming." Claire smoothed out her hair and straightened the hem of her shirt as she walked down the hall and joined the others in the kitchen.

Melody popped four slices of Warburton's white bread in the toaster as Tasha stood by the stove, every burner occupied with bacon and sausages, fried eggs and tomatoes, hash browns, and baked beans.

Liam was leaning over the table, placing butter and marmalade in the center of the four place settings. He was the first to spot Claire, his dark eyes settling on her with a piercing gaze. It lingered for a moment, looking her up and down, then he glanced away without a word.

Claire frowned. Well, his good mood from last night had clearly vanished. Was he trying to intimidate her by looking less than impressed with her appearance?

"Finally," Melody said, turning to Claire with an exaggerated look of exasperation. "We've been waiting for you for hours."

"We have not," Tasha denied at once, shaking her head in amusement at her niece. She shot Claire a compassionate look from where she stirred the baked beans. "Even if that were true, you could have slept for longer. You deserve it after last night."

Claire glanced at Liam. He swiftly pulled his attention away from her again, focusing instead on the fridge as he leaned against the counter, tucking his hands in his pockets. The ridges in his forearms shifted back and forth as he tapped his thumbs against his pants.

"Can I help with anything?" Claire asked, tearing her eyes away from Liam's arms and taking a step closer to the table.

"Will you get the orange juice from the fridge, please?" Tasha instructed. "Other than that, we're just about ready here."

Claire sidestepped the others in the modest kitchen, avoiding eye contact with Liam as she made her way to the fridge and pulled out the juice.

"Do you need the eggs any longer, Mum?"

Mum. How adorable was that? Wait, no. This guy wasn't adorable. He was a pill.

"You can put them away now," Tasha responded, plating the food with Melody.

Liam pushed away from the counter and retrieved the eggs behind him, turning toward the fridge just as Claire walked away.

As she sidled past him, she kept her gaze trained ahead, but his smooth voice made her pause.

"No Mando this morning?" he whispered, motioning down to her shirt. Though his lips remained still, his dark eyes smiled. How did he even manage that?

She glanced up at him, reminded once again how tall he was. "I don't wear pajamas in public."

"But you're fine wearing them in a stranger's bed?"

Heat bloomed in her cheeks as hot as the suns of Tatooine. Apparently, her blush was assuming permanent residency on her face whenever Liam was nearby.

"I didn't know..." But her words refused to formulate as amusement danced in his dark, sugar plum eyes.

She drew a calming breath. She would not be goaded into being embarrassed around him any longer.

"It's alright," he said, finally walking past her. "They were nothing I haven't seen before." His voice dropped even lower. "I believe my six-year-old godson has the same pair."

What. A. Jerk.

Claire scowled after him as he walked away. He took his annoyingly delightful accent with him but left his equally-annoyingly delightful cologne behind. It didn't smell *that* good. It was just like all the other scents that caused a woman to envision a man with rippling muscles chopping down a Christmas tree in one fell swing.

Of course, a man who smelled as good as that could still stink of egotism and spite—which, apparently, were two things this guy had in abundance.

AFTER BREAKFAST HAD BEEN EATEN and cleaned up, the four of them loaded into Tasha's car and headed out for the day. Claire had been more than disappointed to learn Liam would be joining them, but she was determined not to allow him to soil her spirits any longer. She would have an amazing Christmas vacation if it was the last thing she did.

Seated on the right side of the car behind Liam driving, Claire shifted closer to the window, out of sight of the rear-view mirror. The drive to the gardens was only twenty minutes, but she didn't want to see him any more than what was necessary that day.

"So how did the two of you become friends, Melody?" Liam asked from the front as soon as they reached the freeway—or rather, the motorway.

"We roomed in college," Melody responded from where she sat in the back with Claire. "We were put in the same dorm our freshman year, and after that, Claire just loved me so much, she couldn't handle *not* being my roommate."

For a moment, Claire forgot about her decision to not speak around Liam. She didn't want to give him any more ammo than he already had against her, but Melody needed to be corrected.

"Yeah, right," Claire responded. "More like I was the only person who you could convince to room with you again."

Tasha laughed from the passenger seat. "That sounds more like our Melody."

"What?" Melody exclaimed, her jaw dropping in exaggerated dismay. "I was the perfect roommate."

"Oh, so perfect," Claire said. "Throwing parties on the weekdays, forcing me to go get tacos with you at midnight before finals at six the next morning, making me take Fencing and Natural Disasters courses just so you could follow boys around, going to—"

"Alright, alright," Melody said, though she was grinning from ear to ear. "I wasn't all bad, though. I took that Soils class for you so you wouldn't be alone, didn't I?"

"Soils class?" Liam questioned. Claire had almost forgotten he was in the car with them. "Now that sounds like a riveting course."

Claire shifted in her seat, pulling herself farther to the right so he couldn't see her clenched jaw.

"It was the worst class I've ever taken," Melody said. "Seriously. So boring. But I did it for Claire because I'm just that nice of a person."

Claire sent a sidelong glance at Melody, hoping her lowered voice was too quiet for Liam to hear. "You were in the class for a week before dropping out."

"Well, can you blame me?"

"Did you find the class interesting, Claire?" Tasha asked, turning around to face her with a kind smile.

Claire glanced warily at the back of Liam's headrest. "Yeah, I did. It was for my major, so it was required. I promise it wasn't as bad as Melody is saying."

"Yeah, it was," Melody slipped in before Tasha spoke again.

"What was your major?"

"I graduated with a Bachelor's in Horticulture and Floriculture."

"Ah," Liam piped in. "So *you* are the reason we're going to Kew Gardens today."

Claire's defenses started to build one on top of the other, a fence positioning around her heart. First the soils comment, now this. He obviously had no interest in floriculture or anything of the like, but to have him poke fun at her greatest passion in life? She couldn't take much more of this.

Before she could think of a response in her defense, he continued. "Did you manage to use your degree after graduating then?"

She pulled back. It was a fair enough question, but she knew he was wondering what a person could do with such a mediocre major. "Yes, I'm a florist," she stated stiffly.

She could just make out his head moving up and down in response. Had he nothing to say to her, nothing to make fun of?

Oh, of course. He would never do anything to give away his meanness in front of his family.

"Claire's hoping to open a flower shop of her own one day. Aren't you, Claire?" Melody prompted.

Claire could only nod.

"That sounds like such a lovely job," Tasha responded when Liam didn't. "Do you enjoy it?"

How could such a nice woman be the mother of such a terrible boy?

Claire nodded. "Yeah, I love it. It's a lot of work, but it's always worth it at the end of the day."

Tasha sighed airily, facing forward again. "Such a novelty, loving one's job." Then she glanced at her son. "Isn't it?"

Liam nodded in silence. So, he didn't love his job? She supposed that wasn't a surprise. He was probably some big, fancy exec at a high-end company.

"Where are you working now, Liam?" Melody asked, as if reading Claire's thoughts.

"I'm still at Peregrine Productions," he responded.

Each time he spoke, Claire was once again reminded of how much she liked his voice. And every time she was reminded of how much she liked his voice, she had to remind herself of how much she didn't like *him*.

"Ah, that's right," Melody responded. "And you are a..."

"A producer."

"Not for long, though," Tasha responded with another proud smile at her son. "He's up for a promotion."

"Oh, that's exciting," Melody said.

Liam had yet to say a word. Was he not happy with this potential promotion?

"When do you find out that you got the job?" Tasha asked next.

Was she so sure of her son's abilities that it wasn't a question of *if* but *when*?

Another beat passed before he responded. "I imagine when I return to work next week."

Tasha nodded, facing forward as the green scenery passed them by. "I still am amazed that you were able to leave your shoot early. Where were you again? France?"

Again, his head moved up and down.

"That must have been a late flight for you, to arrive home so close to midnight."

Claire's ears perked up. She still couldn't believe her bad luck to have been on the same flight as him the day before. Would he do what it took to prevent his family from knowing the same?

"No," he responded, "I actually arrived in the morning. I just had a few things to take care of before coming home."

Well, that would do it.

Claire glanced sidelong at Melody, whose brow pulled together. "Wait, you arrived on a plane from France yesterday morning?"

"Yeah."

Melody let out a huff of surprised laughter. "So did Claire. How crazy would that be if you guys were on the same flight?"

Liam didn't respond, but from Claire's viewpoint, she could see the whitening of his knuckles as he gripped the steering wheel tighter. Was he uncomfortable with where the conversation was headed? She could really make him pay by stretching out this conversation...

It was a good thing Claire wasn't the vindictive type.

"Yeah," she responded, "that would have been crazy."

"Do you remember your flight number, Liam?" Tasha asked.

He cleared his throat. "I don't, sorry."

Tasha sighed. "I wish we would have known you were coming. Then you might have been able to help Claire around the airport. Apparently, she had some trouble finding her way out of customs." She looked back to Claire with a look of understanding. "I don't blame you. It's a hedge maze in there."

Claire rubbed her cheek, hoping to dispel her blush. She'd

used the excuse of getting lost to avoid mentioning her little carry-on mishap. No doubt Liam had picked up on her lie, just as Claire had picked up on Tasha's insinuation that her son would have helped Claire had he been given the chance. Little did she know her own son.

Well, Claire wouldn't allow Liam to have the first word in this situation—or the last.

"Yeah, that would've been nice to have some help for sure," she said, speaking loud enough for Liam to hear her perfectly. "I really could have used it after some jerk accused me of stealing his luggage."

Oops. Maybe she was the vindictive type after all.

The car silenced. Melody and Tasha's eyes fell on Claire at the same time.

"Wait, what happened?" Melody asked.

"You never mentioned anything about that," Tasha added.

Liam was radio silent.

Claire looked at each of them innocently. Instead of hiding behind the seat, she shifted her body to be visible in the rearview mirror, spotting Liam's temples at once in the reflection.

She knew he would be able to see her if he adjusted a fraction.

Look at me, Liam. You little coward.

"Yeah," Claire continued, maintaining her focus on the mirror, "I had accidentally been handed his carry-on by another passenger on the flight. Later on near the baggage claim, this frail, string-bean-looking guy came up to me, shouting and being super rude."

"No," Tasha breathed. "I can't believe anyone could be so terrible. Especially to a stranger."

"Seriously, what a total jerk," Melody agreed.

"I know." Claire nodded.

Finally, Liam's eyes met hers. She had to admit, the string bean comment was a little much—and absolutely false—but she still had to bite the inside of her cheek to ward off a smile. His scowl would have withered her away like a dried pine branch had she not enjoyed it so much.

She really should have ended the conversation right there. But then, she was only giving the guy a taste of his own medicine. "I wish I could say things ended there, but he ended up accusing me of stealing, then he criticized me for being from the States."

Tasha released another puff of air in dismay.

Melody screwed up her nose. "I wish I would've been there. I could've shown the guy a real American greeting."

"Can you believe that, Liam?" Tasha asked.

Claire focused again on the mirror. Liam's eyes darted to hers, then back away. "No, that's, uh...that's unbelievable."

Claire bit her lip again in order to stop her smile.

"Did you say anything back to him?" Melody asked.

"Well, I could have said a lot," Claire responded. "I defended myself, of course, but I took a more dignified approach. I figured he was just one of those spoiled rich boys who had a bad day, you know? Maybe his butler was late to pick him up."

Tasha and Melody laughed, and Claire was finally able to release her smile. Liam shot her another look, his sharp gaze ricocheting off the mirror to hit her squarely in the chest, but she merely grinned in response.

Hmm. Maybe today would be a great day after all.

SIX

APPARENTLY, LIAM HAD FINALLY BEEN SCARED AWAY from Claire. He spent the rest of the car ride in silence and didn't say another word to her—teasing or otherwise.

Claire wasn't about to complain. She had finally given him a run for his money and was now reveling in her successes as she lived out her best life at Kew Gardens.

The grounds of the botanic center were vast and stunning, even in the seemingly dormant state of winter. A frost had found its place on the ground the night before and now clung to each blade of grass and every bare tree branch in small, crystal blankets. The shimmering white ice provided the perfect contrast to the vibrant red dogwoods and chocolate brown trees scattered around the gardens.

Claire and the others explored the area for hours, spotting stunning Kingfishers swooping overhead and silent roe deer grazing on grass near the lake. Before long, they had visited the Japanese gardens, the Rock Garden and the Grass Garden, the arboretum, the Queen's Garden, and eventually the Palm House before catching a late lunch at the café. Once their bellies were filled and their bodies were warmed, they finally moved to the Temperate House—where Claire had been looking forward to going all day. Not even Liam's continual glances in her direction could put a damper on her mood as she entered the remarkable building.

"It's the world's largest Victorian glasshouse," she said to Melody as they marveled at the expansive, glass structure. The spiral staircase, vibrant green plants, and white pillars holding up the domed structure gleamed as clean as the glass walls and roofing. "They house plants that are under the threat of extinction, as well as some that are *already* extinct in the wild."

Melody, who had humored Claire going on and on and on about every single plant they had seen that day, continued to listen as they moved through the glass structure, observing as many of the fifteen hundred species of plants they could manage.

"This is the yellow fatu, or the *abutilon pitcairnense*." Claire read the words aloud to Melody, describing the yellow, bell-shaped flower. "It's extinct in the wild now, but they're doing their best to make it thrive again." She stopped, shaking her head in amazement. "I just can't get over how incredible this is."

She swept her eyes around the sunshine-filled space and the vibrant green plants overhanging the walkways, the rushing sound of the small waterfall nearby carrying joy straight to her spirits. However, her mood plummeted when she caught sight of Liam a few paces behind her and Melody. Instead of marveling at the glorious work happening around them, his eyes were trained solely on his phone.

Well, that settled it. If she'd had any hope before of finding a sole redeemable quality in Liam Everhart, that well had most definitely dried up now. Where did he get off criticizing her for being on her phone at the airport when he was doing the very same thing himself right now? And how could he be so clearly uninterested in one of her greatest passions?

Yep, that *definitely* settled it. She could never see the value of a guy who could not see the value of a flower.

LIAM MOVED his fingers apart against his phone screen, zooming in on the Cayman sage he'd just taken a photo of, ensuring the quality was high enough to post. The plant's light purple flowers opened out like the mouth of a pitcher of water, the edges of the blossoms crisp and neat against the green-leafed backdrop.

This would be perfect. Kew Gardens was ripe for the picking, and his photography feed was going to benefit marvelously because of it. He usually didn't post photos unless they were taken with his mirrorless Canon camera, but today, his phone would have to do the trick.

He moved on to the next plant, maintaining a healthy distance from Melody and her friend as he focused more on reading the descriptions of the flowers instead of Claire's swaying ponytail.

It really was an impressive thing what they were doing at Kew Gardens, preserving and reviving long lost flowers. What a fulfilling and rewarding job. If only he could say the same about his own work.

"So."

Liam glanced up at the sound of his mum's voice. She stopped beside him, her eyes trained on him instead of the plants.

"So, what?" he asked when she didn't say anything more.

"Are you ever going to tell me what really happened with your work to make you come home for Christmas?"

The phone call Liam had taken in France moments before he had decided to leave flashed through his mind. His boss, Garrett, had shared with him the disappointing news about the promotion, and without thinking, Liam had instantly asked for time off for Christmas, put the associate producer in charge of the shoot, and booked a flight back home.

"Nothing happened," Liam lied. "Hannah took over flaw-lessly, so there was no problem there. And Garrett was more than happy to approve my time off since I'd worked the two Christ-mases before."

His mum studied him with skeptical eyes before looking away. "I suppose that's one redeeming quality the man possesses."

Liam nodded, pulling in his lips to remind himself to say nothing more. Garrett had been stringing Liam along for years with the promises of that promotion. Allowing Liam some time off was his one way of trying to give *something* back for the first time in years.

"And you're sure that's all that occurred?" Mum continued.

Liam hesitated. He didn't like lying, especially to his mum. But he couldn't handle the compassion and words of encourage-ment he'd inevitably receive from her if he told her the truth. He didn't want to be talked down off his ledge. Right now, all he wanted to do was teeter over it with unresolved anger.

Laughter sounded farther down the aisle, gratefully distracting him from the conversation as his eyes pulled to Melody and Claire. Claire said something Liam couldn't make out, pointing to one of the white statues, and Melody burst out laughing again.

What had she said that was apparently so hilarious? Liam found it hard to believe such a bitter woman as Claire could make anyone laugh.

He grimaced at his own bitterness. He was obviously sensitive around the woman since she'd gotten the better of him on the way there that morning. In truth, he envied her. She had a career she loved, and he didn't. She'd used her college degree, and he hadn't. She radiated happiness with her bright smile and charming freckles, and he, well, clearly didn't.

He continued observing her, but when their eyes connected, her smile instantly faded, and she turned away with her nose pointed in the air.

"They seem to be enjoying themselves," Mum said.

Liam nodded, then pulled his attention back to the flowers. He didn't want to look at Claire any more than she wanted him to look at her.

Mum cleared her throat. "Are you ever going to apologize to her for shouting at her at the airport?"

He started. "How..." He glanced back at Claire with a scowl. He should've expected the woman to rat him out to his own mother. "She told you."

"No, she didn't. But it was easy enough to figure out what happened between the two of you after the exchange in the car."

He shoved his hands into his pants' pockets, averting his gaze. This was what he'd been trying to avoid—Mum finding out how horrible of a person he really was. "I was stressed," he said. "And I'd only managed a few hours of sleep the night before. When she took my carry-on, I just...lost it. I was planning on apologizing when we had a minute alone together."

Alright, that was kind of a lie. He wasn't really planning on apologizing, but now that Mum knew about his mistake, he didn't have a choice, did he?

Mum tipped her head forward, motioning to Claire. "I suppose now is as good a time as any, then."

Following her gaze, he discovered Claire standing alone, studying a flower as Melody took a phone call farther down the aisle. The smile slightly curving Claire's lips reminded him of how he'd first seen her at the airport—innocent, peaceful, entirely unsuspecting of the man who was about to disturb her serenity.

He blew out a slow breath. "Fine," he mumbled, then he walked away, knowing his mum was smiling at his back.

She was right. He may as well get this over with.

WHORL HEATH. *Erica verticillata.*

What a gorgeous plant.

"You seem to be enjoying yourself."

Claire's eyes darted up from the pink, tubular flowers as Liam approached, stopping a few paces away from her. Was he finished avoiding her, then? She wasn't sure she was finished avoiding *him*.

"Well, I *was* enjoying myself," she muttered.

Liam didn't respond.

Glancing around, Claire spotted Tasha walking away in the opposite direction, and Melody was still on the phone with whoever it was who'd called her. Dang it. How had Claire allowed herself to have no out around the guy?

She pressed her lips together, averting her gaze from Liam's and moving on to examine the bright red flower from New Zealand.

Kaka beak. *Clianthus maximus.*

"Are you finding inspiration for your little shop back home?" Liam interrupted next.

Claire should have been used to his condescension by now. But her *little* shop? Really?

Instead of rising to his bait, she took an obvious step away from him. "Can I help you with anything, Liam? Something to send you on your way faster, perhaps?"

He didn't respond for a moment, his brow low over his eyes as he observed her. She really didn't like that she found him so attractive. But seriously, even with his bad attitude, she couldn't deny how insanely appealing those dark eyebrows were, or how perfectly they complemented his neatly trimmed beard that was just a touch thicker than everyday scruff.

"I just came over to..."

She waited. "To...what?"

Finally, his gaze dropped, and his square shoulders sloped just a degree. "To apologize. For my behavior at the airport."

Claire's jaw slackened. Was he serious? He was actually saying sorry?

"I usually don't behave in that way," he continued, "and I wanted to express my regret for doing so."

His apology was so eloquent. So...rehearsed. She narrowed her eyes. He'd been speaking with his mom right before coming over, hadn't he?

She glanced over his shoulder and caught Tasha's interested eye before the woman turned swiftly away, focusing intently on the glass ceiling above.

Hmm. Just as Claire had suspected. "Did your mom put you up to this?"

His gaze darted up. "Pardon? No. Well, she may have mentioned it, but I was..."

She shook her head, ending his words. She didn't need to hear any more of his excuses. Whether Tasha found out on her own about Claire and Liam's connection or if Liam had told her, it didn't matter anymore.

"It's fine. I accept your forced apology. Now will you excuse me, please? I'd like to get back to getting ideas for my *little shop*."

She turned away, leaning forward to better see the flowers that resembled small, yellow pinecones.

Wood's cycad. *Encephalartos woodii.*

She'd meant her words as a dismissal, but obviously, Liam continued to miss the memo. He remained at her side, staring down at her.

"What?" she asked.

"Nothing."

He studied her still, his brow lowering as he remained.

"Are you staying here to try to think of another way to make fun of me?" she asked.

No response.

"Should I help you out?" She took another step away from him, focusing on a tree in the distance with small leaves. "You could always poke fun at my American accent. Or continue criticizing my simple dream of owning a flower shop. Or maybe you could tell me more about how shocked you were to find out I actually put my degree to good use."

She glanced at him sidelong, but his expression remained unchanged.

"I wasn't shocked," he finally responded.

She dropped her chin. "Really?" With a sigh, she turned away from him again. "Look, I think it will be better for the both of us if we just agree not to talk to each other again, okay?"

"Are you so incapable of speaking civilly that you need to resort to severing all conversation between us?"

She slowly turned to him. Did he really speak so eloquently all the time, or was it just when he was trying to be rude to her?

Either way, she couldn't make sense of the guy. One minute, he was teasing her for being in his bed, the next, he was criticizing her with all the posturing of a preening peacock.

"See?" she said. "This is exactly what I'm talking about. We just can't help but argue. I don't want to make things awkward for your mom and Melody by showing how much we don't like each other, okay? So let's just stop talking, and things will be better for everyone."

As if to annoy her yet again, Liam didn't respond.

She waited, then in a huff—mostly because she'd been admiring his dark eyes that glistened from the light of the sun shining through the glass roof above—she whirled around, ready to never speak with him again.

But instead of proudly fleeing, she moved forward without looking and slammed right into an employee of the Temperate House, bouncing against her and a large, potted plant the girl held.

As if in slow motion, the teenage girl stumbled back to catch herself, unable to hold onto the plant in the process. Claire reached forward, but it was too late. The girl managed to remain upright, but the pot plummeted to the floor, shattering its base. The plant fell limp on its side, and dirt splayed across the clean, creamy walkway like a permanent, black firecracker.

"Oh my gosh," Claire gasped, a blush searing across her face. "I'm so sorry! I didn't see you."

Guests turned to see what the clatter had been, including Liam, who stood just to the side of the mess.

"It's alright," the employee said with a thick London accent. She stared at the mess on the floor in a daze.

Claire instantly dropped to her knees, moving to pick up the pieces of the broken pot. She grimaced as the girl and Liam hunched down beside her to do the same.

Of course this would happen in front of Liam and so many other people. She wouldn't describe herself as clumsy, but obviously, the world was not quite done humiliating her yet.

She eyed the fallen plant with its long leaves draped across the floor. She was fairly certain she recognized it, but in her state, she couldn't name it.

"Please tell me this wasn't one of the endangered plants," she said, looking up at the employee with a wince.

To her great relief, the girl shook her head. "No, it's just one of the displays for the front of the House." She looked back at the mess. "I'll get a broom. That should make the cleanup easier."

She stood and skittered away, but Claire continued picking up the pieces of the pot, placing them in a larger section that hadn't broken as much in the process.

She worked as quickly as she could, but her fingers fumbled time and time again as she caught Liam glancing over at her.

She could just hear his thoughts.

Typical American.

Clumsy, uncultured, will do anything for attention.

I thought you worked in a flower shop. Isn't this the type of thing you should avoid doing?

People continued to pass by with looks of commiseration, but Claire was more focused on her face being an entire ball of flame, her ears two separate blazing fires competing to see which could burn the brightest. Had Tasha and Melody not heard the commotion? Why weren't they there to help clean up instead of Liam?

She reached for another piece of the blue and white pot. Liam moved for the same piece, but he didn't pull back.

"I got it," she said gruffly, snatching it from his fingers.

This was all his fault. If he hadn't come up to her in the first place, she never would have been frazzled, and she definitely wouldn't have rammed into the employee.

"I'm only trying to help," Liam said as another couple walked past.

"You've helped enough," she muttered, half-hoping he'd hear her, half-hoping he wouldn't.

"What do you mean by that?" He straightened, pulling his hands back from the wreckage with a frown. "I came over here to apologize. To make amends for—"

"For what?" she hissed, checking her tone as another group passed by. "For criticizing a stranger in an airport? For making fun of a guest of your mother's? Or for belittling my decision to major in something so juvenile as floriculture?" She promised she wouldn't allow herself to become anymore affected by the guy, but as angry tears welled in her eyes—borne mostly from sheer humiliation—her control slipped swiftly from her grasp. "Honestly, I don't even know why I care so much about what you're saying. I should expect it based on the type of guy you are."

He narrowed his eyes. "And what type of *guy* am I, then?" he asked, clearly critiquing her choice of words.

That was the final straw. She dropped the last of the pot's pieces into the pile and lowered her voice so no passersby could hear her words. "The type of guy to bring people down, just to make yourself higher. The type of guy who skips out on Christmas with his mom just to earn a few extra bucks." She leaned closer, his eyes as hard as her heart. "The type of guy who thinks only of himself."

She finished, staring at him with the intensity she hoped he felt in her words. But when a flash of pain flickered through his dark eyes, she blinked, finally breaking their contact.

"Here, this will help."

The employee's arrival drew them apart, and Claire and Liam both stood as the girl began to sweep the dirt toward the garbage bin she'd brought with her.

Claire drew deep breaths, attempting to ease the anger that was already being replaced with a nagging regret.

She picked up the pieces of the pot and dropped them into the bin, only then catching sight of Liam leaving the Temperate House altogether.

Instead of feeling accomplished with her success of being rid of him, she blew out a sigh, her heart twisting like the strands of a sour candy cane.

Now *she* was the one who had to apologize. Dang it all.

SEVEN

STANDING IN THE ENTRYWAY OF TASHA'S HOME THE next morning, Claire tapped her foot on the gray rug and flicked her gaze up the stairs again.

The bathroom door was still closed. What in the world was taking Melody so long? Twenty minutes had passed since their scheduled time to leave at eight o'clock, and she still wasn't ready.

With Tasha going to work that day, Melody had promised Claire a touristy day in London with just the two of them. Claire had woken up early that morning at seven, planning on being extra loud as she got ready, just to sneakily wake up Melody, but she was happy to discover her friend already up and occupying the bathroom.

Fortunately, Claire had had the foresight to shower the night before, as Melody had yet to return to their room. Still, doing her hair and makeup with a minuscule hand mirror in the bedroom hadn't been easy.

Claire glanced at the time on her phone before tucking it away with another sigh and readjusting her coat over her arm. In college, she had always hurried Melody to classes, to church, to dances—basically any activity that required attendance. While being late was one of Claire's pet peeves, being rushed just so happened to be one of Melody's.

Still, if Claire didn't find out soon when they'd leave, she was sure she was going to—

Footsteps sounded upstairs, and Liam descended the steps. At the sight of him, dread nudged its way to the center of her chest like a pestering relative delivering unwanted fruit cake for Christmas.

She took a step back from the stairs to allow Liam passage, averting her gaze as she did so. She must look like a total idiot, waiting at the front door like a puppy hoping to be let out to play in the snow.

"Hey," she greeted simply.

He nodded, stated, "Morning," then walked past her without another word.

She stared after him, his thin t-shirt draped pleasantly over his muscular shoulders. Opening her mouth, she hesitated, then closed it again.

She and Liam hadn't spoken to each other since the Temperate House the day before, despite remaining at Kew Gardens until after dark to enjoy the Christmas light display. Afterward, instead of eating Chinese takeout together, Liam had taken himself off to his room, where he had remained the rest of the evening.

Seeing Tasha's disappointment over Liam's avoidance of them was Claire's final breaking point. She knew she was the one reason Liam wasn't eating with them, and she had to make amends before things got even worse. But there was no way she was going to bring up her own faults around Tasha and Melody.

Now, however, without either of them present...

"Hey, Liam?" she called out just before he was about to disappear around the corner to the kitchen.

He stopped, hesitating a moment before turning to peer at her from down the hallway. "Yes?"

Alright. It was time to get this over with. "I just wanted to say sorry for yesterday," she blurted out, her eyes skirting from the wooden flooring to the photos on the wall to the bathroom door once again. "I shouldn't have said those things, and...yeah. Sorry."

Her apology could not have sounded any less elegant—especially when compared to his eloquence yesterday. Was that why it was taking him so long to respond?

Finally, she found his gaze just as he nodded. "Thank you," he said, turning away. "I accept your *forced* apology."

Then he disappeared into the kitchen.

Claire stared at the vacant hallway. Wow. If that wasn't the most perfect comeback ever. Not only had he responded the same way she had during his own apology, she couldn't even call him rude because then she, in essence, would be saying she herself was rude.

How annoying.

The creak of the bathroom door drew her attention up the steps again, and she blew out a sigh of relief as Melody stepped out.

Bring on a full day without Liam.

With a happy smile, she chirped up the steps. "Hey, Melody! Are you re—"

Her words ended abruptly as Claire took in the sight of her friend still in her pajamas, her hair in a stringy mess around her face, and her skin, ashen.

"Melody," she breathed, climbing the steps at once. "Are you okay?"

The bags under Melody's eyes stretched to the tops of her high cheekbones, her lips red and chapped. She barely managed a single step before plopping down on the top of the stairs and leaning forward to rest her head on her arms.

"No," she mumbled.

Her hoarse voice gave Claire reason to pause for just a moment. "Is it a stomach bug?" If it was, would Claire catch it, too?

She pushed aside the selfish thought, knowing it didn't matter, so long as she could help care for her friend.

But Melody shook her head, looking up from her arms as she stared straight ahead in a daze. "No. Food poisoning."

"Oh, no." Claire grimaced, moving to sit beside Melody and putting her arm around her. "Are you sure?"

"Yeah. Aunt Tasha has it, too. We were passing each other on our way to the bathroom all night."

All night? Claire had slept with her AirPods in the night before to drown out Melody's snoring. Was that why she hadn't heard them? And did that mean Tasha was in bed instead of at work?

Then another thought occurred. "Wait. We ate the same thing last night. If you both have it, why don't I?"

Or Liam for that matter? Unless he always looked exceptionally attractive even when sick.

Melody pressed a hand to her closed mouth, squelching a burp before responding in a whisper. "The shrimp betrayed me." Then she hunched forward again with another moan.

Of course. The shrimp from the takeout. Tasha and Melody had both eaten the entire portion together when Claire had passed on accepting any. She'd never trusted those beady-eyed, rubbery creatures. Anything that resembled the insides of the Tauntaun Han Solo killed on Hoth could not—*should* not—be eaten.

Did that mean Liam hadn't eaten any of the shrimp either? She glanced through the bars of the banister, though she couldn't see to the kitchen.

"I'm sorry," Melody said, shaking her head against her arms. "I don't think I can walk around London today."

"Don't even worry about it for one second. We can go another time."

Melody raised her head, though she still leaned forward, clutching her stomach. "No, we can't. You know each day is planned. If you don't get out today, you'll have to miss something else you wanted to see."

Melody was right. Claire really didn't want to pass on the opportunity to see Big Ben and the palaces. But then, she couldn't very well leave Melody and Tasha at home to fend for themselves. It wasn't like Liam would take care of them either. She wouldn't put it past him to ignore the sickies altogether.

"It's alright," Claire said again, as if to reassure herself along with Melody. "We'll just have a day in together. Maybe we could make the Christmas cookies today instead of—"

"Oh," Melody said, delivering an extended groan. "Don't mention any food to me."

Claire hesitated. "Alright, then we'll just...watch Christmas movies or something."

Melody froze, her face dropping a shade whiter as she clutched her stomach. Taking a few deep breaths, she shook her head, her body seeming to relax just a fraction. "No," she said, as if holding her breath. "I'm serious, Claire. I can't have you stay here. I'm going to be spending the entire day on the toilet or sleeping. I can't..." She stopped, groaning again. "You have to go."

Claire watched in dismay, wishing she could help her friend, then Melody's words settled on her mind. "Wait, you want me to go out alone?"

Before Melody could respond, Liam's voice from the hallway sounded through the banister bars. "You won't be going alone," he said smoothly, walking down the hallway and standing at the bottom of the stairs. He looked up at her and Melody with a raised chin. "I'll be going with you."

EIGHT

LIAM'S STATEMENT WAS SO OUT OF NOWHERE, SO insanely ludicrous, that Claire started laughing. "You can't be serious."

His expression said otherwise.

Melody grunted again as she rubbed circles over her stomach. "Would you, Liam? That would be so amazing. I'd feel so much better knowing she didn't have to go alone."

"No, no, no, no," Claire protested as gently as possible. "I can't ask him to do that."

Liam shook his head. "You're not asking me. I'm volunteering."

Claire narrowed her eyes. Was he really volunteering? Just like he'd *volunteered* to apologize the day before?

"I'll feel so much better knowing Liam's with you," Melody said with another grimace. "I would never forgive myself if you got lost alone in London."

Claire frowned. Get lost? How old did Melody think she was?

Before she could respond, Liam motioned to the door. "Come on, then. I assume you don't wish to be kept waiting any longer than you have."

Melody spoke through another groan. "She hates being late."

"I thought she might."

Claire clenched her jaw, her lips pursing in the process.

Brushing aside her annoyance, she turned back to Melody. "I'm not going to just leave you here without any help."

Melody burped behind her closed lips and grimaced. "Believe me, you'll be doing all of us a favor by leaving." Then her eyes widened as she clenched her stomach with both hands. "Ugh. Just end the agony now." She jumped up from her spot on the stairs and raced to the bathroom. "Claire, I wouldn't sit that close to here if I were you. Liam, do whatever it takes to get her out of this house!" Then she slammed the door behind her.

Not wishing to hear what Melody was doing behind the closed door, Claire hopped up and moved down the stairs.

"Ready?" Liam asked as he pulled on his dark coat.

Claire eyed him with suspicion. "Your mother put you up to this, didn't she?"

"Yes, she most certainly did," Liam responded without a hint of shame.

"What did she promise to give you? A crisp ten-dollar bill?"

He straightened his coat collar. "It'd take more than a tenner to get me to spend an entire day with you."

Alright. She deserved that. "Then what?"

He gave her a knowing look. "Why do you care so much?"

"I don't," she quickly answered, raising her chin. "Besides, I think we can both agree that it would be a disaster if we went together. So. I'll be going alone. I just have a couple things to do first."

She brushed past him without awaiting a response and headed to the kitchen. She didn't want to leave Melody and Tasha alone, but Claire had had food poisoning before, and all she'd wanted was to be left alone, just like Melody.

So Claire would go. She'd just be sure to return sooner to check in on them. And she would not be going with Liam.

After retrieving a few bottles of a fruit drink and a couple packages of Jacob's Cream Crackers from the cupboard, she returned to the front door where Liam still waited.

"Here," she said, thrusting one of the bottles and crackers toward him. "Give these to your mom."

Liam scrambled to hold them against his chest, but she didn't wait for his response, going straight upstairs to put the rest of the items on the table next to Melody's bed.

On her way out, she caught sight of Liam entering his mom's room, so she slipped quietly down the hallway toward the bathroom door, hesitating just a minute before gently knocking against the wood.

"Melody?" she said softly.

Melody groaned in response.

"I'm gonna go. Okay?"

"Yeah," Melody said. "Have fun, alright?"

Claire nodded, though she knew Melody couldn't see her. "Just text me the minute you feel better. And don't hesitate to call me if you need anything." She pulled out her phone. "I'll turn up the volume so I can hear it, okay? I'll be home soon."

Melody mumbled a sound of affirmation. "I'll see you later."

Claire hesitated a moment longer before lumbering down the stairs. This was good, her leaving. Nothing else could be done for the poor souls until nature literally ran its course. She didn't need to feel guilty for leaving them. At least, that's what she continued to tell herself.

Slipping on her thick coat, Claire pulled out her hair from beneath it just as Liam descended the steps once again.

"Shall we?" he asked.

Claire's hands dropped to her sides. "I thought we'd decided on not going together?"

"*You* decided that." He placed his hand on the doorknob. "Which presents a problem because I promised my mum, and now my cousin, that I would take you round London to keep you safe."

She scoffed under her breath. What was it with everyone

thinking that she was incapable of traveling anywhere on her own? She'd clearly made it to England just fine, hadn't she?

Still, she didn't want to be rude again, especially if it resulted in Tasha no longer getting to spend time with her son because he was so offended by Claire that he left to stay at his own apartment.

But the longer Claire spent with Liam, the more likely it was that one or both of them would say something mean to each other again. Doing their own thing would be better for the both of them.

She glanced to where his fingers still rested on the door handle. "How about I go alone, and we can just *say* that you went with me?"

Liam studied her in silence.

She hesitated. "Is that a 'yes'?"

Again, he didn't respond. Instead, he stepped off to the side, allowing her passage to the door.

Heavens to Betsy. Had they actually agreed on something? Unable to hide her half-smile, she shuffled past him, retrieving her purse on the way out. "Perfect. I'll see you later, then."

Without awaiting a response, she closed the door behind her with a satisfied sigh. Well. That had been a surprising and welcome turn of events.

Drawing in a deep breath of the frigid, morning air, she walked down the front step of the house, making it nearly to the archway before the door opened behind her.

She glanced back, frowning in confusion as Liam stepped outside, locking the door behind him, then turning to face her with an innocent expression.

"What are you doing?" she asked, stopping just short of the small gate.

He shrugged, pulling in his lips. "Just felt like doing a touch of sightseeing today, that's all."

She should've known she couldn't get rid of him so easily. "So your plan is to trail me all day long, is that it?"

"Well, I did promise my mum and cousin that—"

"Yeah, I'm well aware of what you promised them, thank you."

She looked away but not before she thought she saw a hint of amusement shining in his eyes. Traveling together really would be a disaster. But then, surely for the sake of his mother, they could learn to tolerate each other.

Closing her eyes, she shook her head and finally responded. "Fine, you can come with me." She opened her eyes, looking at him with a narrowed gaze. "But we have to stick to my schedule."

He nodded. "Yes, ma'am."

She ignored his words clearly meant to annoy her. "And I…" She paused, looking around before continuing in a lower voice. "I don't want to hear a single mention about me being in your bed."

He hadn't brought it up before, but she would gladly steer clear of that whole conversation.

His eyes slightly narrowed—or were they squinting with mirth?—before he nodded again. "Yes, ma'am," he repeated.

"And," she said, holding up a finger, the cold air instantly swarming and snapping at her skin, "neither of us are allowed to speak to each other at all unless it's to say something nice."

"Yes, ma'am—"

"And that includes, 'yes, ma'am.' Deal?"

"Yes, m—" He stopped himself, ending with a silent nod.

She sized him up for a moment, wondering if he would actually go along with her rules before realizing it didn't matter. He would be a jerk, or he wouldn't. It was as simple as that.

With a stifled sigh, she walked under the archway and through the gate, stepping out onto the sidewalk as she pulled on her white gloves.

He closed the gate behind them and moved beside her. "Would you like me to show you the way?"

"That's alright," she responded, taking a left from Tasha's house. "I got it."

She had made extensive plans before, saving all of the directions and maps on her phone, not wanting to be at the liberty of Melody's terrible sense of direction. More than that now, though, she just wanted to prove to Liam that she was more than capable of traveling around a city by herself.

He followed her a step behind, so she shifted slightly to the right to put more distance between them.

She was fairly certain they were headed in the direction they needed to be going, but after a few paces, she pulled out her phone just to be sure. Unfortunately, after a few moments of waiting for the map to update, she was shown that she was, in fact, going in the opposite direction of the station they needed to get to.

Her mind raced with how she could play this off coolly. Maybe Liam was no longer familiar with the area, having lived away from home for so long? Or maybe she could just take a quick jaunt around the block without him noticing?

"You do realize you're going the wrong way, right?"

Freaking—

"If you're planning on taking the Tube, the closest station to us is Hammersmith, which is back that way."

Blast his perfect accent. And his perfect beard. And his perfect, black hair that rivaled the thickness of a Ken doll.

"Oh, yeah." She pulled on an innocent expression and turned around. Was her blush super noticeable? "I figured that, but my phone just, you know, sent me in the wrong direction."

"Right."

She walked past him, keeping her pace steady and her eyes focused straight ahead.

"So this is your first time in England?" he asked as they moved through the residential area, bare oak trees towering overhead.

"Yeah," she responded.

"Are you enjoying it so far?"

"Yeah, I am."

Silence followed, and so ended their first conversation without either of them needing to apologize by the end of it. No wonder the exchange had been so stilted.

"So where does this schedule of yours dictate we go first?" he asked next.

She glanced at him sidelong, wondering if he was breaking the "say-nothing-mean" rule, but he merely looked ahead with all the innocence of a beautiful, gorgeous puppy.

She cleared her throat, white puffs of cold air lingering around them as they breathed. "Buckingham Palace."

He nodded, opening his mouth before seeming to think better of what he'd been about to say. Instead of allowing her curiosity to get the better of her, or on focusing on how tall Liam actually was—seriously, he had to be a good foot taller than her, right?—she pulled her attention to the sights around them.

The attached houses shifted gradually to business buildings, and the street they walked along—lined bumper to bumper with compact, neutral-colored cars— led them to a busier street with buses zipping past and bicycles trying to keep up with the pace of traffic.

Claire, having forgotten to keep her map on, pulled out her phone once again, slipping a finger free from the fabric of her gloves to pull up the directions.

Come on, come on, come on. Why was it taking so long to load?

"Do you wish for your phone to take you in the wrong direction again? Or would you rather save time by allowing me to be your guide?"

NINE

CLAIRE STARED DOWN AT HER PHONE, A SINGLE BAR filling out the four available. *International coverage, my backside.*

"Um," she began, watching the pinwheel on top of the map as it went round and round.

Alright. Never mind that Liam thought her inept. If they kept this pace, they wouldn't arrive in Central London until after dark.

"Okay. I guess having you lead the way would make more sense." Her eyes delved into his. "So long as you don't make fun of me for not being prepared."

He shook his head, looking both ways down the busy street, seemingly distracted as he responded. "I already promised you that I wouldn't."

She watched him for a minute, fighting the response she wished to give. *"Yeah, well, a promise doesn't mean much these days, does it? Just ask Richard or my parents."*

Those words would hardly benefit either of them.

Before long, she and Liam crossed the busy street, making their way south until they arrived at the station, the symbol for the Underground—a red circle with a blue bar through the center of it—perched near the top of the building.

"You have your Oyster card?" Liam asked.

From her coat pocket, Claire pulled out the blue card Tasha had given her the night before to use for traveling around the city. "Yep."

He nodded, then they joined the growing line within the station.

Claire was so preoccupied with admiring every new thing she noticed—especially the signs proclaiming "Toilets" instead of "Restrooms"—that when the time came for her to tap her card against the yellow scanner, the blasted thing didn't work.

"Lay it flatter," Liam instructed over her shoulder. "No, flatter. *Flatter.*"

Eventually, he reached around and laid the card on the circle pad himself. Of course the gates swung open on his first attempt. After going through the waist-high gates, Claire swiped the card back from his hands and tucked it safely away.

"You'll need it to leave the next station," he said. "And next time, lay it flat like I told you to."

"I *was* laying it flat," she said, turning on him at once.

But when she saw that familiar twinkle in his eye, she paused. Seriously, what *was* that, that little narrowing of his eyes? It wasn't really a smile, just his lower eyelids squinting up.

Whatever it was, it made his eyes shine, despite their dark tone. And, dang it all, if it didn't make him all the more appealing.

She kept up with his pace as they moved through the station, making their way to a large open area with a glass, domed roof. Two train tracks ran along either side of the center, grey-stoned platform, and large advertisements for ITV's latest shows and Costa Coffee stretched the length of the walls.

"At the risk of breaking one of your rules," Liam began, smoothing out his beard with his hand, "I was wondering if I might suggest a different route than the one you've planned."

Her brow twitched. She wasn't going to panic. She could adapt and adjust most of the time. Some of the time.

Okay, never. She was terrible at adapting.

"We can still see everything on your list," Liam continued, apparently unaware of the turmoil he'd caused within her, "but if there's a better route, one that includes more sites to see, I could show you the way."

Raising her shoulders, she brought the coat up to her ears, hoping to ward off the chill that had come over her since they'd stopped walking. The air wasn't much warmer in the station than it was outside, despite the morning sunlight beaming in through the glass roof.

She had to admit, Liam's suggestion made sense. Having an actual Londoner's opinion on how to get from point A to point B would be super helpful.

"And you're sure we still get to see my list of things?" she asked.

"Of course."

Ugh. She could listen to that accent all day. She just needed to remember that even though she liked the sound of it now, it hadn't always been the bearer of kindness to her.

"Alright," she finally relented. "I guess that would be okay, then. Just so long as it doesn't keep us out too late. I want to make sure we can get back when Melody and Tasha need us."

"Alright, then we'll need to take the eastbound Piccadilly line." Liam stood off to the left side labeled Platform Three. "It should be here in just a minute."

Sure enough, as Claire peered down the end of the cold, dark tunnel, a rush of cold wind fluttered her wavy hair, and a convoy shot forth from the darkness, its brakes squealing in protest.

Her parents had always talked about how much they'd loved taking the Subway in New York. That was another broken promise they'd made.

"We'll take you around New York City for your high school graduation, Claire Bear," they'd said, using the nickname she'd grown to hate.

Obviously, the trip never occurred. Instead, her parents had toured around the Egyptian Pyramids without her while she started work at Peonies & Burlap.

Even though she would have loved to experience riding the Subway with her parents—and the Underground with Melody—she was determined to still enjoy herself, even if she had to hide most of her excitement from Liam.

The train pulled to a swift stop, opening its doors as passengers poured forth like an avalanche, filling every inch of the platform as they exited the train.

"This is Hammersmith," a female voice sounded on the intercom. *"Change here for the District Line. This is the Piccadilly Line service toward Gloucester Road."*

Claire trailed behind Liam as they boarded, taking the last open seats as the female voice sounded again.

"The next station is Barons Court."

Claire leaned as far away from Liam as she could without being obvious, focusing on the white walls of the train. She didn't need to catch another whiff of that lumberjack Christmas cologne he was wearing again today. Why couldn't he smell more like Richard had—of wet dog and body odor?

As soon as the doors closed, the train picked up speed, and the whirring sounded louder and louder. The light from the station eventually disappeared, and the black walls of the Underground flew past the window in a dark blur.

Claire had to turn away from Liam again so he wouldn't spot the ridiculous smile on her lips. She just couldn't help it. This was one of the most exciting experiences of her life.

Those around her had ducked their heads, focusing on their phones or closing their eyes with headphones in their ears. But not Claire. She wanted to drink in every moment, remember and savor every experience she had.

If Melody was there, Claire would have been able to be her usual, giddy self. Instead, she had to check her excitement so Liam didn't think she was a total noob...Even though she was.

After a few stops at a few different stations, and one change of lines from Piccadilly to Circle, the two of them stepped out into the fresh air at Bayswater Station and headed in the direction of Kensington Gardens.

"This way you get to see more flowers and plants," Liam explained.

Claire looked up at him, trying to bring the cold from outside into the warmth that was suddenly entering her heart at his thoughtful gesture.

"You're sure you won't be bored to death?" she asked, recalling the time he'd spent on his phone at Kew Gardens.

He merely shook his head. "Every true Englishman enjoys a good walk around a garden."

She wanted to ask him why he'd appeared so bored at the Temperate House then, but she bit her tongue. She, just like him, had to obey the rules of kindness that morning.

Just before they entered Kensington Gardens through the black, wrought iron gates, the two of them exchanged numbers at Liam's bidding. "Just in case you *do* actually get lost," he said with another twinkle in his eye.

This time, oddly enough, Claire didn't feel so upset.

Despite the fact that she was still missing Melody, Claire couldn't deny how glad she was to have Liam's help, as his route was far better than the one she'd chosen for herself.

Not only did they see Kensington Palace and Hyde Park, but they also visited the Princess Diana Memorial Garden, the Royal Albert Hall, the Albert Monument, The Serpentine, and then, finally, the grand Buckingham Palace—and it had only added an extra hour to their travels.

At each location, after Liam had led her to the areas with the best views, Claire had to sneakily snap a quick selfie when he had his back turned to her. She would have asked him to take a photo of her himself, but after he'd accused her of basically being addicted to social media at the airport, she didn't want him to assume that she was so self-involved she needed a picture of herself at every location, even though she kinda did.

Throughout the morning, neither of them spoke much beyond the occasional question Claire had about a certain statue or body of water. The conversation never strayed to anything personal, and Claire was more than fine with that. She was way too distracted with the sights to dwell on anything else.

Well, she was distracted with the sights, and of course, with Liam's face which had grown even more attractive with the tip of his nose and his cheeks turning all rosy in the cold air.

At half past eleven, they left the palace behind and headed down the Mall. On their way, Claire spotted a red, double decker bus and a few black taxis in the distance.

That settled it. She was in love with London. The atmosphere, the energy of the city, the bustling life around her.

She had loved driving by the gorgeous sights and exploring gardens and tours, but there was something far more satisfying about walking where everyday people walked, about getting a small taste of their real lives—lives that seemed like a dream compared to her own.

If this was what traveling the world was really like, no wonder her parents loved it as much as they did. If only they wished to travel *with* her, instead of merely sharing the details when they returned.

She hesitated before pulling out her phone. She hadn't received any messages from her parents yet. They were probably out of service on the cruise or just busy or something.

But that shouldn't stop her from messaging *them*.

Claire: Hey, Mom! Walking around London today. No wonder you guys love to travel so much. It's so exciting!

She hesitated, then typed out another message.

Claire: How is the cruise going? Miss you and love you both.

She sent the message, then a few of the selfies she'd taken, before sliding the phone back in her pocket and replacing her gloves over her frigid fingertips.

She didn't expect a response back for a few days, if she received one at all. Her parents weren't superb communicators, especially while on vacation. On cruises, they were even worse, even though they always paid for Wi-Fi. Claire just figured they weren't very good at keeping tabs on who messaged them and when.

"Was that Melody?"

Claire glanced up, finding Liam's eyes on her.

"What? Oh, no," she responded. "I was just sending a message to my mom."

He nodded. A beat of silence passed by before he spoke again. "And how does she feel about you being gone for Christmas?"

Claire pulled the ribbons around her heart that she'd allowed to become loosened by her texts, securing them in a tight knot she always held firm when thinking or speaking of her parents. "She's fine with it. She and my dad are actually on a cruise right now, so it worked out really well for me to come here."

She felt his gaze on her, but she wasn't willing to share anything else. Instead, she focused ahead on where the road curved off to the right.

"So where are we headed now?"

LIAM STUDIED CLAIRE FOR A MINUTE, doing his best to hold his tongue. Clearly, she didn't want to talk anymore about her parents, or she wouldn't have changed the topic so abruptly. But what he couldn't understand was *why* she didn't want to.

Still, it wasn't his place to push or prod. Instead, he motioned to the street they were coming up to. "We'll be taking a right on

Horse Guards Road," he explained. "Then a left onto Great George Street. That will take us to Big Ben and the Houses of Parliament and Westminster Abbey."

Claire nodded, her eyes continuing to move all around them, as they'd been doing since the moment they'd left his mum's house.

He'd refused to spend the day with Claire when his mother had first asked him to take her, waking him up early on one of her many trips to the toilet that morning.

"Both of you will be better off outside of this house with Melody and I like this," Mum had said, attempting to appeal to his senses. "And I don't wish for Claire to be alone. She's gone through so much already this Christmas."

Liam had no idea what hardships Claire had been exposed to apart from him being a halfwit, but Mum had continued before he could ask. "Whatever this feud is between you two, you have to overcome it. Forgive and forget, just like your dad and I always taught you."

Of course his guilt had overcome him then, and he'd promised he'd stay with Claire.

"You'll have a good time," Mum had said, then she'd run back to the toilet.

To his utter relief and surprise, he *was* having a good time.

There was nothing so exciting as seeing something from the eyes of someone who'd never witnessed it before. But with Claire, the excitement was manifested over and over again throughout London in such copious amounts, Liam found it hard not to constantly stare at her. She seemed amazed by the simplest of things—from the Underground whirring forward to the gates of Buckingham being opened for the palace guards.

It was charming, really. Made her almost endearing. But that was probably just the excitement of the morning talking. There was no chance he could ever consider the woman who'd been so snippy with him the day before to be *endearing*.

And yet, as they made their way toward Big Ben, the large golden clocktower soaring above them, Claire was exactly that.

Her baby blue eyes rounded like a child's in a Christmas sweet shop, ready to gobble up as many red, boiled sweets as she could.

"Oh, wow," she breathed, her mouth propping open as she stopped in the middle of the pavement, clearly unaware of the people huffing past her as they were made to move around her.

Liam had already stepped to the side, allowing passage to the others as he watched her. All morning, she'd turned away from him when her smile had grown, as if she wanted to hide just how greatly she was enjoying her time in London. She'd also waited until she thought he wasn't looking to snap pictures of herself, though he'd done his best to make her selfies a degree better by stopping at each site wherever she'd have the best lighting and the best backdrop and view.

With how much she'd tried to hide her behavior, he figured she didn't want to reveal this side of herself to a perfect stranger whom she'd argued with probably more than anyone in her life.

But now, from his viewpoint on the side of the pavement, she was so taken with the clocktower that she had clearly forgotten all about attempting to hide her enthusiasm.

Of course, Liam couldn't blame her. Big Ben was one of the greatest prides of London, and for good reason. Yet, instead of admiring the tower again, his gaze dropped to Claire. For some reason, her expression pulled his attention even more than the clock did.

"Excuse me," someone said as they brushed past her.

Finally, her eyes were torn from Big Ben, and she glanced around her, a clear panic in her eyes. Did she not see him?

Not wishing for her alarm to continue, he stepped forward, his eyes remaining steadily on her. "It's a good job I have your number," he said, unable to stop himself from toying with her.

Relief flooded her features at the sight of him, and Liam was left to wonder why that fact made his heart warm.

TEN

CLAIRE BLEW OUT A RELIEVED SIGH AS SHE CAUGHT sight of Liam. She really thought she'd lost him then.

Before she could respond in some sarcastic way—*"Did you hide on purpose just to make me freak out?"*—Big Ben caught her eye once again.

"Remarkable, isn't it?" Liam asked.

She hummed in response. "Does it ever get old? Seeing it every day, I mean."

"You grow used to it. But it's still a marvel to those who appreciate what it took to build it—and what it takes to manage it."

Claire dropped her eyes for half a second to Liam as he focused on the tower with a steady gaze. So he appreciated the building, then. Who would've thought?

The longer she'd spent with him at Kew Gardens, the more he'd driven her crazy. And yet today, he was being so helpful and nice. She, of course, was also on her best behavior. Maybe the ground rules really were helping them both.

After another few minutes of marveling at Big Ben, the two of them progressed across the street toward Westminster Abbey.

She and Liam didn't speak as they moved through the silent

Quire of the abbey, where dark brown stalls holding red, mushroom-shaped lamps lined the black and white checkered flooring. Claire had only ever seen the sight before on *The Crown* and when she'd watched the royal weddings.

Was it pathetic that the only cool things she'd ever seen had been on TV? Probably. Did she care? She was beginning to.

Pushing the unsettling thought aside, she glanced at Liam, his attention focused on the golden backings of the stalls.

She glanced around, the Quire nearly empty apart from the two of them. In an effort not to dispel the silence of the abbey, she leaned toward him with a soft whisper. "Did you watch the royal weddings?"

He shifted his gaze forward, bending down to whisper back. "They had them televised in the office while I was at work, but I didn't watch them for long." He cast a sidelong glance at her. "I'm guessing you did."

"Of course. Why would I not wish to be a part of history?"

He nodded as they stopped midway down the Quire. "Ah, yes," he responded, turning back to look at the stained-glass windows, "because watching extravagant weddings on television is comparable to having seen Winston Churchill giving a speech or Queen Elizabeth I ascend the throne."

Alright, that *had* to be breaking one of their rules. He was totally making fun of her. And yet, when he looked down at her with that same twinkle in his eye as before, her desire to chastise him faded away.

"Or watching George Washington's inaugural address," she responded in another whisper, raising a knowing brow.

He narrowed his eyes. "Who's that, then?"

She stopped her smile before he could see it. "You know, the great man who led my country to victory over a tyrannical king."

He clicked his tongue as if to scold her. "You'd best be careful what you say here. That very king walked these halls."

Claire paused. Wow. She'd never thought of that before. But

she couldn't admit that the idea actually astounded her. Instead, she gave a playful shrug. "Meh."

"Typical American." Liam's lip twitched, but he looked away before she could see if it turned into a smile.

Their time at the airport flashed through her mind, and her defenses rose, though she did her best not to allow them free rein. She didn't want to lose the progress the two of them had made in the last few hours.

"You know, I've been meaning to ask you about that," she whispered, stepping to the side as a group entered the Quire and walked past them.

"About what?"

"What you have against Americans. You do know your mom is from the States, right?"

He nodded at a passerby before responding. "I have nothing against Americans. Most of them, anyway."

He gave her a sidelong glance, and the playfulness in his eyes knocked down one of the barriers around her heart. Still, he hadn't answered her question, nor had he given her any explanation for his words at the airport or beyond.

They took a few steps forward before she paused again, observing the carving across the ceiling that appeared like bare, stone branches.

"So, with your bias," she continued, "I assume you're Team Kate and not Team Meghan?"

He was silent for a minute. "I never would have cast you as a tabloid reader."

"Ew, what?" She scrunched up her nose. "I'm not. I only follow the royal family to covet their wardrobes."

Again, his lip twitched. Would she finally be rewarded with one of those rare, elusive smiles she'd only seen a handful of times? She was beginning to wonder if she should make it a life goal of hers now—to spot one of Liam Everhart's grins.

No, not just to spot one. To *cause* one.

"So," she prodded, "what team are you on?"

A couple walked past them, pointing in the direction of the golden Quire screen.

Liam leaned slightly closer to her, but not close enough for her to smell his cologne again.

Dang it.

"I'm Team 'It Doesn't Matter,'" he responded. Then he raised a brow. "But I'm sure I can safely assume that you are Team Meghan?"

Claire raised her chin. "Nope."

"Wow. So you chose a Brit over a Yank."

"No. I choose them both."

He stared down at her with an incredulous look. "Both? You can't choose both."

Ignoring how lovely the word "can't" sounded in his accent, she shrugged. "Says who?"

"Says literally everyone. That would be like choosing to cheer on opposing Premier Teams. You can't support both Man United *and* Liverpool."

"Why not?"

His lips parted in shock, and he looked at her as if she'd just sprouted a beard and asked him to call her Santa Claus. Had what she said truly been so crazy?

She shook her head. "I just don't think—"

Her words ended abruptly, cut off by the loudest rendition of "Highway to Hell" she'd ever heard, blaring forth from her phone.

"Oh my heck," she sputtered, pulling out her phone in frantic movements, the sound echoing to the highest reaches of the abbey and bouncing back at her with an even greater force.

In her mad dash to end the most embarrassing phone call of her life, Claire fumbled with the phone before it dropped with an even louder clatter to the floor. She reached down at the same time as Liam, but he swiped it from her hands first and instantly muted the ring.

The deafening silence around them pulsed in Claire's ears

even louder than the music had, and she ducked her head in total and absolute shame as she accepted her phone back from Liam.

He remained silent, giving an apologetic nod to those around them, though their accusatory glances were sent in Claire's direction instead of his.

This was just like the Temperate House all over again. What was going on with her? How could she continually embarrass herself in front of this man over and over and *over* again?

"I gotta get out of here," she said, heat rushing through her body.

They hadn't seen half of what the abbey had to offer, but she couldn't bear to remain inside a moment longer.

To her relief, Liam followed after her in silence as they left the church and stepped out into the cold air, standing near a tree with its lower half covered in ivy.

Pressing her face into her hands, Claire shook her head. "I cannot believe that just happened."

She never—*never*—had her phone off vibrate. How could she have been so stupid as to not remember that she'd set it to its loudest volume in case Melody called? And to have it go off in an abbey, of all places. With that song, of all songs.

Liam remained at her side in silence, though she knew he was probably dying to make fun of her again. He had every right to. She was a total idiot.

Groaning, she dropped her hands in surrender. What did it matter if he saw her blush? He'd seen it a thousand times before—at Kew gardens, in his bed, at the airport. "Fine. I give up."

He eyed her curiously.

"Go on." She waved her hands in his direction. "I know you've got a million things to say. Out with it."

He didn't move, his face unreadable as he finally spoke. "Big fan of hard rock?"

She didn't know what she'd expected him to say, but his response—for one reason or another—quelled her embarrassment enough for the humor of the situation to finally burst through her disgrace.

She let out a chuckle, then more laughter rolled forward like the waves of the sea until she pressed her cold hands against her cheeks to cool down. "Ugh," she breathed, dabbing at the laughter-induced tears from her eyes. "What a total disaster."

She glanced up at Liam, and her heart tripped.

There it was, that smile. Liam's entire face had shifted, softened from his usual glower or serious expression to one of utter delight.

His eyebrows had raised, and smile lines appeared at the edges of his eyes, giving him a boyish look. More than anything, though, she was captured by the brilliant smile that stretched across his lips in the most gorgeous way she'd ever seen. She hadn't thought the man could be any more attractive than he already was, but that smile had just proven her wrong. Dead wrong.

Alright. So this guy wasn't that bad. Even if he didn't appreciate flowers like he should.

"For what it's worth," he said, "that's a fine song choice for a ringtone."

Why did his approval raise her spirits? "I set it for when Melody calls."

His smile grew. "I don't think I've ever heard of a song more appropriate for her."

She laughed. "Just not appropriate for an abbey."

She could have sworn she'd heard him laugh, but only his eyes smiled now.

Tearing her gaze away from him—which was basically the hardest thing she'd ever had to do in her life—she stared down at her phone with condemning eyes.

"I guess I better call her back. Maybe she's feeling better and wants us to come get her."

A flash of disappointment echoed in her chest, but Claire swiftly shoved it away in confusion. Melody always made everything a thousand times more fun with her enthusiasm. Why would Claire *not* want her to join them?

Her return phone call went straight to voicemail, and Claire paused. Maybe she was on the other line.

Next, she pulled up her messages and sent a quick text.

Claire: Hey, are you okay? Sorry I missed your call. We were inside Westminster Abbey. Do you need anything? Want us to come back?

As soon as she sent the message, however, her phone buzzed again as she received a voicemail.

"Oh, this is from her," Claire said, lifting it up to listen.

Instead of any words, silence sounded, then a great snore tore through the speakers.

She sniffed out a laugh. "Ah, lovely."

Liam looked at her with a question in his eyes.

She gave him the phone to listen himself, and he put it to his ear, a half-smile on his lips forming when he heard the snoring, too. "Yeah, there's no mistaking that snore, is there?"

She took her phone back, turning it off and tucking it into her pocket. "She must have been playing on her phone, then fell asleep with it unlocked."

Liam shrugged, seeming to accept Claire's guess. "We can still head back if you'd like. Or we could get a bite to eat first. See if she responds by then."

Claire hesitated. They really should be getting back, especially since her list of sights was all but accomplished. Then again, Melody had expressly told them to stay out for as long as they wanted—that she couldn't tolerate any food. And Claire *was* starving, as it was nearing half past one.

"Yeah, let's eat some lunch first," she said, setting aside her looming guilt. "Melody will probably be up soon, then she can let us know how she is."

Together, they moved down the pathway away from the

abbey until Big Ben became visible once again through the spindly branches of the trees.

"Anything you fancy?" Liam asked.

Maybe they should've gone back home. Being around Liam's accent was chipping away at her resolve to not find everything he said entertaining, adorable, and downright extraordinary. If only she could bottle it up and pop it open whenever she was feeling sad.

"I think I saw a Pizza Hut down the road," she responded.

He gave her an odd look.

"What?" she asked. "Do you have something against Pizza Hut, too?"

"No. But there is a time and a place for Pizza Hut. Your first meal in the center of London is not that time nor that place."

Seriously. Everything he said. Adorable.

They passed by a perfectly symmetrical Christmas tree in the courtyard of the Houses of Parliament, a white star perched on the top.

"Alright, then if it's not Pizza Hut, where are we gonna go?"

"Greggs."

"Greggs," she repeated. "And what is Greggs?"

"They're a bakery chain."

She raised her brow, imagining a quaint shop with pastries, colorful tables to sit at, and white chef hats.

"We're having baked goods for lunch?" She could get behind that.

They stopped at the side of the road, *"Look Left"* written in bold letters at their feet.

He led the way forward across the street. "There's more to a bakery than donuts and eclairs."

How that was possible, Claire didn't know. But what she did know was that whatever this Greggs was, she couldn't wait to try it out—especially if it was charming-Englishman-approved.

ELEVEN

THIS WAS GREGGS?

Claire glanced around the small, rectangular shop, raising an eyebrow. She'd been imagining something cozy and quaint, a quintessential bakery. But this looked like nothing more than a miniature grocery store.

The flooring was broken up into black and white checkers on one side and light, slanted wood on the other. Refrigerators lined the back of the store, holding various drinks, sandwiches, and salads, while the other side of the shop displayed stands with plain baguettes and a wide variety of chips.

It was clean, she'd give it that. And the smell inside *was* fantastic. But Liam had made it sound like a high-end, not-to-be-missed bakery. This had to be just a fast-food joint.

"This is better than a Pizza Hut?" she asked as they joined the line that stretched to the back end of the store.

He nodded. "Trust me."

Claire hmphed under her breath. Trust him? She barely knew him. She'd been disappointed by people she'd known for years, all of whom she should have been able to rely on. Why would he be any different?

The line behind them grew as they inched forward across the

shop. Apparently, everyone in London had had the same idea to eat lunch there that afternoon. The food couldn't be that bad if there were this many people here to eat it, right? Then again, there were some fast-food chains that always had eternal lines that spoke *nothing* of the value of their food.

"So what's good here?" she asked.

"Nearly everything," Liam responded. "I'd recommend getting one of the savory pastries at the front."

Claire peered past the line to where the cashiers stood behind glass pastry displays decorated with snowflake window clings. The pastries did look appetizing with their glistening, golden crusts. But then, who knew what was inside each one? She wasn't crazy mistrusting of foreign food, but what if they held some weird British concoction she couldn't stomach, or what if she ended up with food poisoning like Tasha and Melody?

Pulling her lips to the side, Claire glanced to the refrigerated sandwiches instead. Those would probably be her best bet— something that let her see exactly what she was eating.

She glanced at each one, trying to decide what looked the safest.

"Excuse me, are you in the queue?" a woman behind her asked.

Claire glanced to where the woman motioned forward, only then noticing the line having moved past the refrigerators.

"Oh, yeah. Sorry."

Without thinking for fear of embarrassing herself again, Claire swiped the sandwich that looked the most neutral, grabbed a bag of chips and a bottle of water, then stepped up behind Liam.

He must have heard her movements, as he turned around in the next moment and settled his eyes on the sandwich.

"What did you decide on, then?" he asked.

"Um." She held up her stash. "A sandwich and chips."

His brow furrowed. "You'll enjoy the crisps enough, but you

won't like that sandwich. You'll be better off putting it back and getting something else up front."

The line shifted again, and he faced forward without another word.

Claire frowned at the back of his head. Why did he do that, speak so authoritatively? Just when she was starting to like him—or tolerate him, rather—he had to go and speak all high and mightily.

"How do you know I won't like"—she paused, looking down to read the ingredients as the line moved forward again—"rye bread, mature cheddar, and Branston pickle?"

Truth be told, she didn't know what half those ingredients were. But she liked cheese as much as the next person, rye bread most likely tasted like wheat, and Branston pickle probably resembled dill pickles, which she enjoyed, as well.

Yeah, she'd be totally fine with this sandwich.

Liam, however, wasn't convinced. "You won't like it because you don't enjoy shrimp."

She paused, wrinkling her nose at the angled container the diagonally cut sandwich rested in. "Wait, this has shrimp in it?" Then another thought occurred. "And how do you know I don't like shrimp?"

Had he heard her admit as much the night before?

"No, it doesn't have shrimp in it." He clarified. "And I know you don't like shrimp for the simple fact that you are out here with me instead of being sick all over my mum's house."

Oh. That made sense. "So that means you don't like shrimp either?"

He nodded. "I never trust anything so transparent. Person or otherwise."

His smiling eyes almost made her forget all about how annoyed she was with him. Almost.

He faced forward again. "We seem to have similar tastes in food, which is how I know you won't enjoy that Branston pickle sandwich. You'll regret not putting it back. Just as you'll regret not getting one of the hot pastries."

Ugh. There was nothing worse than a person thinking he knew her better than she knew herself.

Gripping her sandwich tighter, she raised her chin. "I think I'll take my chances, thank you."

Liam merely shrugged, then approached the cashier to purchase his food.

As he ordered what she could only assume were his blessed savory pastries, Claire became distracted with the other side of the glass window, where donuts, cookies, and muffins were presented in neat, enticing rows—biscuits with a tree cutout on the top, cupcakes with red, white, and green frosting, and mince pies she'd never eaten but had only read about in Regency books.

Well, if she didn't like her sandwich—which she would if it was the last thing she did—at least she'd have something sweet as a backup.

After Liam finished his purchase and told Claire he'd wait at the door for her, Claire moved forward with her less-than-appetizing food.

"Will this be all for you, ma'am?" a young man with a London accent asked.

"No, can I also get a..." She paused, reading out the descriptions of the pastries on the red, snowflake-covered sign. "Christmas ring bun?" Would Liam want one? Or would he think a cupcake with a plastic ring on it childish? "Actually, can I get two of those?" Better to be safe than sorry.

After purchasing her food, she turned to meet up with Liam, catching a glimpse of a square pizza slice amidst all the other savory pastries. Dang it. If she hadn't been so prideful, she could've bought that instead of her rye sandwich.

Scolding herself for already proving Liam's words right about her regret, she found him standing near the doorway.

"Ready?" he asked, motioning for her to go first.

Together, the two of them made their way down the street

across from Big Ben, Claire taking extra care not to become so distracted by the beautiful sight to be left behind.

Deciding to brave the cold instead of finding a crowded place indoors to eat, they followed the busy pathway along the Thames, passing by a red telephone booth.

Claire eyed it longingly. That would be one picture she'd be sure to get without it having to be a selfie—but she'd save it for when she and Melody were together.

Moving past the bridge and makeshift booths, they finally found an empty bench at the side of the road facing the river. She walked up the two steps of the stone pedestal—which the bench was fitted on to see above the barrier to the river—then settled on the far side of the bench.

The cold from the seat instantly filtered through her pants, so she crossed her legs to warm up at least one thigh. The air was bitingly cold, but the sun beaming through the leafless branches of the trees above warmed her shoulders enough to take the edge off of the brisk breeze.

Liam sat down beside her, a foot of distance between them as he rifled through his bag of food. Claire did the same, looking up at the view from the bench as she did so. The London Eye was situated almost directly across from them, the perfectly circular observation wheel vibrantly white in the early afternoon light. Claire glanced to her right, where Big Ben was only just visible through the bare trees, and she shook her head again, amazed that she was actually sitting here for lunch.

"One day, Claire Bear, we'll tour around all the big cities together," her parents had promised when she was just a child. *"London, Prague, Rome, Paris. It'll be a dream."*

It was a dream. But she never would have thought she'd be living out that dream without her parents.

"How's your sandwich?" Liam asked.

Claire refocused her attention on the present, looking to Liam, who'd already tucked into his lunch. The muscles in his jaw flinched pleasantly as he took another bite, steam wafting up from the pastry into the cold air.

She cleared her throat. "Oh, I haven't tasted it yet." And she didn't want to at all. Would it be bad if she just went straight for her ring buns?

She glanced to Liam as he took another bite of his food. The scent made her stomach growl. Did it taste as good as it smelled? "How's your...What is that?"

He swallowed, raising his pastry. "Sausage roll."

She nodded, turning away before she could catch another whiff of the food that already smelled better than hers looked.

With a deep breath, she rooted out her meal and peeled back the plastic covering to the sandwich. No delectable scent tickled her nose. That was not a good sign.

With uncertain fingers, she lifted the sandwich, doing her best not to eye it warily before taking a bite.

Instantly, an overpowering assortment of spices, sweet-and-sour-something, and an odd crunch invaded her mouth. There could be only one culprit for such a taste. Branston pickle—which turned out not to be a regular pickle at all. Of course. Of course this would be disgusting.

She managed only three chews before swallowing hard and ending in a barely muted shudder.

"I did warn you," Liam said from her side.

She looked over at him, annoyed with herself for not being able to hide her disgust. "What are you talking about? This is amazing."

"Then let's see you take another bite."

Claire would rather jump in the frozen Thames. "I will in a minute. I just want to savor what I've already eaten."

He blew out a quick breath through his nose in a sort of scoff. "You're a terrible liar."

She eyed him for a minute, considering continuing in her lies before she looked back at the sandwich. What was the point of lying about it? Such food didn't deserve any false praise.

"Fine," she said. "I give up. It's awful."

Liam smiled with his mouth closed as he chewed, then swallowed. "It's the relish. I've heard it's an acquired taste, though I have yet to acquire it myself."

She eyed her sandwich again with as much disdain as her stomach was sure to be feeling right now, having to actually house a bite of the disgusting food.

With tentative fingers, she peeled off the top piece of bread. She couldn't live off of chips and a cupcake for lunch, so she'd need to salvage whatever she could of this sandwich if she was going to have enough energy to get back to Tasha's house.

"What are you doing?" Liam asked as she used the plastic edge of the container to scrape off a bit of the relish.

"Trying to make this somewhat edible."

His eyes remained on her task. "There's no need." He rummaged through his bag for a minute, then produced a small, white paper bag with Greggs's four-square logo on the center of it. "You can have this."

"What?" She pulled back. "No, I'm not going to eat your food. I've got plenty."

"It's alright. I purchased this one specifically for you."

Had he really been that confident that she wouldn't like the sandwich? Obviously, he had. She stopped leaning back, though she still didn't reach for the bag. What had he bought for her?

"Go on. You'll like this one."

As he wiggled the bag up and down, the scent caused the hunger ache in her stomach to grow until finally, she relented with a sigh and accepted the bag from him.

"Thank you," she mumbled, her fingers warming instantly from the hot pastry.

She set it in the center of her lap, cleaning up her now-deconstructed sandwich. Pausing, she held it up for Liam. "I don't suppose you'd like any of this?"

His eyes gleamed. "I think I'll pass, but thank you for such a generous offer."

She grinned, tucking away her garbage before finally peeking into the white bag Liam had given her.

"So what is this?" she asked, eying the square, flat pastry with suspicion.

"Shrimp."

TWELVE

Instantly, Claire's eyes flew to Liam's, but the smile he tried to hide amidst his chews gave away his teasing instantly. Staring out at the Thames, he finished off the last of his pastry before continuing.

"It's a Sausage, Bean, and Cheese Melt. Very neutral tasting. Very safe for your American tongue."

She ignored another teasing look. "It's not going to give me food poisoning, is it?"

This time, it was his turn to give her a glance of annoyance. "No, it will not," he said firmly.

He reached into his bag and pulled out the same pastry for himself. Claire watched him take a bite before finally doing the same with her own.

Instantly, the flavor of the baked beans and cheese filled her mouth with warmth and a happy, homemade flavor. A soothing heat filtered through her body an inch at a time, a pleasant contrast to the cold air nipping at her limbs.

If the inside of Greggs didn't appear like a typical, cozy bakery, the food certainly made her feel like she had been in one anyway.

"It's nice, isn't it?" Liam said.

She eyed the warm beans inside the pastry from where she'd taken her bite. "It kills me to admit it, but yeah. This is amazing." Then she dove in for more. "I will say, though, the name is pretty unimaginative."

"It's British," he defended. "Straightforward. To the point."

She swallowed another bite. "In America, it'd probably be called something like the Big, Cheesy, Half-Pound Melt Meal."

He gave a short laugh, but she missed the sight of it as he wiped his mouth with a napkin.

The two of them sat together in silence, watching tourists take pictures of one another at the edge of the concrete barrier to the river where a ferry ambled down the brown water. Claire couldn't deny the strange sense of peace settling over her as she sat there with Liam. She'd been picturing the worst day ever with him, and now...was she actually enjoying herself?

"Was the Eye part of your plan for today?" Liam asked as he finished off the last of his melt, crumpling up his paper as he motioned across the river.

"No, we hadn't planned on it," Claire responded, crossing her legs at the ankles and bouncing them to get some warmth into her. "Melody said it was a waste of time."

"I figured as much," Liam said, still looking at the Eye. "We went once as children, and she was clawing at the walls to get out. She can never stay in the same place for long."

Claire smiled. "Yeah, she hasn't changed at all. I guess that's why she's the life of the party wherever she goes. And what makes her good at her job."

"Is she still working as an event coordinator?"

Claire nodded.

"I assume she loves it as much as you love your job?"

Claire glanced to him, finding his gaze on her. He'd remembered her saying that she liked her work?

"I think she does," she responded.

He nodded, looking out across the water again. This time, his eyes lost their mirth as they took on a faraway look, focusing on something in the distance.

Claire narrowed her eyes. His mood had changed so abruptly, just like in the car to the gardens. Was it talking about jobs that always got him down?

"What about you?" she asked, wanting to test out her own theory. "Do you love your job?"

His jaw twitched, and he took a moment to respond. "I used to."

Claire wasn't sure what to say. Clearly, for one reason or another, his work was a taboo subject. Had it always been, or only just recently?

"You're a producer, you said?" she asked, hoping to pull information from him in a roundabout way.

He nodded.

So much for getting more out of him.

"And what does that entail?" she asked.

He drew a deep breath, still staring in the distance. "I essentially do all the work required to create a production our company has been hired out to do."

"That sounds exciting."

He continued in a soft tone, his eyes still captivated by something over the river. "I thought the same when I first started. But now, it's just ..." He ended in a shrug.

"A grind?" she guessed.

"Exactly."

She grimaced. She had no idea what that would feel like. Her job was exhausting but rewarding. She wouldn't be able to handle doing something for a living that made her utterly miserable.

"That's where I work," Liam said, motioning across the river. "The tall glass building to the left of the Eye."

Claire followed his gaze to the structure in the distance. "Wow, your view must be incredible."

"It is. But I spend most of my time traveling or in meetings on the lower floors, so I hardly get to enjoy it."

She studied him for a minute, trying to understand him. She had a myriad of questions floating through her mind—Why did he work somewhere he was so miserable? Why didn't he just quit? What was it exactly that he hated?—but before she could ask a single one, he clapped his hands on his thighs.

"Ready to go on?" he asked.

She hesitated, wanting to pry more into his life, but she nodded all the same.

After cleaning up their lunch, Claire tossed her good-for-nothing sandwich in the garbage bin to the side of the platform, then stepped down and spooked off a few pigeons who had wandered toward them during their meal.

"So which way is Trafalgar?" she asked.

He pointed to the street in the opposite direction of Big Ben. "That way. But don't you want to see a better view of Big Ben first?"

Not realizing there *was* a better view, Claire instantly agreed. She didn't think she could ever be tired of seeing the structure.

As they made their way back up along the Thames, Claire raised a finger. "Oh, let me know how much the sausage-bean-cheesy-melty thing was so I can pay you for it."

He shook his head. "It's no trouble."

"Are you sure?" she asked, furrowing her brow.

He nodded, but Claire wasn't about to agree. Instead, she pulled out one of the buns from her extra grocery bag and extended it to him. "Fine. Take this as payment then."

He was about to protest when she thrust it toward him. "I bought another one for me, too."

Finally, he accepted the bun, and together, they removed their cupcakes from the wrappers and enjoyed them as they walked.

Claire took the nickel-sized Santa head ring off of the bun first, then took a bite through the red, white, and green sprinkles. Instantly, the sweetness infused her tastebuds, and she smiled.

"Alright," she said after swallowing, "I'm officially a Greggs convert."

"Glad to have you join."

"Although I think they should definitely consider giving up selling those sandwiches."

His eyes shone in response.

As they passed by more crowds of tourists and traversed down Westminster Bridge, Claire realized that once again, Liam was right. This view *was* better. They stopped midway across the bridge and turned around to see the Houses of Parliament stretched out behind the clock tower, Big Ben leading the way forward like a stalwart officer.

She pulled out her phone and snapped a few pictures before glancing to Liam, the wind biting at her exposed fingertips. Would he ever turn away long enough for her to take a quick selfie?

Instead of turning away, however, he faced her with an outstretched hand. "Alright, let's see your phone."

She eyed him. "Why?"

"Because I've seen you take about a hundred selfies today, and you deserve at least one photo with the whole of a building inside of it."

Claire's lips parted. Well, that was just great. So much for being sneaky—and so much for not embarrassing herself again.

He wiggled his fingers for her phone once more, and she awkwardly relented before taking a few steps back toward the wall of the bridge.

Liam backed up a few paces, as well, turning the phone on its side.

Claire wasn't sure why she suddenly couldn't remember how to smile naturally. Could it have something to do with the fact that Liam's eyes were focused solely on her?

"There," he said, looking at the phone. "That one ought to work."

Claire took a step toward him, glad she'd gotten that over with before a short, middle-aged woman came up to Liam with a warm grin.

"Would you two like one together?" she asked, her knitted cap hanging halfway off her head.

Claire froze as Liam's glance skirted from her back to the woman. "Oh, no thank you."

But the woman held out her hand for the phone. "Come on, then. You'll regret not having one together with such a lovely girlfriend."

"Oh, she's not my..." Liam stammered. "We're not..."

Claire watched him become more and more flustered. Well, this was new.

Oddly enough, the more uncomfortable he grew, the more Claire's confidence solidified. With an amused grin, she took the phone from Liam's hand and placed it in the woman's.

"We would love one together," she said. "Thank you."

She grabbed Liam's arm and pulled him toward the wall of the bridge once again.

"Sorry," Liam mumbled as he stood rigidly beside her.

Claire only smiled all the wider.

The woman looked at the phone, then shook her head. "Closer," she said, motioning for Liam to stand nearer to Claire.

Liam blew out a breath, taking a minuscule step toward her.

"Closer, luv," the woman said again.

"Just take the picture," Liam mumbled under his breath.

Claire laughed. "Come on," she said, sliding her arm under his and around his back. "She's not going to let up until you come closer."

He hesitated only a moment before draping his arm over Claire's shoulders, then all at once, her confidence vanished.

"What a lovely couple," the woman said to herself as she took the picture.

Claire's mouth dried. Her heart hammered against her chest as if she'd just sprinted through the whole of London, heat pooling throughout her body. With the weight of Liam's arm around her shoulders, the press of his fingers against her upper arm, and the smell of his tantalizing cologne wafting beneath her nose, she could no longer breathe.

She never should have pulled him toward her. But then, how was she to know she'd have this reaction to Liam—*Liam*, of all people. The guy who'd been so rude to her at the airport, who'd made fun of her over and over again, who...who had given up an entire day to take her around London just so she wouldn't get lost. Who had laughed with her and bought her lunch and took her photo when she wasn't brave enough to ask.

"There you go," the woman said, finally lowering the phone and offering it back to Claire.

She and Liam pulled apart, and Claire took the phone with a gracious smile before the woman departed, leaving Claire and Liam to their own, silent discomfort.

Had he possibly felt the same pull to her as she had to him? The same quickening heartbeat and shallow breathing?

Swiftly, she rid herself of the absurd notion. Why would *he* be attracted to *her*?

As if to prove her point, Liam stifled a yawn, averted his gaze, and tucked his hands into his coat pockets. "To Trafalgar Square, then?"

She nodded, and the two of them made their way back across the bridge, the cold wind across the Thames no longer bothering her as heat continued to pulse through her body.

If only the bean and cheese melt had been the cause of such heat because she was all too aware of who the real culprit was.

THIRTEEN

After Trafalgar, Liam returned home with Claire to a quiet house. She gave a quick wave in departure, then slipped up the steps to her room, leaving Liam downstairs to edit a few of his photos from Kew Gardens, though his mind continually traveled over the last few hours he'd spent with Claire.

He was surprised by how much he'd enjoyed his time with her. They *had* both been on their best behavior, but toward the end of their day out, he'd begun to see what he believed to be was the true Claire Frost.

He smiled again at the memory of her song choice blaring out across the abbey, and the way her lips had twisted at her first taste of Branston pickle. He had to admit, she was a lot of fun to tease.

But then, that was the problem, wasn't it? He shouldn't be having fun with anyone. That would just make it all the harder to go back to the mundanity of his job next week.

Today would have to be the anomaly. And tonight, well, he would take part in simpler activities—updating his photography page, watching movies, going to bed early. All the things that wouldn't be too difficult to say goodbye to once work started again.

Getting an early start on his so-called "simpler activities,"

Liam popped up to his room for a quick kip, waking up in the late afternoon to voices downstairs.

Following the sound, he found Mum, Melody, and Claire in the sitting room.

All three women looked at him as he came around the corner, but his gaze settled on Claire first. She sat on the couch opposite his mum and cousin, her blue eyes peering up at him, her thick, blonde hair draped over one shoulder, just as it had when they'd been forced to take that photo together.

Claire had fit far too perfectly in the crook of his arm—and her long curls had smelt far too much like flowers—for it to do him any good.

"There you are, Liam," his mum greeted with a weakened smile. "We were wondering when you were going to come down."

Liam could count on one hand the number of times he'd seen his mum sick. Even when she'd become ill when he was a boy, she'd still wake up to make his school lunches and be ready when he came home to listen to how his day had gone.

"How are you two feeling?" he asked, noting Mum's face had regained its color while Melody's had faded to an even lighter pallid.

Melody mumbled incoherently, shifting to the side and clutching her stomach.

Mum smiled compassionately before responding. "I'm feeling better than Melody." Then she motioned to Claire. "We were just listening to Claire recount the day you had together. It sounds like you were able to see everything on the list."

He moved farther into the room, sitting on the arm of the couch Claire occupied, a few feet still between them. "Yes, we were on a very tight schedule."

Claire glanced up at him but remained silent. Ah, so she only had the courage to speak to him when the others weren't around.

"So what will you be seeing tomorrow, then?" his mum asked next.

Liam's eyes snapped to Claire's. Tomorrow? Had he been roped into spending all of tomorrow with her, too?

"The museums," Claire responded. "So long as Melody is feeling up to it."

Something akin to relief—or was it disappointment?—rushed through him. So Claire and Melody would be spending the day together tomorrow, not Claire and Liam.

Melody groaned, drawing the attention to her again. "I hope I feel better. I can't handle another day like this."

Liam looked at his cousin, her face still white with bags under her eyes. "What are you talking about, Mel? You look much better than this morning. Very...chipper."

Melody rolled her eyes toward him. "If by looking 'chipper,' you mean that the fluids are only coming out of one end of me instead of two, then yes. I am feeling chipper." Then she closed her eyes and groaned. "Speaking of, if any of you need to go to the bathroom, go now, or you'll have to wait a half hour for me to be done with it."

Liam grimaced, catching Claire's cringing eye. Unable to help himself, he leaned toward her, whispering, ""Highway to Hell," indeed."

To his delight, Claire pressed a hand to her mouth, stifling a laugh, but it still sounded at the back of her throat. Liam fought a smile as his mum and Melody both looked up at him.

"What?" Melody asked, glancing between him and Claire.

Liam stood, moving to the adjoining kitchen. "I was just asking what the plan is for tea."

"Ugh, nothing," Melody said, flapping her head back against the couch. "Everything sounds disgusting."

"So you'd take issue with my making a bacon butty, then?"

Melody made a gagging noise, but Claire looked up at him, smiling at his teasing.

It had been a long time since he'd been able to make someone smile. He'd forgotten how good it felt. At work, he was too busy getting productions completed and putting out figurative fires to do much joking at all.

"I'm with Melody, I think," his mum responded, shifting on the couch so her back was no longer turned to him. "You and Claire could always go out to eat, though."

Alarm bells rang inside of him. He was supposed to have already done his duty with Claire. Was he really going to be roped into spending the evening with her now?

He closed the fridge, averting his eyes. "I wouldn't want to leave you and Melody out. What if I picked something up that we all wanted, then we could eat it together here."

Claire was looking at him. He could feel it. But he wouldn't meet her gaze.

"No, seriously," Melody said, exhaling heavily as she stood from the couch and faced him. "I'm not eating tonight, so you and Claire can do whatever. Now, if you'll excuse me, I have an appointment with the toilet." She wandered down the hallway, murmuring to herself along the way. "If I haven't lost at least ten pounds by the end of this, I'm going to be livid."

Mum stood with slightly less dramatic flair. "I really feel the same way," she said, pressing a hand against her stomach. "I don't have much of an appetite right now. And," she paused, looking over her shoulder before continuing in a lower voice, "I think anything you bring back here will just set Melody off. She is still feeling awful." Mum shifted her gaze to Claire. "She ate so much of that shrimp."

"Seriously pounded them," Claire responded with a grin.

They shared a quiet laugh, and Liam glanced between them just as Claire caught his gaze.

Blast. He wasn't supposed to be looking at her. He didn't want her to see how desperately he was trying to get out of spending more time with her.

It wasn't that he didn't want to. He just enjoyed it too much.

"Really," his mum continued, looking back at Liam, "you won't be leaving us out. I'm headed to bed, and as soon Melody's done with her *appointment*, I'm sure she'll be going back to sleep, too." She glanced to Claire. "Go have some fun, alright? Someone might as well."

Then she moved to the hallway without another word, leaving Liam to stand mutely in the kitchen.

Claire stood, straightening the cushions that had shifted on the couch. "You don't have to feel obligated to take me to dinner, you know."

Liam cleared his throat, pulling on a look of sincerity. "I don't feel obligated."

She scoffed. "I saw your face, Liam. It's fine. You spent all day with me. You don't need to spend the night with me, too."

He raised a brow. "Spend the night with you? I could be wrong, but I believe that's beyond the scope of what my mum suggested."

Her cheeks pinked exactly as he'd hoped they would.

"You know what I meant," she said. She slipped her phone into her back pocket, then pulled on her soft pink coat.

He hesitated. He'd obviously offended her by not wanting to go out to eat with her. It was a shame, really, after the progress they'd made that day. "What are you going to eat, then?"

Shrugging, she secured the coat buttons. "Pizza Hut?"

Her suggestion produced a laugh before he had the chance to check it, and she smiled in response.

"No, I'll find somewhere else that's closer," she continued. "I'll see you later."

As she walked alone down the hallway, Liam's stomach turned at his own selfishness. This woman had traveled all the way to England to spend time with her friend who was now bedridden. Was he really going to make her eat alone?

With a stifled sigh, he followed her to the door. "Alright, we'll go together. If only I can be sure you really don't eat at Pizza Hut."

"No, it's okay, really," Claire said, holding up her hand as he put on his own coat. "I don't want you to feel obligated to—"

"I don't," he interrupted. "We both need to eat. We may as well go together."

She eyed him hesitantly. "Are you sure?"

He opened the door, then motioned for her to precede him. "I am."

And he was. Because as much as he didn't think it would be wise to spend more time with Claire, he refused to do anything that would require him to apologize to her again.

He'd had enough of that to last a lifetime.

FOURTEEN

AFTER A QUICK DISCUSSION ABOUT WHERE TO EAT THE fish and chips Claire was anxious to try, the two of them took the Underground toward the center of London.

"It's about a thirty-minute ride without delays," Liam said as they settled down beside each other on the black-cushioned chairs of the train.

Claire nodded, biting her lip to keep from smiling as the train whooshed ahead to the next station. She would never grow tired of traveling this way.

"You know you don't have to hide your fascination from me."

She swung her gaze toward Liam, a knowing look in his eyes. Honestly, she shouldn't have been surprised that he'd seen her excitement. After all, he'd noticed when she'd snuck selfies and cringed at her sandwich. Why wouldn't he notice this, too?

"I just didn't want you to have yet another thing to make fun of me for," she defended.

His brow twitched. "Why would I make fun of you for enjoying riding the Tube?"

She shrugged. "Because I'm so uncultured to have never ridden anything like it before."

His eyes searched hers for a moment, narrowing slightly

before he looked away. "I don't think you're uncultured. If anything, it makes me like you more."

Claire stiffened, a warmth blossoming from her heart like a crocus breaking through the cold, winter snow. He...liked her?

No. No, he probably meant that he just liked her as a person, nothing more.

Shaking her head at her nonsense, Claire trained her gaze on the darkness rushing by the window. She needed to be careful. Liam's smooth voice seemed to always put her in a silly trance, making her think things she would never normally consider.

"Mind the gap between the train and the platform," the male voice spoke overhead as the train slowed to a stop.

A few more passengers filtered in, taking the open seats down the row from them before the doors closed.

"So are you enjoying your time in England so far?" Liam asked as the train whooshed ahead.

"Oh, absolutely. My parents always told me how amazing it was here, so it's nice to see it for myself finally."

"Your parents have been before, then?"

Dang it. She hadn't meant to bring them up.

Gluing on the typical smile she always wore when speaking of her mom and dad, Claire nodded. "Yeah, they used to travel everywhere on business, but England was always one of their favorites."

"Wise people, your parents," Liam joked.

Claire smiled, though frustration snapped in her chest like flames popping in a fireplace. She shouldn't have made them sound so good to him. But then, wasn't that what she wanted, to hide how life really was growing up with absentee parents? Anyway, that was a long time ago, and since then, she'd grown into a well-adjusted adult, despite it all.

Or so she liked to think.

"What do they do for work?" Liam asked next, leaning forward to remove his coat.

She leaned farther away from him, though her eyes locked

onto his shoulders that worked beneath the thin fabric of his button-up shirt.

"Um," she said, her mind growing fuzzy as his cologne clouded around in delicious wafts from heaven. Was she floating to the top of the train, or was his scent just that intoxicating?

Liam leaned back in his chair, resting his coat against his legs and brushing hers in the process.

Her breathing stinted. What had he asked? Right, her parents. That would bring her back down to earth. "They started up their own data analysis company after I was born, traveling all over the world to do consultant work for other businesses. They retired a few years ago, though."

"Which is why they're on a cruise."

"Yep. They really like going during Christmas. That's where they've spent the last three Christmases, actually."

Liam glanced at her. "*They've* spent their Christmases on cruises?"

Freaking—There was another stupid slip. She shrugged flippantly. "Yeah, well, I don't really like cruises all that much. I went with them last year and was sick the entire time even with meds, so I didn't really want to go again."

"The next station is Shepherd's Bush Market."

The train slowed, and Claire crossed her legs away from Liam, leaning against the side of the chair to avoid pressing into him.

"Did your parents know you were sick?" Liam asked.

"Oh, yeah," she said with a little laugh. "I could barely leave my bed."

"So did you choose to come to England after they had already decided to go on the cruise?"

"Yeah, they'd been planning to go for months."

He was quiet for a minute, the tram's squeaking and jingling marking the air before he spoke again. "So...they knew you wouldn't be able to go with them, and they still chose to go?"

Claire cringed, hearing the question behind his words—the question he really wanted to ask.

Your parents didn't care enough about you to spend Christmas with you?

She rushed to explain, desperate not to sound so pathetic that her own parents didn't want to be with her. "It's no big deal. We've actually spent more Christmases apart than we have together, so..."

Oh, perfect. That made her sound *much* better.

"The next station is Latimer Road."

"Mind the gap between the train and the platform."

Liam stared at her with a curious eye, but to her relief, he didn't push her for more information. She struggled to concoct another topic of conversation, but as the train rushed from station to station, the two sat in continued silence. As was always the case with her parents being mentioned in conversation, Claire's mind was blank, a shattered vase below wilted flowers.

"The next station is Paddington."

When the doors opened again, a large group filtered onto the train, filling the rest of the seats and the center aisle. The warning beeps sounded, and the last passengers managed to slip on just before the doors closed. A woman with a swelling belly and a toddler clasping onto her legs glanced around for a place to sit, taking hold of the bar near the doorway to prepare for the train's launch.

Within a matter of seconds, Liam stood and motioned for the woman to take his seat. With a relieved smile and a quick, "Thank you," she sat down beside Claire.

Claire glanced up at Liam, who focused straight ahead, as if he hadn't just done the most benevolent thing in the world.

The woman's toddler tapped her mom's leg, and Claire listened as she whispered in the most adorable accent she'd ever heard. "Mummy, I want to sit on my own chair."

"I know, poppet, but there aren't any left."

The little girl pressed her lips bravely together, doing her best to stop her tears, but Claire's heart twisted.

"Would you like my seat?" she asked, leaning forward with a friendly smile.

The little girl shied behind her mom, though she delivered a tiny nod.

"Oh, you don't have to move," the mother said with a hand to her belly.

But Claire was already scooting forward. "It's totally fine."

The woman smiled graciously once again, then Claire stood. As the mother helped the toddler into the seat, Claire glanced around for a rod to hold onto, surprised at how swiftly the carriage had filled up at just one station.

Nearby, Liam motioned her forward, shifting to the side and raising his hand farther up the bar to allow her more room.

"Thanks," she said, careful to place her hand a good foot away from his.

He nodded in silence, then Claire caught him smiling at the little girl with a quick wink before he focused straight ahead again.

Looking away, Claire did her best to breathe in the other less-than-pleasant smells around her, instead of Liam's intoxicating scent which shifted toward her like the pleasant waves of the sea.

"The next station is Edgeware Road."

Thank heavens. The train would be sure to empty then.

But of course, the opposite happened as more people pushed and prodded their way into the carriage. Liam shifted his hand from holding the rod to grasping onto the loops above their heads. His arm flexed, the muscles pressing into the folds of his sleeve, and the top of his clavicle became visible as his shirt popped open near the collar—just as it had at the airport. Only this time, she had a perfect, prolonged view.

Claire blew out a slow breath. Alright, so she was just going to resign herself to death by attraction, was that it?

She focused her gaze on the floor as the train sped forward, her feet braced apart to avoid any movement.

The stations had always seemed so close to one another, but by the time the next was called, an eternity had passed.

"The next station is Baker Street."

"Mind the gap between the train and the platform."

If only Claire *could* mind the gap and get off this freaking train.

She closed her eyes. Okay, she was being dumb. Yes, she was insanely attracted to Liam—his silent confidence and caring behavior. But that didn't mean she couldn't stand next to him without losing her cool, right?

But as the train stopped again and more people filtered on, Claire was shuffled even closer to him, a mere's spaghetti's width between their sides.

Ooh spaghetti. That sounded good. But no, they were having fish and chips for dinner. Which sounded just fine. Like the buns she'd eaten for lunch. Not the Branston pickle. Not the rye bread.

Of course, at the moment, she didn't really care about what she'd eaten for lunch. All she was really doing was trying to distract herself from Liam's powerful stance right beside her.

She shifted her footing as the doors beeped closed, and a sudden pressure in her upper calf drew her attention to where the zipper of her boot pressed into her skin.

Finally, something else to focus on. She raised her foot a fraction to reach down and readjust the zipper, but when the train whooshed forward, she lost her balance and fell directly toward Liam.

She yelped, landing against his solid chest as his free arm instantly wrapped around her back to steady her. Her head spun from his touch, warmth pulsing from her heart to spread throughout her limbs.

Without hesitation, she scrambled from his grasp, clasping onto the rod with both hands and shifting her hair back with a flick of her head.

"You alright?" Liam asked in a tone as smooth as honey glazed ham.

With an averted gaze and burning cheeks, she ran her tongue

over her teeth. "Yep. Just needed to embarrass myself here, too, you know. Gotta hit all the spots in London apparently."

The grin she was rewarded with would have made all the embarrassment in the world worth it, had her legs not weakened at the sight.

FIFTEEN

AFTER WHAT SEEMED AN ETERNITY, CLAIRE AND LIAM finally reached Aldgate Station. Claire was the first to put some distance between them, hopping from the train onto the platform with so much swiftness, she nearly toppled into the people in front of her.

She couldn't help it. She was too attracted to Liam—like, unhealthily attracted to him. How else could she explain knowing him for only three days and having such strong reactions to being merely near to him? Falling into his perfectly solid, perfectly lovely, perfectly manly chest had been a wakeup call.

Thank goodness it was only physical attraction. If she liked him any more than as a friend, she'd be in for a world of hurt when she left England, and that was something she didn't want for herself. She already missed too many people from her life as it was.

What she really needed to do to keep herself safe was to remember all of the things she didn't like about the guy. That would be easy enough—she'd just think about how rude he'd been to her at the airport and how often he'd made fun of her since.

And yet, as the evening progressed, she found it more and

more difficult to remember those brief moments, as Liam Everhart seemed to be on a mission to prove he was an anomaly among the men in her life, past *and* present.

First, as they'd strolled down the long, cement platform between the two train tracks, a musician's jazzy rendition of *Jingle Bells* had echoed down the station, so Liam had tossed a few spare pound coins into the man's saxophone case as they walked by.

It wasn't that big of a deal, really. He'd be selfish if he *hadn't* dispensed a few coins. But then, as they sat down for dinner at Honeysett's Fish and Chips, he took to asking her question after question about Peonies & Burlap, about what her typical day of work looked like, and about how she found herself falling in love with flowers in the first place.

"It's kinda morbid," she'd said, but he'd urged her on anyway. "I was at my great-aunt's funeral when I was just a little girl, and I was more interested in the floral displays than I was the actual service."

Liam had chuckled, then he'd spent the next half hour asking her how she was making her dream come true of owning her own shop one day.

If Claire didn't know any better, she'd have thought he was trying to impress her, what with all of his perfect conversational skills, but she knew he didn't like her in that way. He'd seemed hardly ruffled by her falling into him on the train, or when their knees bumped into each other beneath the table as they ate. More importantly, how could he be attracted to *her*, an apparently accident-prone American who he'd been forced to hang out with all day long?

It was more likely that his mom had coerced him into speaking about Claire's life, just like she'd coerced him into spending the day with her. There was no other reason for him to appear so interested in her.

Especially when the saucy waitress who'd been eying Liam up all night returned to their table to deliver their separate checks, which Claire had insisted on to avoid the appearance of her being a freeloader.

"I'll be right back for these, then," the waitress said with another smile in Liam's direction.

Liam smiled in return, and Claire averted her gaze once again. Richard had always flirted with the waitresses when they went out. Not that Liam was flirting, per say. But there was no way he wasn't flattered by the brunette-and-red-lipped-beauty's attention.

Richard would always say on their dates, *"I'm not flirting, Claire, I'm just being friendly."*

Yeah, friendly. Then he must have just been being "friendly" by inviting his ex to stay with him overnight at the Christmas Lodge, too.

Clearing her mind from her gloomy thoughts, Claire reached for her small purse atop her coat on the chair beside her, only to discover the purse wasn't there. Her stomach plummeted as she shuffled aside her coat and cast her eyes to the chair beside her, across the table, and all around the floor without a single sight of the purse.

Had she left it on the Underground? Or had someone swiped it without her noticing?

"What's wrong?" Liam asked across from her.

She frowned. "I can't find my purse."

His eyes roved across the table. "Did you have it with you when you left my mum's?"

Mum. He was so wonderfully British.

Focus, Claire.

"Yeah, but..." Wait. *Had* she had it?

She closed her eyes, picturing the moment she'd attempted to leave Tasha's in a mad dash so Liam wouldn't feel obligated to join her. Then, as clear as day, she visualized the purse she'd left behind on the table beside the couch.

Dang it all. She'd taken her traveling Oyster card out of the purse for ease of access, housing it in her coat pocket instead. If only she would have left it in the purse, she could have realized she'd actually left both at home earlier.

Slowly, she met Liam's gaze with a wince. "I think I left it there."

"It's no problem," he said at once, reaching for her tab.

There he went again, being all benevolent.

"Well tell me what it costs, and I'll just Venmo you the money."

"It's fine. Really." He slipped his card into his own black folder, then a few pound notes into hers.

She pulled out her phone, shaking her head as she tapped on the app and waited for it to load. "No, come on. I'm gonna pay for my own meal."

The waitress returned, and Claire didn't notice—or rather, *tried* not to notice—as the woman's coquettish smile and lingering gaze landed on Liam before she left with the payments.

Annoyed that Liam still hadn't told her the cost—or was she annoyed that he'd smiled at the waitress again?—Claire tapped impatiently on the table. "Come on. How much was it?"

"Uh, seven hundred quid," he exaggerated.

Quid. That had to mean money, right?

She dropped her chin. "You'll be sorry when you wake up to find that much money in your account tomorrow."

He narrowed his eyes and pursed his lips as if in confusion. "No, I believe *you'd* be the sorry one in that situation."

She laughed, then pressed her lips together and shook her head. "Fine. I think it was twenty pounds, so I'll just pay you that."

She looked down at her phone, only to discover the app had delivered a "Failure to Upload" message.

She growled in frustration. Stupid crap service.

"Having some trouble?"

She glanced up, amusement playing on his lips.

With a wave of her hand, she slipped her phone into her back pocket. "It's fine. I'll just pay you when we get back to your mom's house."

He didn't respond as the waitress returned to their table. Claire had never received faster service in her entire life.

"There you are," the woman said, placing Claire's tab on the table beside her and handing Liam's directly to his hands.

He took the folder with a nod and a, "Cheers."

Good grief. Why didn't he just marry the girl if he loved her so much?

"Did the two of you enjoy your date?" the woman asked.

Wow. Hint, much? Claire had a mind to pretend she was dating Liam, but unfortunately—no, *fortunately*, he wasn't Claire's to claim.

"Oh, we're not on a date," Claire responded when Liam remained silent, taking his card back and slipping it in his wallet.

The woman's face brightened, and she shifted to face Liam directly. "In that case." She pulled out a small slip of paper from her shirt pocket and slid it across the table with her red nails. "Call me sometime."

She gave a little wink and sauntered to the opposite side of the restaurant.

Claire watched her with half-hooded eyes. "Wow."

"What?" Liam asked, looking up from where he signed his name on the receipt.

"Nothing. Just..." She motioned to the slip of paper with the girl's name and number still on the table. "I guess this sort of thing happens to you often, then?"

He glanced down at it, then a half-smile spread across his lips. "Perhaps."

She stared at him, then rolled her eyes. Men. They were all the same.

And yet, when they left the restaurant and Claire secured the buttons on her coat, she spied Liam discreetly tossing the slip of paper into the garbage at the side of the restaurant.

She narrowed her eyes, her mind swirling. He'd just...thrown it away. But why? The girl had been so obviously into him. And she wasn't unattractive, by any stretch of the imagination. How —*why*—was he not interested in her? Did he not like brunettes? Was he more into blondes?

Her stomach did a funny turn.

"What?" Liam asked, pausing as he straightened the collar of his coat.

Only then did Claire realize she still stared at him.

He must not have realized that she'd seen him toss the number. Instead of confronting him about something she had no business to, Claire shook her head and tore her gaze away.

Night had fallen long ago, bringing with it the frigid cold of early winter. Claire tightened her scarf around her neck and tucked her hands into her coat pocket as she followed Liam in silence down the street. Their way was lit by streetlamps, Christmas lights draped over shops and fresh greenery, and glowing lights from cars and buses beeping their way down the busy road.

People passed them by on the sidewalk, bundled up against the cold, carrying red and green shopping bags and gifts wrapped with flawless bows.

Claire loved this time of year. Everyone seemed to put their best foot forward, sharing extra smiles and greetings and well wishes. But something had always occurred to taint her outlook.

Parents. Boyfriends. No family.

Not this year, though. This year was going to be different. She'd taken charge of the narrative, was unwilling to allow anything to bring her spirits down—her parents being MIA, Melody being sick, Liam being coerced into spending the day with her.

After all, why should any of those things dictate how she felt? She was in England, for heaven's sake. Not on some cruise, not being cheated on, not being looked over by her parents' work.

Instead, she was walking around London near...Near what exactly?

She glanced around, hoping to see a landmark or any recognizable buildings, but she found nothing.

"Where are we?" she asked. "I mean, in regard to, like, a well-known site."

"The Tower of London is just down there," Liam responded, pointing to a street they approached.

"Oh, really?" All other thoughts fled from her mind as she peered down the street, hoping to catch a glimpse of the historical site. Yellow lights lined the busy road, the hazy glow expanding into a soft fog that now slipped across the sky, but the Tower was nowhere in sight.

"I was surprised that wasn't on your list of things to see today," Liam said.

"Well, it was originally. But Melody said it wasn't that impressive."

Liam stopped walking, turning to face Claire with a slack jaw. "The Tower of London is *not that impressive?*"

Claire paused in the middle of the sidewalk, turning to face him. "Yeah, she said not to waste my time."

Liam ran his fingers through his thick hair, the strands somehow remaining back, despite his tousling them. "Leave it to my cousin to convince you to miss out on one of the most incredible places in London." He blew out a frustrated sigh. "Alright. Come on. We're going to see it right now."

SIXTEEN

LIAM TOOK A LEFT DOWN THE SIDE STREET, STRIDING across the pavement. Claire hadn't thought he was serious. He really wanted to prolong the evening with her?

"Wait, isn't it closed?" she asked, jogging to catch up with him as the frigid air infiltrated her lungs.

"Yes, but at least you'll get to see the outside of it."

A sudden lightness overcame her, and she fought off a smile. She'd been so disappointed when Melody had pushed the Tower from their schedule. Catching a glimpse of it would be better than nothing.

"Not that impressive," Liam muttered, continuing in a louder tone as they progressed down the street. "The history there alone is mind-blowing. Not to mention the architecture." He stopped walking abruptly, and Claire followed suit, trying very hard to match his serious expression, though his unexpected ferocity was nothing short of adorable. "Do you know, there are carvings in the Beauchamp Tower from the people who were imprisoned there hundreds of years ago?"

He didn't wait for a response before he continued, walking down the street once again. "It's nine hundred years old, for heaven's sake. How old must a building be to be 'impressive' to

Melody? I mean, the horrific history there must be shared and respected by everyone, if not for history's sake, then for the sake of those who were forced to give their lives within those walls. You know?"

When he finally stopped, his scowl directed down at Claire, she raised her hands in a gesture of retreat, still attempting to hide her amusement. "No need to blame the messenger. *I* wanted to see it, remember?"

He paused, her words seeming to sink in as he shoved his hands in his pockets and continued in a lower voice, though his brow still hung heavily over his dark eyes.

"You're right, of course," he said. "Leave it to Melody to be far too opinionated about a subject she knows next to nothing about."

Claire bit her tongue for as long as possible, but her desire to tease him won out. "Far too opinionated. Hmmm. I wonder if that's a family trait?"

She watched him from the corner of her eye, his gaze shooting to hers before his shoulders visibly lowered and that smile-not-smile touched his lips. "Touché, Claire."

How she loved her name on his lips. No, no. In his accent. No, in *any* British accent, not just his. It just sounded so delicate, so feminine. She'd never really liked her name before, but in that accent...Mmm. She could get used to such a sound.

With Liam clearly feeling better about life as he stopped his rant—which, to be honest, sounded more like a song than anything due to that accent—the two of them made their way to the tower, stopping first to use the public restrooms.

To add insult to injury, Claire once again had to borrow money from him.

"Just add it to my tab," she said, trying to embrace being at the liberty of her embarrassment around him.

"That's seven hundred and *one* pounds, then," he joked, and she grinned all the way to the stall.

Afterward, they walked around the outside of the wide, light-stoned structure, Liam pointing out the different towers and sharing a few facts Claire had never heard before. They took a moment to watch the ice skaters in the moat, gliding across the temporary, frozen rink, before taking in more of the sights. By the end of their makeshift tour, Claire was enraptured—not only by the history, but by how impassioned Liam was with the whole site.

"Alright, you've convinced me," she said. "I'll make Melody go there with me before I go back home."

Liam gave a firm nod. "Excellent. Then my work here is done."

She smiled up at him, then looked beyond his shoulder to where a concentrated set of lights glowed across the Thames.

"What's that?" she asked, motioning with a nod of her head.

Liam turned, following her gaze. "Christmas by the River. It's one of the markets they hold every year."

"Wait, a Christmas market?"

He nodded. "It's quite festive. Very Christmassy. Have you ever been to one?"

"No. Well, there are a few random street gatherings where I live, but nothing like an actual European market." Claire narrowed her eyes to see it better, though she couldn't make out much more from the distance. "My parents have been to a bunch in Germany and Switzerland. Next to cruises, that's where they loved spending Christmases the most."

"Were they traveling for work then, too?"

Claire bit her tongue. What was it about this guy who managed to bring out all these memories she'd done her best to suppress for years?

Then again, perhaps this was her chance to prove that she was more than fine with her parents' decisions.

"No, they were just visiting some friends in Europe," she explained. "I got to stay back in Colorado with my aunt and uncle."

'Got to.' More like 'had to.' Claire used to beg her mom and dad to let her go every time, and every time, it was the same answer.

"We're sorry, Claire Bear, but the Winthrops only invited your dad and I to stay. We'll go one day when you're older. We promise."

Claire was still waiting for that promise to be fulfilled—and about a thousand others. She just couldn't understand why, after seven—or was it eight?—visits, they still hadn't brought her with them. Still, they'd always bring home little trinkets for her as they showed her all the photos of the markets, sharing how magical and dreamy they had been and how wonderful of a time they'd had.

"Do you want to have a look?" Liam asked.

At his offer, a strange guilt niggled at her conscience. She'd waited so long to go with her parents, always picturing seeing the markets with them. But then, would that ever happen?

Liam waited for her response, an easy expression on his face, and she knew at once what her answer was. Seeing the Christmas markets with her parents was a childhood dream. But seeing them with this insanely attractive man right now? It was an adulthood dream come *true*.

"I would love to," she responded, and Liam's eyes warmed.

Together, they made their way across the stunning Tower Bridge, its grey stone towers lit with green lights and blue, curved cables.

Instead of allowing Liam the opportunity to ask more about her parents, Claire urged him to speak more about the Tower of London and the bridge until they finally reached the market.

Hungrily, her eyes took in the sight. Backed up against a domed, glass building, countless wooden stalls lined the Queens Walk pathway, boasting a variety of foods, drinks, and handmade goods for sale.

Each miniature chalet's pointed roof was decorated with rows of shimmering white lights like stars in the night's sky. At the front of each roof, green shrubbery was packed in tight with more white Christmas lights, flocked, pointed pinecones, and silver bells.

As they walked down the row of huts, Claire marveled at the beauty, constant waves of people meandering down the smooth boardwalk, munching on chips, curry, and various pastries and sipping mulled wine and hot cocoa as they mingled with friends.

"It's like a postcard," Claire breathed. How could this be even better than she'd imagined?

Liam nodded, his face lit by the warm light coming from within the huts. "There are a few other markets around London, but this one is my favorite. My family used to come every year."

"I can't even imagine having such an incredible tradition," she said as they passed by a group of girls at the side of the walkway. They huddled together to take a selfie with Tower Bridge in the background.

"I'm sure you have your own traditions that are just as memorable," Liam offered.

Claire almost scoffed. Her most consistent family tradition was to not be together, and they were having a pretty good run at it.

They progressed down the pathway, passing stalls filled with nutcrackers, art displays, and hanging garden features before Claire spotted a hut offering warm drinks.

She stopped, motioning forward with a nod of her head. "Would you mind if I added a few more pounds to my tab?"

Liam didn't hesitate, heading straight for the booth to purchase two hot chocolates and delivering one of them to Claire. They continued their stroll, the warmth from the cup seeping through Claire's gloves as she held her drink in between her hands.

They passed by another stall boasting more than a dozen different types of cheeses, then another with crocheted mittens, scarves, and hats.

"Oh, wow."

Claire stopped, glancing up at Liam's exclamation. "What?"

His eyes were focused on the crocheted items. "I've found just the thing for you."

She watched, intrigued as he reached for one of the hats—a green beanie crocheted into the shape of Yoda's ears. "You have to purchase this to complete your bedtime ensemble."

Instinctively, Claire's defenses rose, creating that familiar fortress around her heart as she was brought straight back to her humiliation at being discovered in Liam's bed.

But when his lips curved up, his eyes doing that delightful squint, her embarrassment was washed away in the thrill of his attention.

"You're the worst," she said, fighting off a grin.

"What are you talking about?" His smile grew. "This is perfect for you. Come on. Let's try it on."

Claire was about to dodge out of the way, but as he reached toward her, closing the distance between them, her feet rooted to the pathway.

He gently placed the knitted cap over her head, then stood back to examine it. Claire did her best not to fidget, but as his dark gaze roved over her, her anxiousness increased.

Finally, he pulled his lips to the side in disappointment.

"Hmm," he mused. "I'm not sure about it, to be honest. While it's adorable, it *is* a bit wonky."

Claire didn't even bother to attempt a comeback, her mind focused on one thing. Adorable. He'd called her adorable.

No, he'd called the hat adorable. Yikes. She needed to get ahold of herself. Pulling off the beanie, she placed it back on the stand. "I'll decide for you. The hat's not gonna happen."

She walked away from the stand as she shook her head, though a secret delight swelled in her chest, swirling around like the glitter inside of a snow globe.

Liam caught up with her, his grin even wider.

"You're never going to let me live that down, are you?" she asked.

"What, you lying in my bed with your *Mandalorian* pajamas?" He tipped his head toward her. "How could I forget it? They were amazing."

She narrowed her eyes, looking away as her heart warmed again. He'd promised that morning not to mention her being in his bed, but for some reason, she didn't have the desire to remind him. "They *are* amazing. And anyone—*you*—who has a problem with them can...eat my beskar."

He chuckled, the rumbling sound echoing in her ears like a baritone choir. "I don't know why you're under the assumption that I don't like them," he said. "I'm a big fan of the show myself. Although, I can't say that I own that exact pair of pajamas."

She rolled her eyes, doing her best not to smile. "They're warm, okay? That's why I brought them. And I definitely wasn't planning on wearing them in front of anyone other than Melody."

"Ah, I am of the privileged crowd then, I see."

How was it that everything this man said made her melt like a mini marshmallow in hot cocoa?

"So," he continued, "I have to ask, as this is a fairly important distinction. Do you like the show for the story, or do you like it because of Baby Yoda?"

Claire glanced up at him with raised brows. "You mean Grogu?" she asked, using the creature's actual name.

He looked at her, impressed. "Ah, you've passed my first test. Most don't."

Her heart swelled to bursting. "I'm a diehard fan, I'll have you know. Just like with Harry Potter. I don't claim to be crazy knowledgeable about the lore and everything, but...I'm pretty much in love with the Mandalorian."

"In love. Wow."

Claire raised her eyebrows, nodding with a serious expression.

"Now, are you talking about being in love with the show, or with Mando?"

"You mean Din Djarin?"

He met her gaze with another pleased look. "Second test, passed."

She laughed, shaking her head. "I'm in love with the show." Then she paused. "Aaaaand a little in love with Mando himself. He's super hot."

Claire didn't know what had come over her. Perhaps it was the magic the Christmas Market had swirled within the air, or the sugar from the hot chocolate getting to her head.

Or maybe, just maybe, she was simply overcome with euphoria as she earned smile after smile from Liam—all because she was *finally* being herself.

Whatever it was, she was going to chase that feeling of joy because it didn't come very often.

SEVENTEEN

LIAM NEVER SHOULD HAVE BROUGHT CLAIRE TO THE Tower of London, nor should he have encouraged her to see the Christmas Market. He'd known from the minute she'd fallen into him on the train that every moment he would spend with Claire Frost that evening would be a struggle, and he'd been absolutely correct.

Not a struggle in the normal sense, with the two of them arguing and losing patience with one another. But a struggle in that he could no longer deny his attraction to her. A struggle in that every time she spoke passionately about flowers or her job, every time she skirted around her struggles with her parents, he became more and more intrigued by everything she said.

And that just wasn't going to work for him.

He'd done his best that night to relax, to allow himself the freedom to just enjoy his time with this spunky, unique woman who liked listening to AC/DC and watching *Star Wars* and *Harry Potter* films.

But his trepidation continued to rear its head. He didn't have time to like anyone, nor the energy to carry on a long-distance relationship. But surely this tiny, minuscule, inconsequential crush he'd seemed to develop that afternoon would fade as soon as morning came. Melody would be better. Claire would spend the day with her. Mum would be back at work. And Liam would be allowed some time to himself to take photos.

So maybe tonight he could relax. Maybe tonight, he'd allow himself to flirt and converse and be happy. Perhaps Heaven knew he needed this momentary joy after the week—and years—he'd suffered with very little happiness at all.

"Did I weird you out?" Claire asked, clearly misreading his silence.

"No, you haven't *weirded* me out," he finally said, mimicking her word, the r's sounding strange on his tongue. "I'm merely trying to grasp what you said. And the fact that you're telling me that you're in love with a man hired out to kill people. Sorry, no. A *fictional* man hired out to kill people."

She grinned in response. Why was it so satisfying to make her smile?

"Unless," he continued, "you're saying the actor is attractive and not the actual Mandalorian?"

"Oh." She seemed to think for a minute. "Well, Pedro Pascal is definitely easy on the eyes. But I think I prefer Mando."

He laughed, surprised with her response. "You can't even see his face."

Then she looked at him like *he* was mad. "With a helmet like that, who needs to see his face?"

He'd always heard that women loved a man in uniform. He supposed Mandalorian armor could count for that, as well. "Alright, walk me through this. How can a *helmet* be attractive?"

She peered straight ahead, focusing on nothing in particular, apart from the image she clearly had of Mando in her mind. "Well, when it's combined with those amazing pauldrons over his broad shoulders, and of course that cape just billowing in the wind, he's already a keeper. Then you take into account the helmet, which has all your basic, typical 'hot guy'"—she did air quotes with her fingers—"features. The ones women swoon at, you know? Nice, angled jawline. Defined cheekbones. Heavy brow. Narrowed eyes. You just can't get better than that, you know? If a guy has all those features, I know I'd kiss *my* willpower goodbye."

She finished her explanation, grinning up at him as he watched her with amusement. But as their eyes connected, her gaze roving over his features, her smile suddenly faltered, and a blush blazed across her freckled cheeks.

She tore her gaze away, pointing out the Tower of London across the river. "Oh, look. There's the Tower again." Then she veered off course and headed toward the barrier between the pavement and the Thames.

Liam followed slowly behind her, completely aware that she was changing the subject, though he had no idea why or for what reason her demeanor had changed so suddenly.

Unless...Had she been thinking that maybe Liam possessed some of those features that she found so irresistible? Or had she realized that he was nowhere near what she wanted in a man?

Both possibilities made his chest tighten for reasons he didn't wish to explore.

Joining Claire near the stone barrier, Liam quietly sipped his hot chocolate as the world slowed around them. A fog had rolled across the river and now hovered above, blurring the tips of the bare tree branches in the darkness and cloaking the world in a hazy color.

Down the pathway lit with spherical lamps, a street musician played out "Silent Night" on his violin, and a ferry floated down the river, his lights reflecting in the river's ripples.

In that slowing down, Liam's thoughts had a moment to catch up with him, and they weren't exactly pleasant. How could this woman be the same one from the airport? How could he have misjudged her so greatly?

Now, more than ever, he regretted his cruelty toward her.

He took a deep breath, leaning over the edge of the railing. "Claire," he began, her eyes on him in an instant, though he couldn't meet her gaze in return. "I've been meaning to say this for a while, but I just...I want to apologize for how I treated you at the airport."

She tilted her head to the side. "You already did."

If only that were true. But he could hardly count his past words as sincere. "I just wanted to reiterate it again. I had just received some disappointing news from work, and I hadn't eaten or slept, so I..." He broke off, shaking his head. This was the worst confession known to man. "Anyway, I just wanted to apologize again for being shirty."

He ended, introducing an awkward silence between them as he shifted his footing against the pathway and stared hard at the dark water catching the light from the lamps.

"Well," Claire began, "I think this goes without saying, but your apology is more than accepted."

Liam glanced toward her, their gazes catching as the Christmas lights danced in her blue eyes.

"Thank you," he said softly, watching her for a minute, her hair fluttering in the cold, winter breeze, her small nose painted pink at the tip.

"So are you ever going to tell me what the disappointing news was that your job gave you?" she asked.

Liam stared, dragging his mind to focus on her question instead of the pleasant way her freckles dotted her nose. "Oh, it was nothing." He never should have mentioned his blasted job.

"Come on," Claire pressed. "You got to hear everything about my work for, like, an hour. I don't even get to hear one tiny thing about yours?"

She had a point, but still he hesitated. He hadn't spoken of the news to anyone, fearing that saying it aloud would finally settle in stone what had happened. But then, it already *was* settled. Keeping his disappointment in, attempting to process the news all by himself, was probably the thing upsetting him the most.

Claire intentionally bumped against his shoulder with her

own, a small smile curving her lips as a subtle nudge for him to continue.

Fine. That settled it. Not just because of her encouragement, but because he wanted something else to focus on besides the warmth in his heart that continued to steadily grow each time they touched.

"It really is nothing," he said, staring across the Thames. "I'd been promised a promotion for a few years, and I didn't get it. That's all."

Claire's brows pulled together. "Oh, I'm so sorry."

He shrugged, attempting to blow off the disappointment as simply that—a disappointment, instead of the life-altering, soul-crushing, heart-wrenching thing that had occurred.

"It's alright," he said. "It's life, I suppose."

But Claire shook her head. "No, that's so awful. To be promised something for so long." Her eyes took on a faraway look. "There's nothing worse than when promises fall through. Especially when they're made by people you should be able to trust."

Liam studied her, noting that the look on her face now was the same as when she'd spoken of her parents on the Tube. Was she thinking of them now? Were they the ones who'd disappointed her with unfulfilled promises?

"So is that why you took time off?" she guessed next.

Liam would much rather discuss her family issues than his work problems. But then, perhaps if he answered her questions, she'd be more willing to answer his own.

Slowly, he nodded. "I'd like to profess complete altruistic reasoning behind my returning home, but yes. Part of the reason was to be with my mum. But most of it was because my new boss —the person now in the position I was supposed to have—started this week, and I just couldn't handle being there."

"Like salt in the wound."

"Precisely."

"I don't blame you for taking time off. I wouldn't want to be there either." Claire shook her head again, her frown increasing. "Did they hire someone inhouse or..."

"No, it was an outside source. A woman from a different company." He glanced at Claire sidelong. "From the States."

Her eyes dawned with recognition. "Ohhh. So that's why you were so...you know."

He rubbed self-consciously at the back of his neck. "Yeah."

"Wow," Claire mused. "So an American stole your job *and* your luggage. No wonder you hate us."

Her teasing glance eased only a small amount of his guilt. "I have nothing against the lot of you. I'm sure who they hired is no doubt highly qualified for the position."

"But still," Claire continued. "Even if she is qualified, to have *your* promotion just handed to someone else must be unbelievably disheartening."

Liam didn't know how to respond. Claire was absolutely spot on. But how? How could this woman who hardly knew him, know exactly how he felt?

"How long have you worked there?" she asked next.

"About eight years."

"And how long have they been promising the promotion?"

"The last three."

She turned on him with a raised brow. "Three years? That is so long to just hold that over your head. No wonder you're so upset." She paused. "I take it you haven't told your mom yet."

He winced. "No, so if you wouldn't mind..."

But Claire was already shaking her head. "Oh, don't even worry about it. I won't say a word."

He nodded his gratitude. "I'll tell her soon. I just...don't want to disappoint her."

Claire stared up at him, her brow pursed before she shook her head and looked away.

"What?" he asked.

"Nothing."

"No, come on."

She took a slow sip of her hot chocolate. "I just...I mean, I know I don't know you or your mom very well at all. But from the short time I *have* spent with her, I already know that there's nothing you could do that would disappoint her." Then she turned her blue eyes on him. "She loves you."

There was a hint of sadness in her tone, but she looked away too quickly for Liam to be sure.

He knew Claire was right, though. His mum did love him. And yet... "Unfortunately, I *can* disappoint her. As is evident by my absence over the last few Christmases."

Claire looked up at him with a curious gaze. "Can I ask why you did stay away? Was it just work, or..."

Yes, there was a big *or*. But he didn't need to open up *that* can of worms. "A lot of it was due to my work schedule, but it just keeps getting worse. After I didn't get the promotion, I decided to come home so at least I wouldn't be failing in *every* regard in my life."

He stopped, averting his gaze in embarrassment. He hadn't meant to share so much.

"So you don't like how busy your job makes you, then?" she asked, her eyes delving into his.

Did this question mean something to her? "No," he answered truthfully. "Before, I loved it. But now, I travel so often that I hardly have time to do what I actually enjoy."

"Which is..."

She waited in silence, and Liam hesitated for only a moment. He'd already opened up about everything else that evening. Why not his passions next?

"I enjoy wildlife and landscape photography," he said with a flippant raise of his shoulder. "I'm only an amateur photographer, but I've always been interested in taking photos of the animals and scenery around the UK."

"That sounds amazing," Claire said, her smile brightening.

Either she really thought so, or she was an excellent liar.

"I always thought so, too," Liam said. Her enthusiasm,

whether real or not, picked up his heart. "I first got a job at Peregrine Productions because they produced a lot of wildlife documentaries, so I got to film and photograph the animals. Now, the company has grown so big, they're mostly hired out to film exercise equipment and health food videos."

Claire raised a lip to reveal that her disappointment matched his own. "So you haven't been able to take any photographs lately?"

He held his tongue, not wanting to share too much about his photography feed on Instagram. "I dabble here and there, but nothing too serious. I don't really have the time. That was actually one of the reasons I'd wanted the promotion. As an executive producer, I wouldn't be required to travel as often, so I'd have more time for what I actually enjoy." He shook his head, realizing he was whinging again. "Anyway, that's life, isn't it? Disappointments happen."

Claire looked away, her lips half-curved. "I dunno."

"What do you mean?"

She drew a deep breath, staring up at Tower Bridge, the spires strong and firm, glowing a bright green. "Like you said, life is full of disappointments. But also, life is what you make it. If you keep being disappointed by the same thing over and over again, you have to ask yourself if something needs to change, you know?"

He stared down at her as she continued, apparently unaware that he was hanging onto her every word.

"I mean, there are some things in life you can't change," she said. "And there are some situations where we need to learn to let go and just deal with the disappointments as best we can. But in other situations—like a job, for instance—we can either choose to keep being disappointed, we can choose to see the good in what we have, *or* we can choose to leave it behind and find something better." Her eyes met his, unwavering. "Something that will lift you up instead of drag you down. Something that brings you lasting joy."

When she finished, Liam stared down at her, his mind swirling with thoughts, though his tongue remained empty.

Lasting joy.

When was the last time his work had brought him *lasting* joy? Had it ever? The only thing in life that had done that was taking photographs, and how often had he gotten the chance to do that in the last few years?

"Or," Claire continued, her eyes on the Thames, "I could just be an insane person trying to convince you to be crazy along with me. Either way, in my experience, crazy is much more fun than corporate."

Liam couldn't help his smile, though her words left him unsettled. Unfortunately, quitting wasn't so simple for him to do. There were other things to consider—wasting eight years of his life at a single job, being just as miserable in another career, the what-if of receiving a promotion if he could just stick it out a little longer.

Still, she'd spoken a truth to his mind he hadn't considered for many, many years.

Why *was* he staying with that job?

"Can I ask you another question?" Claire asked.

Liam glanced toward her, unable to say anything but, "Yes."

"Why did you throw away that number?"

Liam stared, narrowing his eyes. "What number?"

"The waitress's. From the restaurant."

Recognition dawned, surprise filling in the spots his confusion had left behind. "Oh. I don't know."

Claire gave him a dubious look. "Come on. She was gorgeous. And so obviously into you. There's no reason for you to have thrown her number away unless you have a girlfriend or something." Then she paused. "*Do* you have a girlfriend?"

Liam hesitated, finishing off the last of his hot chocolate and tossing the cup into a nearby rubbish bin. "No, I don't."

She nodded, seeming satisfied as she shifted her body away

from the river to face him, her side resting on the barrier. "Then why did you throw the number away?"

He turned to face her, too. Why was she so interested? "I have my reasons."

"And they are…"

"I'll tell you if you agree to answer a question for me."

She narrowed her eyes. "And what question is that?"

"I don't have one yet. But when I do, you have to promise to answer it."

Without a second thought, she nodded. "Fine. Deal. Whatever. Now tell me."

He smiled at her obvious impatience. "So anxious, I see."

"I'm not *so* anxious. I'm just curious, that's all." She turned away as if to prove her point.

Alright, so she *was* a terrible liar. That was good to know.

"I threw away the number for two reasons," he began. Claire turned toward him with invested eyes, apparently forgetting her decision to appear uninterested.

"Number one, that woman didn't know that you and I weren't dating until the end of the meal. If she was flirting with an unavailable man—even a *potentially* unavailable man—I'm fairly certain she wouldn't hesitate to flirt if she was unavailable herself."

Claire's lips parted, and she stared up at him, clearly speechless.

"What?" he asked, pulling back.

"Nothing. I'm just…surprised."

"Why? Because I'm not a total pig?"

She shook her head. "No, not you. Just…men in general, I guess. I can't tell you the number of dates I've been on where the guys haven't hesitated to flirt with the waitresses."

Liam paused. Had she meant to call their dinner a date? He supposed he *had* paid for her.

"So what was the second reason?" she asked.

"Unfortunately, it is far less noble. I just don't have time for a relationship. My work hours would never allow it."

Like the slow descent of fog rolling over the Thames, the light faded from Claire's eyes. She turned away, pulling out her phone. "It's getting pretty late. We should probably head back now."

Liam hesitated. He'd clearly offended her. But how? What had he said to upset her? Was it about his job or his lack of time for a girlfriend?

Instead of pursuing the reasons that were lost to him, Liam followed her back through the market, the magic from the evening gone.

It was probably better for the night to end this way. If the spell Claire had placed over him had continued much longer, he was sure he would have spilled the fact that there was actually a third, more potent reason for throwing that waitress's number away.

But no good would come from telling her—or even thinking about it himself—that the reason he'd tossed the number away that evening was because every other woman that night had paled in comparison to Claire.

EIGHTEEN

THE RIDE BACK TO BROOK GREEN WAS LONG AND painful. Claire could think of nothing to say to Liam, blaming her silence on how exhausted she was from all the sightseeing they'd done that day.

She was so desperate to put distance between her and Liam that when they finally arrived back at Tasha's—the house silent with only the bathroom light glowing at the top of the stairs—she'd delivered a quick departing wave, then darted up to her room.

Quietly, she dressed for bed, slipping beneath her blankets on the mattress without a sound to avoid waking Melody, who didn't stir in her bed just to the side of Claire's.

Flashes of car lights illuminated the window as they drove past the house, and Claire watched them for a moment with a deep sigh.

She could only pray Melody was better by tomorrow. It had felt like weeks since they'd spent any time together, although it had only been a single day.

An outrageously long, surprisingly fun, annoyingly confusing day.

She hadn't expected to be so affected by Liam's words at the end of the night, but she'd been derailed, her thoughts ending up in some empty, dried-out field in the cavern of her memories. Which was utterly ridiculous, now that she thought about it. After all, she didn't like the guy beyond his very attractive physique, remember?

But hearing how he prioritized work had brought back unwelcome memories from her past, memories she'd just as soon forget all over again.

Pulling out her phone, she tried to deaden her thoughts by taking part in some mindless scrolling on Instagram now that she was connected to Wi-Fi. After watching a few German Shepherd puppy reels, cake decorating timelapse clips, and gorgeous English garden slides, she pulled up her own photos.

She hadn't posted since the airport. Maybe she ought to share some images of the flowers at Kew Gardens or perhaps some of her selfies from around London. That should keep her mind off of whomever she was trying to keep her mind off of.

Shifting on the mattress to lay on her side, she started from the end of her day and worked backwards. She swiftly skipped past the images she'd snapped of the Christmas Market and the Tower of London, Liam's calming voice and delectable accent echoing in her mind.

Yeah, this wasn't her smartest idea. Maybe she'd just skip to Kew Gardens instead where she only had unpleasant memories of the guy. But as she swiped past one more photo, her eyes locked onto her and Liam standing in front of Big Ben.

Her instinct told her to exit out of the picture. No good would come from staring at the two of them with their arms around each other. And yet, after a quick glance to ensure Melody was still asleep, Claire gave in to temptation and zoomed closer until she and Liam were front and center on her screen.

She'd felt Liam's discomfort matching her own in that moment on the bridge, and yet, as she traced his face with her eyes, he looked nothing but the perfect picture of relaxation. His arm was draped easily around her, his smile revealed more in his eyes than his lips, and his head tilted ever so slightly toward her.

Her heartbeat quickened as if he stood beside her in that moment, but she bit her lip, forcing herself to come back down to earth.

He'd said that he didn't have time for a relationship because of his work, that he was too busy with his job to focus on anything else—just like her parents. They hadn't had time for their own daughter because of their job, and now because of their retirement. What was with people, choosing trivial things like careers and cruises instead of their own family?

But then, Liam wasn't her family, and she wasn't his. Her stomach swirled with regret. She shouldn't have reacted so emotionally to him that night. He didn't deserve that, especially after the entire day he'd sacrificed for her. Really, she should be thanking him for reminding her, albeit inadvertently, that she shouldn't get too wrapped up in her attraction to him. This was just one more notch to add to her arsenal of reasons why she shouldn't fall for Liam Everhart.

Although, she probably, most definitely should have been more grateful to him for what he did for her today.

She closed her eyes, laying her phone down on her stomach. She'd been in such a hurry to escape him that she hadn't even thanked him. Had he noticed? Did he now think she was just a spoiled, selfish American?

With a sigh, she opened her phone again, swiped away from the photo of her and Liam, and pulled up the thread he'd started between them.

Her thumbs hovered over the buttons for a minute before she typed out a quick message.

Claire: Hey, Liam. Thanks for today...

No, that was stupid. She could come up with something cleverer.

151

Claire: Hola, Liam!

Nope. That wasn't going to work either.

Claire: Thanks for today. It was fun.

Now she sounded as excited as Dwight Schrute wishing Kelly Kapoor a happy birthday.

With an aggravated sigh, she chastised herself for overthinking a simple message, then typed out the first thing that came to her mind.

Claire: Hey, Liam! I just wanted to say thanks for today. I had a great time!

Holding her breath, she finally sent the message, then clasped the phone to her chest. Would he respond, or was he already asleep? Would he "like" the message or just ignore it altogether?

Tired of the barrage of questions she now assaulted herself with, Claire pulled up Instagram again, determined to post her photos. Then another thought occurred.

Did Liam have an Instagram account?

After a bit of sleuthing—and by "sleuthing," she meant searching out his name on Instagram and every other social media site she could think of—her search came up empty. Not even Melody was friends with him.

Determined not to fail on this apparently very crucial task, she pulled up Tasha's Facebook profile, but there was no sign of Liam anywhere. Even scrolling down his mom's page, she discovered nothing. Until, that is, she caught sight of stunning photo of a baby fox cub nestled in the grass in front of a den.

Claire paused, admiring the photo before seeing that his mom had reshared the post from an account on Instagram named "Everhart Photography."

Her heart picked up, and she hid her smile as she clicked on the page, Instagram automatically pulling up.

Finally, Claire was rewarded for all her hard work.

As clear as day, *William Everhart* was listed above the bio. That's why her search for 'Liam' hadn't pulled up anything.

Her eyes widened as she caught sight of his more than one hundred thousand followers. Though after a quick scroll through his feed, she could see easily why he'd gained such a following.

His bio read:

Amateur Photographer / Wildlife Enthusiast
For prints, click the link below

She scoffed. Amateur photographer, her foot. He'd said he dabbled in photography, but the photos she observed were anything but "dabbling."

She felt like a kid on Christmas morning, hungrily eying the beautiful photos of hedgehogs, foxes, birds, and deer, mixed with stunning shots of the sea, moors, tarns, and the countryside.

She couldn't believe he had downplayed his talent so greatly. Or was he really that humble that he didn't think the photos were as incredible as they were?

Scrolling back to the top of his page, she went too far and accidentally refreshed it. A new post appeared, and her heart jumped.

Without hesitation, she clicked on the photo of the red flower, recognizing it at once as the Kaka beak from Kew Gardens.

Her breathing stopped as she read the caption.

"Visited Kew Gardens yesterday. Such important work being done there to preserve gorgeous flowers such as the Kaka beak from New Zealand. As you know, I typically don't post photos taken with my phone camera, but I needed to spread the word about this phenomenal location. Visit today. You won't regret it."

Claire read the words over and over, realization sinking deeper and deeper into her heart. Liam hadn't been staring at his phone due to boredom at the gardens. He'd been taking photos of flowers—the same flowers Claire had admired.

She shook her head in frustration. She'd been dwelling on her assumption that he didn't like flowers to keep herself grounded around him. Now what was she going to do?

Before she could answer her own question, her phone buzzed, and a message slid down from the top of her phone, revealing Liam's name.

Her heart fairly lurched from her chest. Quickly, she clicked on the message and read his words.

Liam: It was my pleasure.

Claire read it again. It was his pleasure. Did he really mean that? More than likely, he was just being nice.

Well, that was great. He'd responded, she'd done some good stalking, and now she could finally rest.

She lowered her phone to her chest and closed her eyes. But when her stomach grumbled, she thought of the last time she ate food, and when she thought of the last time she ate food, she thought of Liam...and the fact that she hadn't paid him back.

With another sigh, she pulled up her phone again, swearing it was for the last time.

Claire: Don't forget to tell me how much I owe you for dinner.

She paused. He'd paid for a lot more than that. Sending one message after another, she continued texting him.

Claire: And for the hot chocolate.
Claire: And for the beany cheesy thingy.
Claire: And for my trip to the toilet.

Finally, she stopped, smiling at her own joke until the three floating dots appeared at the bottom of the message thread. She pulled in her lips to prevent her smile, then glanced to Melody, ensuring she was still sound asleep.

Liam: Haha I told you, you don't need to worry about paying me back. It's my treat.

Haha. Did that mean he'd laughed at her teasing? Still, Claire hesitated, not sure if he was trying to be a gentleman or if he really was okay paying for her.

Claire: Are you sure?

Instead of a message, Liam sent a GIF of Kuiil on *The Mandalorian* saying his signature phrase, "I have spoken."
Had she died and gone to heaven right now?

Claire: Alright. You've convinced me. Thank you so much again.

Liam: You're welcome. Here's another treat for you to give you sweet dreams.

She waited anxiously as the dots appeared again, then Liam sent a GIF of Mando.

Liam: Check out those pauldrons.
Liam: #sweetdreamsaremadeofthis

Claire laughed at the back of her throat, causing Melody to stir at the noise. Swiftly, Claire hid her phone until her friend settled again, then she moved to respond.

Claire: You sure do know how to make a girl blush.

He reacted with a laugh at her message then sent his final text.

Liam: See you tomorrow.

Her spirits lowered just a fraction at his ending the exchange, but she shook the thought from her mind. This was better. She didn't need to text him after spending the entire day with him.

Claire: Goodnight!

She turned the phone off and tucked it under her pillow. She would go to sleep now. And she wouldn't think about Liam down the hallway.

Thank goodness she would be spending the day with Melody tomorrow. Her friend was sure to be as vocal as usual so Claire wouldn't have time to think about Liam—or compare her time with the both of them. Because as of right now, Claire was finding it extremely difficult to believe that a day out with Melody would be as incredible as her day out with Liam had been.

NINETEEN

To Claire's relief, Melody was finally feeling more like herself the next day. With Tasha already at work and Liam who-knew-where, Claire and Melody set off for their day around London. They stopped by a few museums and the Tower of London—under much duress from Melody—before they headed to Covent Garden.

Peppermint and chocolate permeated the air as Claire followed Melody around the indoor Apple Market, browsing high-end, handmade goods ranging from jewelry and watercolors to prints and soaps.

Claire was grateful for the sheer number of things to look at, as it helped distract her mind from straying to Liam. What was he up to today? He was gone from his mom's house before Claire and Melody had left that morning. Was he taking photos? Working from his own house, even though he'd taken time off?

She shook the thought from her mind for the hundredth time, looking to Melody for a distraction, but her friend was staring down at her phone again.

Claire had just assumed she'd been messaging back and forth with her family all morning, but as Melody's secretive smiles continued to grow as the day progressed, Claire's suspicions rose.

"Who are you messaging?" she asked with narrowed eyes. Normally, she didn't like to pry, but Melody was hiding something—as was made evident when she turned her phone off and faced Claire with wide eyes.

"What?" she asked. "Oh, no one. Just a friend." Then she bumped her elbow into Claire's. "So you still haven't told me about your day with Liam yesterday. How was it?"

So much for Melody being a distraction.

Claire stifled a sigh. She'd already answered that question at the Tower of London, but Melody had been too distracted with her phone to listen.

"It was good," she said truthfully.

Because her time with Liam *had* been good. After her back-and-forth the night before, Claire had woken up with a clearer mind. Yes, she was attracted to Liam. Yes, she had a teeny, tiny, minuscule crush on him. But the fact that he was married to his job, and the fact that he lived in England, would make her keep him at arm's length if it was the last thing she did.

But there was no chance she'd share all of that with Melody.

"Was Liam in a good mood?" Melody asked next, her eyes on the red, oversized ornaments hanging down from the glass roof above them.

Okay, Claire needed to play this cool. Melody could usually tell when something was wrong with Claire from a mile away. Before Claire had even broken up with Richard, Melody had guessed what was going down that same night. Luckily, for Claire's sake, Melody was inordinately distracted today.

Raising a flippant shoulder, she replied. "Yeah, I guess so. I mean, he was pretty moody in the beginning, but he seemed to warm up after that."

She could have said the exact same thing about herself.

"That's good," Melody said. She pulled out her phone, grinned, texted, then put it away again. "Yeah, I was worried that he'd be in a total mood all day. Aunt Tasha said he's been crazy stressed lately."

"With his job?" Claire guessed without thinking.

Dang it. She shouldn't be revealing that she knew that much about him.

Luckily, Melody had just pulled out her phone again. "Um, yeah, I think that's part of it. But Aunt Tasha says she thinks he's having problems with his girlfriend again."

The blood rushed from Claire's head like snow falling off a roof's peak. Those words shouldn't have affected her at all. After all, she'd already established why Liam wasn't good for her. But she'd asked him specifically the night before if he had a girlfriend. Had he just flat-out lied to her? Was that the real reason he'd thrown away the woman's number?

Just as soon as the blood had fled from her face, it all came rushing back in a sea of warmth. How could she have been so naïve as to believe his reasonings? Of course a guy that attractive wouldn't be single.

Then again, what reason did he have for lying about such a thing? He had said he didn't have time for a relationship. Could his mom just be confused? Or was he in the relationship and didn't want to announce it to anyone yet?

"Claire?" Melody asked, breaking through her thoughts. "Are you alright?"

Claire blinked. *Get a hold of yourself.*

She pulled on a smile and nodded. "Yeah, of course," she responded too chipperly. "I didn't know Liam had a girlfriend. That's...swell."

Swell? Any other word would have been better than *swell*.

"Well, he kinda does," Melody said, staring down at her phone again. "Aunt Tasha said he's been dating a girl on and off over the last few years. She thinks that maybe something happened between them to make him stress out more."

Oh. So they weren't dating then. The tightness in her stomach eased but only slightly. Still, she would hang onto the discomfort, if only to remind herself that she wanted no more baggage than she already had this time of year.

Honestly, it didn't matter if he had a girlfriend or not. She was done thinking about him. Instead, she focused on the décor, the market, and Melody, who raised her phone again, beaming at what she read.

Alright, it was time to do some prying. "So who are you messaging?" she asked again.

Melody glanced up, a residual smile on her lips. "I already told you. Just a friend."

Claire wasn't buying it. "From Colorado or England?"

"Um, England. Hey, do you want to grab some of those cookies we saw on the way in? They smelled so good."

Claire followed her past the rest of the stalls, allowing a moment to pass before she continued. "You do know that the more you try to sidestep my questions about your *friend*, the more I'm going to press until you answer me."

Melody looked over at her, her mouth open as she clearly attempted to respond, then she pursed her lips and sighed. "Fine. He's just an old friend of mine. His parents are good friends with Aunt Tasha."

Ah, it was a *he*, then. "So what's his name?"

"Dean," Melody replied, her gaze taking on a look as starry-eyed as Ariel looking up at the statue of Prince Eric she'd thieved. "You remember me talking about him."

She ended her words in a statement, but Claire struggled to place the name. Honestly, Melody had had so many male "friends" in her life that there was no way Claire could keep up with them all.

"Anyway," Melody continued as they approached *Ben's Cookies*, "we met my first time in England when I was ten. Since then, we've seen each other every time I've come over. It's not that big of a deal."

She ended in a shrug, but Claire saw right past her fake flippancy. "So you'll be seeing him this trip, then?"

She whispered a warning for her spirits to keep up, to be prepared for Melody's typical enthusiastic self, who jumped from person to person regardless of anyone's feelings but her own.

Melody shook her head. "No. Well, yes. He was supposed to spend Christmas with his family in Scotland, but they had to cancel because the dates were double booked or something. Anyway, he'll be going with his family the day after Christmas, so they'll be at Aunt Tasha's for her Christmas Eve party."

"Oh, that'll be fun," Claire responded. That was much better than she'd expected. She thought Melody was going to ditch Claire for the guy.

"Yeah, it'll be good to see him," Melody agreed, staring down at her phone. "Even if it is just for a little bit." Her smile faded somewhat, then she faced forward. "Ready for those cookies?"

Just as Melody could read Claire, Claire could read Melody, and Melody was clearly not happy with only seeing this Dean guy once during her trip.

"Did he ask to see you before Christmas Eve?" Claire asked as they entered the small shop, a variety of cookies placed behind a glass display shelf.

Melody nodded, keeping her eyes trained on the sweets. "Yeah, he asked if I could go with him to the Winter Wonderland in Hyde Park. It's this huge carnival thing with rides and food and stuff. It's, like, the best Christmas Fair in all of London."

Claire cringed. The fair sounded a bit too much for her own taste—especially when compared to the market she'd been to with Liam last night. But then, that made perfect sense for Melody to love it.

"Dean also had some extra tickets to see the *Nutcracker* tonight since his mom's a patron there," Melody continued. "But I told him I was busy."

She sent an easy smile to Claire, then asked the cashier for three dark chocolate cookies. Claire smiled in return, though it failed to raise her heart that had steadily declined until it rested in the pit of her stomach.

Melody was trying hard—that much was obvious—and

Claire appreciated it. But then, what sort of friend would Claire be if she didn't at least encourage Melody to meet up with this guy she obviously had a thing for?

After purchasing a couple milk chocolate chip cookies herself, Claire followed Melody from the store, stepping into the cold air once again.

Melody took a bite of one of her cookies, then stared down at her phone with another smile.

Fine. Claire wouldn't put it off any longer. Curse her guilty conscience. "Why don't you just go with him tonight?"

Melody looked up from her phone, at least having the courtesy to appear shocked. "What? No way. I already told him I was busy. Besides, I'm not going to ditch you again."

"You didn't ditch me," Claire corrected. "You were sick. And really, it's totally fine. I want you to be able to see him more than just once. I mean, you came all the way here."

And if Claire was being honest, Melody may as well go be with Dean, since she was on her phone with him all day anyway.

Melody frowned, looking between her phone and Claire. "But what would you do?"

Claire shrugged. "I'll just hang out with Tasha."

"No, she's working late tonight since she had to take yesterday off. It would just be you and Liam again."

Uh, nope. Nope, nope, nope. That definitely wasn't going to fly. "Don't worry about me, Melody. I'll be just fine. Really." And she would be. She'd just sneak out and go eat dinner somewhere by herself. Or she could buy a stash of McVitie's Chocolate Digestive Biscuits and eat those for dinner in her room while watching *Home Alone*. Mmm. That sounded like a lovely evening. Either way, she'd rather be alone than force Liam to spend any more time with her.

Melody's frown deepened, then her gaze shot up, and she gasped, wrapping her fingers around Claire's arm to stop her in the middle of the square. A large Christmas tree propped up in an oversized barrel towered beside them. "I've got it. Why don't we just double? To the fair and the ballet? I'll go with Dean, and you can go with Liam!"

Claire blinked, staring at Melody in silence. Had Melody lost her mind? "I'm not going to go on a date with someone who has a girlfriend." Or who might have a girlfriend. Or who might not have a girlfriend.

"He's probably not dating her *now*," Melody defended.

Claire gave her a look, then Melody glanced away with a sigh. "No, you're right." Her eyes brightened again in an instant. "Then we won't call it a date. We'll just be hanging out. That's probably better for Dean and me anyway."

Still, Claire shook her head. She refused to put herself into any more situations with Liam. Never, ever again.

"Melody, I promise, it's fine if just you and Dean go. You'll have a better time, anyway. I'll just stay at Tasha's."

Melody paused, narrowing her eyes. "You must have really hated your time with Liam yesterday to not want to be with him again."

Claire froze. Dang it all. That was not the message she'd wanted to send to Melody. Her friend would no doubt confront Liam about it, and then where would Claire be?

"No, no," she said, hastily correcting her. "I really had a good time with him. But he already gave up his entire day yesterday to hang out with me. I'm not going to ask him to do that today, too."

Melody grinned, raising her chin. "You're not asking him. I am." Then she pulled out her phone and started tapping her thumbs against the screen.

As Claire realized what Melody was doing, she launched forward, attempting to take away her phone, but Melody dodged out of the way.

"Please don't, Melody," Claire pleaded. "He'll think I put you up to it."

Melody frowned, not looking up from her phone. "Why the heck would he think that?"

Claire paused, mutely shrugging.

"You overthink things too much, Claire." Then with a roll of her eyes, she added, "Don't worry. I'll make it abundantly clear."

Claire watched in dismay, her stomach churning. "You make it really hard to like you sometimes, you know?"

Melody smiled. "I know." Then she put her phone away with a satisfied sigh. "There. Done. Now we just wait to see what he says."

Crossing the courtyard of the market, Claire shook her head. "And if he's busy and can't go tonight?" Please, please be busy.

"Then we can just go together with Dean."

Claire's brow pulled together. As happy as she was for Melody to be able to do what she wanted, Claire couldn't help but regret her encouragement. Melody was just too pushy sometimes. Claire didn't want to be a third wheel any more than she wanted to be shackled to a guy who may or may not have a girlfriend.

The next few minutes dragged by until Melody read her next text from Liam with a broad smile. "He can make it!"

Well that was just great. "What did he say?"

Melody showed Claire the text.

Liam: Sure. Sounds fun.

Well, *he* sounded less than enthused.

Before Claire could even react, Melody looped her arm through hers and pulled her ahead. "We are going to have the *best* time. You will love Dean. He's sooo dreamy."

Ah, excellent. Claire couldn't wait to meet Dreamy Dean and spend another evening trying not to fall even harder for Liam.

One thing was for certain, she was going to make it perfectly clear to Liam that tonight was *not* a date. She'd hate for him to think she was like the waitress from last night—flirting with a guy who was unavailable.

Even if that was *exactly* what she wanted to do.

TWENTY

LIAM SHUFFLED TOWARD THE EAST SIDE OF HYDE PARK, the large gate to Winter Wonderland looming above in all its flashy, Christmassy glory. Normally, the pop-up fun fair boasted thrills for all ages, including rides, street vendors, circus performances, and ice sculptures.

But having fun at the fair was conditional on the people one went with and, of course, the ability to withstand pressing crowds.

Unfortunately for Liam, neither factor was in his favor that afternoon. Honestly, if it weren't for Claire going, there was no chance he'd have ever considered coming at all.

"Liam! Over here!"

Liam followed the sound of his cousin's voice, finding her as she wildly waved her arms overhead. Dean Wilson stood by her side with his typical smirk, and Claire looked on with a shifting stance. Her eyes were on Liam until he met her gaze, then she promptly looked away.

His heart quickened at the mere sight of her, but he told it to settle down. There was no room for any of that nonsense today. He was there for one reason and one reason alone—to save her from Melody and Dean's absurdity.

"Took you long enough," Melody said as they met up near the front line. "We've been waiting for, like, an hour."

"Sorry about that," Liam said half-heartedly. "The Tube was busier than normal."

"How've you been, Liam?" Dean said, reaching forward to shake Liam's hand. His brown hair was slicked back with a faded buzz at the sides. "It's been a while."

Liam returned his handshake, then tucked his fingers back into his pockets. The temperature had dropped significantly from the day before due to the clouds cloaking the sun with dark gray blankets. "I've been fine, thanks. And yourself?"

"Much better now that I have your beautiful cousin on my arm," Dean responded, his dark eyes all over Melody. Then he glanced to Claire. "And, of course, meeting this gorgeous bird has been an utter delight, as well."

Liam gauged Claire's response carefully, pleased when her smile revealed discomfort more than anything. It was no wonder. Dean was ridiculous.

It went without saying that Liam had never liked the guy. Where Liam had finished school, Dean had dropped out. Where Liam had worked hard to make a living and stand on his own two feet, Dean was still living with his parents and couldn't keep a job if his life depended on it. But none of those things mattered as much as how Dean treated the women in his life. He was always dating multiple girls at a time and spoke about them like they were possessions to be collected instead of actual people with hearts and souls of their own.

Unfortunately, Liam's parents had been friends with Dean's since college, so they had been forced to be civil for years.

Melody tugged on Dean's arm, pulling him toward the entrance where the queue stretched back a few meters. "Alright, I'm done waiting. Come on, we already purchased the ticket for you, Liam. Let's go already!"

Dean laughed, following her at once as Claire and Liam fell in step behind them. Claire once again averted her gaze from Liam, seeming inordinately focused on the sign they neared, Santa holding a list on one side and a woman ice skating on the other.

Wanting to begin his rescue of Claire sooner rather than later, he leaned toward her. "Were you really waiting for long?"

She still wouldn't meet his gaze. "No. It was only a few minutes."

Her answer was stinted, and he couldn't help but wonder if it was his presence or Melody's behavior that was preventing her from being the normal, chatty woman from the day before.

Melody laughed ahead of them in the queue, turning around to face Liam and Claire. "Oh my gosh, you guys. You have to hear Dean's story about the Airbnb they just rented. Go on, Dean. Tell them. It's seriously the funniest thing you'll ever hear."

The story turned out to be one of the dullest in Liam's life, but he smiled politely through the retelling. Claire did, as well, but he couldn't decipher if it was genuine or not.

As the queue moved forward, Melody continued boisterously laughing at everything Dean said, shifting her body away from Claire and Liam until there was something she wanted to say to them. Claire, however, remained silent.

"Did you have a good day today?" he asked as Melody and Dean showed their tickets to the worker standing nearby.

Claire nodded, her eyes brightening. "Yeah, we actually—"

"Come on!" Melody interrupted again, waving them forward as she and Dean moved into the fair.

Liam thought he heard a sigh coming from Claire's lips, but she smiled and followed Melody in silence. Liam did the same, though he wanted to give his cousin a piece of his mind. Was she so oblivious to Claire's unhappiness? No, Melody just cared more about her own pleasure than anyone else's.

But then, this was exactly why he'd come today. He had been a text away from saying no to Melody's request for him to come to the fair and the ballet later on, but the second he heard that Dean would be with them, he knew there was no way he could ever leave Claire to their mercy.

"Oh, look at the littles!" Melody squealed next, dragging Dean and the rest of them toward the bumper cars first, where kids rode around in penguin carts. "Aren't they adorable?"

"So sweet," Dean agreed, his eyes focusing solely on Melody. "But I think I see someone even more adorable than those children."

"Oh, you are so funny," Melody said laughing. "Isn't he funny, Claire?"

Claire smiled with a succinct nod, then looked over her shoulder. If she was anything like Liam, she was looking for a distraction before she became sick all over the pavement.

"Oh, I just want one of those babies so bad," Melody continued.

It was no wonder they'd entered through the Red Gate instead of one of the other three entrances. Melody had clearly wanted to walk through the family section to impress Dean with her love of children.

Liam would hate to break it to her, but Dean wasn't a fan of kids, as he'd been apt to announce to the men during every Christmas Eve party he'd attended of Mum's.

Focus on Claire.

He turned toward her as Melody pulled them to the next station, where kids rode around in circles atop plastic reindeers.

"So you were supposed to visit a few museums today, right?" he asked.

Claire glanced to Melody, as if to ensure she was occupied enough not to interrupt her again, then she finally responded. "Yeah, we got to go to the Natural History Museum, but we ended up going to the Tower of London instead of the Tate Modern."

He raised his eyebrows. "So you managed to get Melody to budge, then."

Her lips curved. "Barely."

Was it bad for Liam to hope that Melody had a terrible time there, since she was making him have a terrible time at the fair?

"Dean, you goose!" came Melody's voice above the sound of children's laughter. "Don't you dare say such a thing. You'd be an amazing father. I just know it."

Liam refused to look at them again, though they followed them to the next section, the Santa Land Train Station. "So were you more impressed with the Tower than Melody was?"

The light shone a bit brighter in Claire's eyes, though they were a mere fraction of what they'd been the day before. "Oh, yeah. I seriously loved it. It's definitely been a highlight of the trip so far."

Liam had to check his smile. Why did that make him so happy to know that she'd loved something he'd recommended again?

"And did you go back to Greggs for lunch?"

She hesitated, though her smile grew. "Um, not exactly."

"Oh, don't tell me. You finally made it to your blessed Pizza Hut?"

Her grin was dazzling, brighter than any star, brighter than the sun, warming him through to his soul.

"I should've known," he said, shaking his head in feigned disbelief.

"But I still loved—"

"Oh my gosh, a carousel!" Melody's loud voice carried out across Santa Land, cutting off Claire's words again. "Okay, everybody, quick. Let's go there before the line gets bigger!"

Claire fell silent again, and Liam frowned in frustration. He'd finally made some progress, and now he was back at square one. Melody was a good person. He knew that. But whenever she was around Dean, she became unbearable.

A buzz in his back pocket distracted him for a minute as he followed the others through the crowds of parents wrangling their children. With Claire no longer speaking, he pulled it out to read yet another message from another coworker.

Andrew: Mate, sorry to hear about the promotion. I
couldn't believe it. Let me know when you want to go out

for a bite. Maybe catch up on a few things. I'm glad you took time off, at least. You deserve it.

Liam typed out a quick response, then tucked his phone back into his pocket, determined to never open the blasted thing again. Watching Melody and Dean snogging would be better at this point.

While the message was nice, it had to be the tenth of its kind Liam had received that day from different workmates as the promotion had officially been filled as of that morning.

He appreciated the sentiments he received, but he couldn't take the pity any longer. What he wanted now, more than anything, was a distraction. Something to keep his mind off of the disaster that was now his work life.

"Hurry, hurry, hurry!" Melody cried out.

Dean hurried. Claire and Liam did not.

When they finally reached the carousel, Melody slipped right in front of a woman and her young son. Disapproval marked the mother's brow as she pulled her boy back to avoid him getting rammed to the side. Melody and Dean, of course, were completely oblivious to the whole affair.

By the time Liam and Claire reached the queue, three more families had filed in front of them, so Melody tried to wave Claire and Liam forward to join them at their place in the queue.

Liam shook his head, not wanting to displace even more families than they already had. But would Claire want to join her friend?

"Do you want to move up to them?" he asked as the queue continued to grow.

To his relief, Claire shook her head. "No, that's fine. To be honest, I'd just as soon leave the line altogether."

That was something he could get right on board with. "I'm with you. Let's wait over there until they finish with their kiddie ride."

After telling Melody where they'd be—Melody barely

acknowledging their words—Liam led the way to stand to the side of the Santa Land Chill Space shelter.

"Will this do?" he asked, ensuring they were well out of the way of the families moving in and out of the doors like clockwork. Kids rode on the train across from them, and the air was filled with the stomach-warming scent of cinnamon and sugar.

"Yeah, this'll work great," Claire responded. "Anything is better than standing near those two any longer."

His heart lifted. *Here* was the real Claire. Did that mean that Melody was the culprit to her silence, then, and not he?

"I take it you haven't been enjoying your time with them," he said.

"No, I haven't. Thank-freaking-heavens he only joined me and Melody for the last half hour." She blinked, seeming to think better of her words. "I mean, he's super nice, but..."

Liam held up a hand in the air. "You don't have to explain to me. I've known him for most of my life, and *I* can barely stand him. Or Melody, for that matter. At least when she's around him."

"Right?" Claire responded, the ice melting from her eyes one slab at a time as she peered up at him with ease. "I seriously love Melody. And I usually have such a great time when I'm with her. It's just that...whenever she's around guys, she just turns into this airheaded attention-hog."

"So she's like this with more men than Dean?" That was encouraging. At least Dean and Melody deserved each other, then.

"Oh, yeah. You should've seen her in college." She paused, smiling politely at a family with a double pram before continuing in a lower tone. "She used to make me go with her to all these stupid parties where I'd end up alone by the dessert table while she just made out with random guys."

Liam grimaced. Unfortunately, he wasn't surprised.

Before he had the chance to respond, Claire pressed on, her

words coming out in a constant stream, as if the dam had broken and the water couldn't help but spurt out.

"I'm used to being second choice with everyone," she said, her eyes focusing on Melody as she leaned her head against Dean's arm. "And really, it's not that big of a deal. But she just pushes and pushes and pushes until she gets exactly what *she* wants, you know?" She waved her hand in the air toward Liam. "I mean, today is the perfect example. I told her not to invite you, but she just went ahead and did it anyway. Then I told her to make sure that you knew that this wasn't a date, and who knows if she even did that. I just can't with her sometimes."

She stopped, shaking her head as she did so.

Liam chewed the inside of his lip, not sure how to proceed. So Claire hadn't wanted him to come today, then. Was she still upset about whatever he'd said last night?

"Sorry," Claire muttered as his silence continued. "I guess I just needed to vent or something."

He eyed her rosy cheeks, made all the redder by her blush. Why was it so important for her to ensure that he knew this evening wasn't a date?

"If it helps," he began, "she did clarify that we'd just be hanging out together."

Her shoulders visibly relaxed. "Okay. Good. I just wanted to be sure."

Liam nodded. Alright, so Claire was happier now. But what about himself? "You know, if you didn't want me to come here today, you could have messaged me yourself."

Honestly, it would be easier not to be there. Never mind that he was only trying to help her. If she didn't want him there, he'd just as soon back out.

Claire's blue eyes landed on him in an instant, and she frowned. "What? Why wouldn't I want you here?"

"You just said you told Melody not to invite me."

Understanding lit her eyes, and she instantly shook her head. "No, no, no. I'm more than happy to have you here.

Honestly. I'd much rather talk to you than the back of Melody's head or Dean's glazed-over eyes. I just felt bad asking you to give up another one of your days off, you know?" She ended in a shrug. "I just didn't want to put you out again."

Well, blast. Not only did she balm his pride, she'd also somehow convinced him to want to be there with her, too. Everything would have been so much easier had she just told him to leave.

Melody's laughter bellowed toward them, and they both turned as she neared the front of the line, hopping up and down as she clung to Dean's hand.

In an effort to distract them once again from his cousin's ridiculousness, Liam shifted his body toward Claire. "For the record, you aren't putting me out."

She gave him a dubious look. "So you were just more than happy to stop whatever it was you were doing with your spare time to hang out with some rando from America?"

"Well, I *was* rather sad to step away from watching my saved clips of the royal weddings..."

Her eyes shimmered as a barely restrained grin lit her expression.

"Really, though," he continued, "I was happy to come today. If only to save you from having to spend more time alone with Dean and Melody. They really are a bit much together."

Claire nodded with a heavy sigh. "Well, thanks for agreeing to share in my misery. They are nauseating. But, for what it's worth, I'm still having a nicer time here than I would've been having home alone at Christmas."

Liam paused, wondering if he'd heard her right. Her parents were on a cruise over the holiday, but was there nowhere else for her to spend Christmas?

"You really would have been home alone?"

Claire's mouth hung open like a nutcracker's. Obviously, she hadn't meant to let that slip. "Yeah, but it's not that big of a deal.

I've done it before, and it's actually really peaceful. But this year, I dunno, it's nice to be somewhere other than home."

Liam nodded, his heart reaching out to her, if only to cloak his own pain. Spending two Christmases by himself in a hotel room, drowning himself in production after production, may have numbed his pain for a time, but it was also very, very lonely and *anything* but peaceful.

"So what do you do for Christmas normally?" he asked gingerly. He didn't want to impose, but a fraction of him wanted —*needed*—to know she had some happiness at Christmas to fall back on.

She seemed to hesitate for a minute, then pulled on a tight smile. "I used to stay with my grandparents through all of December when I was a kid, then after they died, I was invited to go with my aunt and uncle up to their lodge for Christmas."

"That sounds nice," he said, praying that it was.

She nodded, her eyes taking on a faraway look. "It *was* nice. They always had this huge tree they cut down themselves set up in the center of the front room. We'd stay up late every night, playing games and eating fudge and peanut brittle around the tree. It was always really fun."

"So did they not get together there this year, then?"

Her expression fell, but she picked it straight back up with a shrug. "No, they did. Their family is just getting so big now with their kids marrying and having children of their own. There's just not much room for me anymore."

Liam's chest burned. Really? Her uncle had no room to invite his one niece to stay at his massive holiday home for a couple days? It wasn't Liam's place to judge, but how could all of the adults in this woman's life be so selfish?

Before he could respond—though he still didn't know what to say—Claire pointed abruptly to the carousel. "They're finally getting on."

Liam glanced to where Dean and Melody rushed past children to mount two horses situated side-by-side. They laughed together as they held each other's hands across the aisle, preventing anyone else from moving past them.

"Are Christmas trees a thing here?"

Liam paused, shifting his gaze back to Claire as she changed the conversation. "Yeah, of course they are. Why?"

She shrugged, focusing on the carousel as the ride began to slowly turn round. "Since your mom doesn't have one up, I thought maybe they weren't."

Instantly, Liam's heart twisted. He knew exactly why Mum didn't have a tree up, and he knew it was his fault. But how could he admit that aloud? "I think her job has taken its toll on her this year," he lied. "She more than likely just doesn't have the time."

Guilt cinched tightly around his chest, tied in an impossible knot. He should have come home for Christmas before. He should have been there for her. Yes, he'd been grieving in his own way, but what sort of son abandoned his own mother when she had no one else?

"Do you think..." Claire hesitated, *Jingle Bells* blaring out from the carousel's speakers.

"Do I think, what?"

Finally, she pulled her eyes up to search his. "Do you think your mom would be okay with us surprising her with a tree?"

Liam stared hard at Claire, unable to remove his eyes from her.

"If it'd make things worse, we don't have to," Claire rushed on. "I wouldn't want to offend her or make her sad or anything. But we could have it set up for her when she comes home from work, then we could all decorate it tomorrow morning together."

Liam tried to press down his heart, but it refused to obey, rising up like a bird dreaming of flight. "I don't think she'd be offended at all. In fact, I think she'd absolutely love it."

Claire's face brightened, her wrinkled brow smoothing as she peered up at him. "Do you think Dean and Melody could be convinced to leave here early to get a tree, then?"

Liam turned, his eyes skimming the spinning carousel until he found his cousin.

His stomach turned. "Um, no, I don't think we'll be able to convince them at all."

He pointed toward Dean and Melody, who were now snogging from atop their horses for all of Santa Land to see. Liam had been wrong before. He *wouldn't* rather see his cousin and Dean kissing.

"Ugh, gosh." Claire pulled a face. "They've been with each other for a freaking hour. I hate to think what they'll be doing by the end of the night." She shook her head, turning to Liam with a frown. "Alright. I've got a better plan. What if we ditch those two disgusting animals and get the tree ourselves?"

Liam smiled at her ferocity. He liked this version of Claire much better than the one made to be silent around Melody. "Are you sure? There are actually a lot of fun things we could do here."

But Claire shook her head. "No, I think I'd rather do something nice for your mom."

It took everything within him to have his heart keep its shape as it threatened to melt like an ice sculpture at her words.

"Melody might be offended," he warned.

"Yeah, right," Claire huffed. "She'll be glad to have free rein with the guy. She knows I judge her and all her boyfriends for their PDA. Besides, we can make amends by agreeing to go to the ballet tonight." Then she paused. "Unless *you* want to stay here?"

He smiled, tossing his head toward the exit. "Let's go," he said, and Claire's eyes sparkled.

As the two of them made their way from the park, Liam tried to convince himself that his anticipation for the day had grown exponentially because he was doing something for his mum, not because he was going to have the next couple of hours with Claire all to himself.

But deep down inside, he knew the truth just as much as he knew he was in trouble *because* of that truth.

TWENTY-ONE

JUST AS CLAIRE HAD SUSPECTED, MELODY HARDLY seemed shaken up about being left alone with Dean.

Melody: Are you sure you don't want to stay??

Claire: Yep, totally. You guys have fun. We'll meet up for the Nutcracker, k?

Melody: Okay, sounds good. Thanks, Claire! You're the best! Tell Liam thanks, too.

Claire thumbsed-up the message, shaking her head. She should have expected this the moment Melody had mentioned Dean. Claire was always second choice when it came to her friend's men. Still, sometimes, Melody drove her nuts. It would be good to put some distance between them today.

Of course, that meant that she would be spending all of her time alone with Liam now, who just might have a girlfriend. But Claire and Liam were merely friends coming together to do something nice for his mom. That was all.

She glanced toward him as he hung up his phone again from

yet another tree farm, the both of them standing off to the side of the Winter Wonderland entryway.

"Any luck?" she asked.

"Unfortunately, no. Every lot is booked solid. The earliest delivery options are for tomorrow afternoon."

Claire let out a disappointed sigh. She'd really wanted to have that tree tonight. And she *really* didn't want to go back into the fair. But with no car—Tasha's at her work and Liam's back at his house—they were running out of options.

"What about a taxi?" she asked.

"No, they wouldn't allow it atop the car."

She tapped a finger to her chin. "The bus?"

"Not likely."

"The Underground?"

His eyes squinted in a smile. "I'm fairly certain that's illegal."

"Fairly certain or absolutely?" she pressed.

"We can't take a tree on the Tube."

She rolled her eyes with pretend annoyance. "Fine. I guess we'll just be boring and wait until tomorrow to have it delivered."

"Sorry," Liam said, looking down at his phone. "Short of carrying it all the way home, I think waiting might be the best option."

Claire looked up at him, the cogs turning in her mind as she waited for him to meet her gaze.

When he did, he pulled back. "What?"

"That's the best idea you've had all day."

"What idea?"

"You. Carrying it home."

He was silent for a minute before a scoff escaped his lips. "You can't be serious."

She opened her mouth in a wide, encouraging grin. "Come on, it'll be fun!"

"And what would be fun about it exactly?"

"I dunno. Just the adventure of it all."

But Liam shook his head. "I think I'd rather not."

Claire pulled her lips to the side, thinking of another route. "Well, if we don't have the excuse of getting a tree, then, I guess we'd better go back in there."

She motioned with her thumb over her shoulder to where Winter Wonderland still blared with music, laughter, and a kissing Dean and Melody.

Liam cringed.

"Or..." Claire took a sliding step toward him with raised eyebrows. "We find the closest tree lot to your house and bring the Christmas spirit into your home for your mom."

Liam looked down at her with a wary gaze.

"You know she'd appreciate it," Claire said, giving her best, innocent grin.

Finally, he closed his eyes and drew a deep breath. "Fine. Fine, let's just get one."

Claire clapped her hands together with excitement. "Yay!"

Liam turned around, but not before she caught the sight of a smile turning up his lips.

Together, the two of them walked to the nearest Underground station, Claire's steps much lighter than they'd been all day. Spending a day with Liam was proving to be much happier than being forced to watch Melody and Dean kissing on a carousel.

Choosing the tree lot closest to Tasha's house, the two of them carried on lighthearted conversations until they arrived at McBride Christmas Trees, a wooden fence around the lot with white lights looped down from post to post. A few families milled about. Workers in green sweaters and brown beanies sawed off the bottoms of the trees and wrapped them tightly in white rope.

As they made their way to the Norway spruces at the back of the lot, Claire breathed in the deep pine scent permeating the air. The last few years, she'd only managed a fake tree in the corner of her apartment. She'd nearly forgotten how much she loved the smell of a live one.

After choosing a tree already wrapped—and willing to risk

any imperfections that might come along with it—the two of them purchased the pine then made their way out onto the street.

Liam heaved the tree onto his shoulder as Claire ensured others around him allowed him a wide berth.

"So how far away are we from your mom's house?" she asked as they stepped down the street.

"Quarter of an hour," Liam said, his eyes focused straight ahead.

"Are you going to be able to make it?" she teased, securing her scarf more tightly around her neck as the brisk wind picked up again.

"I'm going to have to, aren't I? It's not like you can help with those tiny arms of yours."

Why did his taunting thrill her to her core, when before, she'd just wanted to smack him upside the head? "I'll have you know that these tiny arms can lift more than you think. I have a lot of practice at the flower shop."

"Are you saying this tree weighs the same as a bouquet of baby's breath? Because my shoulder would like to tell you otherwise."

She laughed. "No, but I do have to heave fifty-pound bags of soil and huge floral arrangements daily. So..."

"Alright. Well I'll give you a chance to prove your strength when I need a break. I'm anxious to see in what way you'll embarrass yourself again today."

Claire paused. Did he mean he was anxious as in, looking forward to it, or anxious as in, stressed about what she would do?

Her heart lowered a fraction. "Well, you don't have to worry about that. I've made a pact to never embarrass myself again. That way you won't have to be embarrassed by me, either."

Liam glanced at her sidelong, his brow twitching. "I'm not embarrassed by you."

She scoffed. "Likely story."

They stopped at a crosswalk, and Liam lowered the tree to the ground with a grunt. "What reason would I have to be?"

She watched him, confused by his sincerity. "Because of all the things I've done in front of you."

"And why should any of that embarrass me?"

Claire didn't know what to say. In all honesty, she didn't know why her actions *should* embarrass him. And yet, when she'd made a fool of herself in front of Richard or any one of her exes, it was always about them looking away with red faces more than her. One time, Richard had even gone so far as to leave to "take a phone call" when she'd shattered a jar of pickles in the middle of a grocery store aisle after he'd tickled her sides.

And yet, as she thought of each moment she'd shared with Liam, she couldn't remember one time where he'd left her side by choice. He'd helped her pick up the vase at Kew Gardens until she'd shouted him off, he'd turned off the phone at the abbey, he caught her on the Underground, and he even paid for her trip to the bathroom without a second's thought.

But, why? She couldn't make sense of it. He couldn't be doing it all just to impress her. Was he just that innately...kind?

"Claire?"

Her name on his lips broke her from her thoughts, and she realized he'd already picked up the tree and was making his way across the street.

Swiftly, she caught up to him, and the two of them continued toward Tasha's house.

Halfway there, Liam stopped, shifting the tree to his other shoulder. "This is absolutely ludicrous," he muttered.

A man with a long brown coat did a double take at Liam as he passed by. "You know there are services for that now, mate."

Liam nodded. "Yeah. Just doing this for...you know." He tossed his head to Claire, who stood by him with a silent smile.

The man looked at Claire, then tipped his cap. "Good luck."

As he continued past them, Claire grinned, definitely more amused than she ought to be. "We're just having so much fun."

Liam didn't respond, though the twinkle in his eye remained.

After a few more shifting of shoulders, and another unhelpful

comment from a passerby—"Why didn't you have it delivered?"—the two of them finally arrived at Tasha's.

Liam propped the tree up in the corner of the front room,
then moved to the attic to find the decorations. Claire remained
downstairs, finishing a few dishes and tidying up the area Melody
had left behind before wandering to the bottom of the stairs.

"Do you need any help?" she called, eying the empty steps
that had been pulled down from the open attic.

"No, I'm almost done," came Liam's muffled voice from
inside.

She nodded, though she knew he couldn't see her. As she
waited, she allowed her eyes to wander about the space, folding
her arms as a cold draft came down the hallway. The pictures
along the wall caught her attention, and she stepped forward to
give them a closer look.

The first few were of Tasha and her late husband's wedding,
while the next revealed a young Liam—probably four or five—
standing beside his parents. She smiled at his woolen jacket, flat
cap, and hair cut straight above his eyebrows.

The ladder from the attic squeaked, and she glanced up as
Liam descended with a box and a tree stand. He looked down at
her with a smile, which she returned before pointing to the photo.
"Is this you?"

He glanced to the wall as he moved down the stairs. "Yeah. We
were camping in the Lake District. It was my dad's favorite place
to go."

She looked back to the picture. "You look so much like him."

"So I've heard." He came up to stand beside her, a solemn
expression on his face.

Claire hesitated. She wanted to know more about his dad, but
she was never sure how much was *too* much to ask.

"Were you like him in other ways?"

"We were fairly similar. I definitely discovered my love of the
outdoors because of him. He'd take us camping every weekend he
could."

She glanced up at him, but he averted his gaze and motioned down the hallway. "Shall we?"

Claire trailed after him, more questions about his father resting at the tip of her tongue, but she swallowed them one by one, not wishing to upset Liam by bringing up an obviously painful subject.

"Hot chocolate?" he offered as he deposited the box on the couch.

"Yeah, please."

He put the kettle on, retrieving two mugs as Claire fought against her judgment to ask him anything too intrusive. Her eyes caught sight of a camera on the counter, its sleek, black exterior contrasting from the tattered, orange neck strap draped to the side of it.

"So what were you doing today?" she asked, pulling her gaze away from the camera. "Before we roped you into hanging out with us, I mean."

Liam pulled out a purple tin of Cadbury's Drinking Chocolate, dumping a few spoonfuls into each mug. "Oh, I was just... milling about. Checked on my apartment. Took a few photos."

Ah, so he *had* been taking photos. Just as she'd suspected. "Took a few photos," she repeated, nodding her head. "And how did that go?"

He shrugged. "It was alright."

"Did you get any good shots?"

"Nothing spectacular."

Claire dropped her chin, no longer able to keep up the façade. "I stalked you."

He looked up at her as the kettle started to scream. "Al...right?"

She nodded, feeling no shame whatsoever. "Do you know what I found out?"

He watched her in silence.

"I found out that you are a big, giant liar."

He narrowed his eyes. "Am I?"

"Yep." She pulled up her phone, found his Instagram account, then showed him the screen. "A big. Giant. Liar."

He stared at the page for a minute, unflinching, then he turned away and took the kettle off. "You *have* done some stalking."

"Yep."

"I still don't understand how I'm supposed to have lied to you, though." He poured the water into the mugs and stirred them slowly one at a time.

"You said you *dabbled* in photography," she replied, looking at his feed and spotting a new image she hadn't yet seen. She clicked to view the photo bigger, marveling at the buck deer backlit by the morning sunshine and a golden fog. "I mean, this is incredible. Is *this* what you took today?"

He glanced up at the image, then put the spoon into the sink. "Yeah."

She stared at it again, shaking her head. "It's seriously amazing. And look at these comments. They all want to know when prints will be available." She glanced up as he retrieved a glass bottle of milk from the fridge. "Are you going to sell them?"

He shrugged again, swirling the milk into the mugs until the liquid edged closer to the rims. "When I have the time."

She shifted through a few more photos. "I really am so impressed. The only thing I can't understand is why you'd choose to stay at Peregrine Productions when you have this other option to make money—not to mention something that you're crazy talented in."

When Liam didn't respond, she lowered her phone and looked up at him, wondering if she'd said too much.

He stared down at his hot chocolate, blowing into the drink as steam drifted past his lips. "It's a bit more complicated than that."

She lowered her phone, taking her own steaming cup into her hands. "Can I ask how?"

He took another sip. "I've spent so much time building up

that career. Quitting now just seems like I'd be throwing away eight years of my life." He raised a shoulder. "Ever since my father died, I just...I don't know. I'm afraid of wasting any time at all, so to erase eight whole years seems careless."

Claire grew silent, hanging onto Liam's every word. She had no clue what it would be like to lose a father, let alone one who'd actually loved his family.

"I'm sorry," she said softly, not knowing what else to say. "I didn't know all that was holding you back, but it makes sense."

"But it doesn't make sense," he countered. "What *would* make sense is quitting so I don't waste more of my time at a dead-end job that doesn't care about me or my family."

He ran his fingers through his thick hair, and Claire pushed aside the thought that accompanied his movement—*Was his hair as soft as it looked?*

"Do you know the real reason my mum didn't have a tree up?" he asked next.

Claire shook her head, listening intently.

"Because she didn't have the heart to do so," he replied, staring at the pine still propped up at the back of the front room. His dark eyebrows hovered low over his eyes, and his lips thinned. "My dad died a few weeks before Christmas three years ago. I was there for his funeral, but I was sent on a work trip over Christmas that same year. Agreeing to go provided me with a distraction, so the next year, I did the same." His lip curled in disgust from his own actions. "I later learnt that she didn't put any decorations up either year because she couldn't bear to do it alone." He paused, finally looking to Claire. "So how is that for Son of the Year Award?"

Instead of feeling disgust, which she was sure Liam had been expecting, Claire's heart broke for Liam and Tasha both. "I'm sure your mom doesn't blame you," she said softly. "And not that it really matters, but I don't blame you either."

His eyes locked onto hers as she continued.

"You were both grieving," she said. "And sometimes, it's easier to grieve on your own. It's okay if that's what you needed to do to come to terms with something so heartbreaking."

Liam blinked, and she thought she saw a shimmer of emotion in the dark depths of his eyes, but he looked away too swiftly for her to be sure.

"Thank you," he said softly, clearing his throat. "As you can see, there are a few things I've got to work out if I'm ever going to make any lasting decisions about my life." Then he took another drink of his hot chocolate.

Claire opened her mouth to say more, but she closed it right back up and took a sip of her drink, as well. She wasn't going to risk saying anything more about the subject she didn't know enough about.

"What?" Liam asked, clearly noticing her hesitate.

Claire shook her head. "Oh, nothing."

"No, you had something else to say."

She hesitated. "Life will pass you by if you wait for the stars to align. Because stars don't align for us. They live out their days in the same way *we're* supposed to—on the path that will help us shine the most."

Liam's eyes found hers again, and a warmth within their dark depths slipped past her chest to nestle deeply within her heart.

"Wise words to live by," he said, his smooth tone as warm and soothing as a crackling fire.

"Something my parents taught me," she said, taking another drink. "I only wish I hadn't learned it at my cost." She ended with a short laugh, though it fell flat when Liam didn't join in.

He must not have gotten her depressing joke.

His eyes narrowed, and she knew she opened a door she'd tried to keep closed.

"How do you really feel about them being on a cruise instead of with you for Christmas?" he asked.

TWENTY-TWO

CLAIRE CONTEMPLATED BRUSHING ASIDE LIAM'S questions without so much as a response, but as she thought back to how open he was about his fears and concerns, about how he dealt with his dad's death, a light broke through the barrier around her heart. Maybe she could give a very small explanation as to what her life really was like with parents who were basically Kate and Peter McCallister.

Except her parents left her home alone on purpose *and* never felt badly about it.

"I'm alright with it," she began uneasily. "I mean, it's hard that they don't have service to message me much." Or at all. "But I really do hope they're having a good time. And honestly, they were gone so often when I was a kid that it's basically second nature now."

"So you never got to travel with them anywhere?"

"I went with them to Yellowstone once on a family vacation. My cousin is a ranger up there. But the rest of the trips they took were for business, so they couldn't exactly bring me along."

Liam hardly looked convinced, which didn't help her desire to remain unaffected by her parents' lack of attention throughout her life.

"They'd always bring stuff home for me, though," she continued. "Souvenirs and stuff. So that was...nice."

Of course, she would have much preferred being with her parents to receiving gifts from them. But at least they thought of her enough during their travels to bring tokens back for her.

"That's good," Liam said weakly, clearly not believing in his words or her own.

"It really is fine," she said, not wanting the conversation to carry on any longer than it had. "I've learned that life is much easier to handle when I focus on what I have rather than what I don't."

Liam downed the last of his drink, then placed the cup in the sink. "You're like a walking self-help book."

Claire laughed. "That's because I've read enough of them to last me a lifetime."

Their gazes met, more questions floating around in his eyes, and she cringed. What was her deal? Why was she oversharing so much?

Refusing to be the subject of any further questioning, Claire turned toward the front room. "We should probably get that tree set up before the sap gets onto the floor."

She knew Liam wanted to continue their conversation, but she had never been more grateful for his silence as they made their way toward the tree.

As Liam lifted the pine, Claire directed him to where it would sit in the tree stand, then they switched places as she held the tree upright, and Liam twisted in the screws. The smell of the pine tree wafted around, sharing its Christmassy scent to every corner of the room.

"Is it straight?" he asked, his voice muffled as he lay down on his side, his upper half hidden beneath the branches.

"As far as I can tell," she said, looking more at the long stretch of Liam's legs than the direction of the tree.

Alright, she wasn't just *looking* at his legs. She was absolutely checking him out. But she shouldn't be doing that if he had a girl-friend, right?

She bit her tongue for as long as possible until the words pushed past her lips likes blades of grass breaking through a first snow. "So do you take photos alone usually? Or do you go with a friend...or a girlfriend?"

That was *super* subtle.

Liam grunted as he shifted to the next screw. "No, I typically go alone." Then he shuffled to the side and poked his head out to stare at her between a few branches. "And to answer your fishing, no, I don't have a girlfriend, like I told you last night."

Instead of her typical embarrassment at having been called out, relief flooded through her limbs. Until, of course, Melody's words slunk back into her mind. "That's not what your cousin seems to think."

Again, Liam's head popped back out, but Claire focused ahead on the dim light outside. The sun was swiftly setting, the only light in the front room coming from the fire burning in the hearth and the soft light from the kitchen.

"And what does she think?" Liam asked.

His no-nonsense tone made her pause. Was he defensive because he did have a girlfriend—or because he was annoyed with Melody? "Oh, nothing, really."

Liam pulled back to the third screw. "That's good. Because Melody knows very little about my life."

His gruff tone drew her attention back down to him, but all she could see were his legs and torso—a nice, tapered torso that was revealed even more as he raised his arms.

"Are you upset with Melody or something?" she asked, an odd swirling occurring in her stomach as she stared at him.

"No." He grunted as he tightened the screw. "I just don't appreciate definitive statements from uninformed people." He poked his head out again, and she pulled her eyes from his torso. "What makes her think I have a girlfriend, anyway?"

"She just said that you had been dating someone on and off. She and your mom think that that's why you've been in a mood."

His frown deepened. "When have I been in a mood?"

She secured the tree with one hand while using her other to make a numbered list with her fingers. "The airport. Kew Gardens. Around London—"

"Alright, alright." He ducked back beneath the tree, grunting as he shifted to the final screw. "I can see why she'd say that, but that's not why—"

"I know," she interrupted. "It was because of your job."

"Exactly. Wait, you didn't tell her…"

She shook her head. "No. I promised I wouldn't."

"Thank you." He grunted again. "Anyway, I wouldn't be in a *mood* because of that relationship."

Claire hesitated. *That* relationship? "So you were dating someone, then?"

Liam didn't respond for a minute. "It's true that I dated a woman on and off for a few years. But when I say dated, I mean that we went out on a few dates. We were never anything serious. I haven't even seen her since the summer when she was dating someone else."

Claire couldn't explain the weight that lifted from her shoulders as he spoke. He'd said himself he didn't have time for a girlfriend. But if he worked somewhere else, would he have time then?

She gave a firm shake of her head. She would not even finish that thought.

Liam shifted beneath the tree. "So now that you've done your fishing, am I allowed to do mine?"

Her heart thumped. "I guess."

"Do you have a boyfriend waiting for you back home utterly distraught that he can't spend the holidays with you?"

She stretched her lips into a grim line. "Oh, I'm sure he's finding comfort in the arms of someone else right about now. Same as when he was with me."

Liam stuck his head out. "He cheated on you?"

Somehow, his accent made the word sound worse. "Yep."

He huffed and disappeared once again. "Men are pigs."

She smiled. "You're a man."

"*Some* men are pigs."

Her grin widened. "It was fine, really. He gave me the perfect out of a relationship I never should have been in. He was more of a way to..."

"Pass the time?" Liam offered.

"As horrible as that makes me sound, yes."

"It doesn't make you sound horrible. It makes you sound human." He grunted, then wiggled his way from beneath the tree. "There. That should do it."

Claire cautiously released her hold of the tree. When it remained upright, she beamed. "Perfect."

"Mum will love this."

"You think she'll be up to decorating tomorrow?"

"Absolutely." He stretched out his arm to reveal his watch on his wrist. "We ought to be getting ready soon. Though we should probably eat before we go."

"Oh, I know this great place to eat pizza—"

"Don't," Liam cut her off, holding up a finger in the air. "Don't you dare."

She laughed, and his eyes brightened with that smile she'd grown to lov—slightly tolerate.

Instead of eating out again that night, Liam suggested spaghetti at home, so the two of them whipped up the simple meal together, hanging a few garlands around the house as the noodles boiled before sitting down across from each other at the table.

Their conversation consisted of flowers, photographs, and the sites around London before they cleaned up and made to get ready for the ballet.

Halfway down the hallway, however, Claire paused. "Oh, the tree needs to be watered."

"I can see to that."

But she was already backing up into the kitchen. "No, that's alright. You go on ahead. I'll do it."

His footsteps shuffled down the hallway as Claire found a plastic pitcher and filled it up with water, making her way to the tree before sidling under it as a few drops spilled.

After an annoying struggle, Claire awkwardly emptied the pitcher into the stand, then moved to pull back. Somehow, however, the pitcher handle hooked onto the end of one of the screws and refused to budge.

She grunted, struggling to get it loosened, but the pitcher held fast. Squinting to see the culprit of her grief, she noted a piece of metal jutting forth at the end of the screw, so she tried to push the pitcher around the hooked edge.

Unable to move far enough to unsnag the handle, she shuffled farther beneath the tree, holding onto the branches for more leverage. In her movement, she somehow managed to forget her grip was on a freewheeling tree instead of something sturdier. She tugged hard once again, finally unhooking the pitcher just as the tree teetered forward.

"No, no, no," she swiftly repeated as soon as she caught sight of the tree's movement, but the pine toppled forward without any regard to her pleading.

Dropping the pitcher, she covered her face with her hands, bracing until the pointed needles fell across her body, and she yelped.

LIAM PAUSED in buttoning up his white dress shirt. Had he imagined that shout? Or had something happened to Claire?

He strained to hear further, but silence met his ears. Unable to appease his worry, he left his room, noting Claire's door and the bathroom door still ajar. She hadn't come upstairs, then. Was she still watering the tree?

He moved down the stairs quietly, hoping to hear any clue as to what had happened, but no further sound came. Only when he rounded the corner did he finally see what had occurred. Claire was on her back, her hands covering her face, her shoulders shaking—was she crying or laughing?—and beside her, lay the tree.

He rushed forward, worry tensing his stomach. "Claire?"

She froze, her hands still covering her face.

"Are you alright?" He sidestepped the tree, pausing above her when she said nothing.

Another moment passed before she responded, her voice muffled in her hands. "Yep."

He looked again to the tree still on its side. "What, uh...What happened here?"

She remained where she was, still hiding her face. Had she tripped over the tree somehow? Hurt her nose by falling?

"Oh, you know," she replied, her voice steady. "I was just watering the tree when the pitcher got caught on the stand, so naturally, I pulled the whole thing down on myself. But, hey. Good news. The pitcher's no longer stuck."

She waved an elbow to the right of her where the empty pitcher also lay beside her.

He reached down, heaving the tree up from its side as he took note of the water that had spilled across the floor and was now seeping into Claire's side, darkening the fabric of her shirt. He pressed his lips tightly together, trying to hold in his growing smile. He needed to make sure she really was okay before he allowed himself to fully register the humor of the situation.

"Are you sure you're not hurt?"

"Yep. I managed to wiggle my way out from under it, so I'm good."

He made sure the tree was secure, then turned to face Claire.

"If you're not hurt, why are you still on the ground, hiding your face?"

"Well, I couldn't really stand up before because I was laughing so hard."

So she *had* been laughing. That was good news. "And now?" he pressed.

"Now, I'm not getting up or showing my face because I swore you'd never see me embarrassed again."

A smile broke out across his lips. If this woman wasn't the most adorable, most thoughtful, most charming...

"Come on," he said, offering her his hand. "Let me help you up."

"Nope. I'm good."

He dropped his hand to his side. "You don't want my help?"

"Oh, I'd be fine with your help. But I'll just get up when you're gone."

He shook his head in amusement, but when he caught sight of the scratches on her arms, his smile faded. "You *are* hurt."

He crouched beside her, reaching out to smooth a finger over the white abrasions the needles left across her smooth skin, but instead of ensuring the cuts weren't too deep, his attention was swallowed up by the energy skittering up his arm from her skin against his.

Swallowing hard, he pulled back and shook the feeling from his hands, glancing instead to her face she still covered. "Did you get scratched on your face, too?"

"No."

As if she'd tell him the truth.

The blood thinned in his legs from his crouched position, so he knelt instead, resting a hand near her shoulder. In his movements, his knee pressed against her hip, but he swiftly shifted away.

"Just let me see your face once," he said, "then I promise I'll leave you be."

He watched her closely until she finally raised her hands out to the side of her, though she kept her eyes closed. "There, see? I'm all good."

Liam smiled at first, her ridiculous actions making her all the more endearing. But as he continued to stare down at her, the light from the fireplace flickering across her features, the humor slipped away, and a stirring swelled in his chest that he couldn't dampen.

Just as she'd said, her face wasn't scratched. Instead, it was flawless. Her skin smooth across her high cheekbones, her arched lips curved ever so slightly at the ends, and her hair—those full, gorgeous waves splayed out behind her head and across the floor. What would his fingers feel like, swimming through those currents?

His hands itched to feel just a strand of the silky swells, but he knew if he gave into that one desire, he'd give into an even greater desire he had—the desire to kiss her perfect lips that now called up to him, beckoning him closer.

How he wished to answer them.

CLAIRE FOUGHT to keep her eyes from opening, but as Liam's silence continued, she shifted, unsettled. Why wasn't he saying anything? Had he somehow left without her hearing a sound?

Slowly, she peered up through her lashes. A jolt of energy shot through her stomach when she found Liam kneeling beside her, his face directly above hers as he stared down at her.

When had he moved so close to her? And why was he watching her so intently? "What's wrong? *Did* I get scratched?" she asked, the fire's light casting dark shadows across his features.

"No," he said, his deep voice sinking into her soul. "You're... you're perfect."

Her heart leapt at his words, her cheeks aflame as she fought the sudden urge to hide again. She was still ripe with humiliation after being body-slammed by a pine tree. Add Liam's compliment, and her blush was done for.

Time stood still as he looked down at her, his eyes slightly narrowed, as if deep in thought. She wanted to ask him what he was thinking, but her breath caught in her throat as he leaned closer to her. His knee rested against her hip as he slowly moved his left hand to the other side of her.

He was only doing so for balance—or so she tried to tell herself. But as his gaze washed over her, she could see the desire in his eyes, desire that matched her own.

He hovered directly above her, like a lion standing over his prey. Only, Liam wasn't a lion. His raised shoulders were powerful, his stance protective, but the softness in his eyes as they caressed her features made her feel less like prey and more like a treasure—a treasure to be cared for, watched over.

A treasure to be loved.

She drew in a deep breath. Love? He didn't love her, nor did she love him. That would be impossible after only a few days together.

And yet, she couldn't deny the pull she felt to the man above her. She wanted him to kiss her. She wanted to feel his lips, to breathe in the scent of his cologne more fully. She knew it was stupid. Foolish. Idiotic. Insane.

But what did it matter if she could have her desire met this minute?

His eyes dropped to her lips, and he leaned toward her, her heart rapping against her ribcage with anticipation. His perfect face drew closer and closer until her eyes closed, and she drew in a final breath before his kiss would be hers.

TWENTY-THREE

THE FRONT DOOR TORE OPEN, AND MELODY'S SHOUTS echoed down the hallway. "Claire? Claire!"

Liam jumped up in a heartbeat, heading for the kitchen as Claire scrambled to her feet, turning toward the tree and pretending to straighten the branches.

"In here," she responded, her voice sounding far too strangled. She couldn't help it. Her lungs still struggled for a solid breath.

"Oh, good!" Melody cried out. "I'm so glad you guys are home. I am in serious need of your help, Claire."

With her head still spinning, Claire drew a deep breath. She'd almost kissed Liam. *Liam*, of all people. And he had almost kissed *her*.

What had either of them been thinking? Or was that the problem—that they hadn't been thinking at all?

"I just can't decide what dress..." Melody stopped, coming around the corner.

For a split second, Claire wondered if Melody had read the room, somehow sensing the chemistry between Claire and Liam that had scattered to pieces and now floated fractured in the air

197

around them. But as Melody's eyes focused on the tree instead of Claire or Liam, relief flooded through her body.

"Aw, did you guys get that for Aunt Tasha?" Melody asked. "She's going to love it."

Claire glanced to Liam, who ducked his head in the fridge. There was no way he was hungry. Was he hiding his face, or was he trying to cool down?

"We just finished putting it up," Claire said, folding her arms to keep her limbs from shaking. All that adrenaline that had built up to kiss Liam was now leaving her arms as weak and flimsy as a daffodil's stem during a spring snowstorm.

"Perfect," Melody said. "Because like I said, I need your help deciding what to wear. And..." She paused, raising her lips in a sign of hardly veiled disgust. "You're taking a shower, right? You look kinda sweaty and red."

Claire's blush screamed, and Liam shifted to stare into the freezer next. "Yeah, of course I am," she said, leaving the tree behind and walking toward Melody. It was time to get the heck out of here.

"Liam," Melody began as Claire walked past her, "you'd better hurry, too. The ballet won't wait for any of us."

Liam merely hummed, his head still in the freezer as Claire left the kitchen.

Thank goodness for Melody's timing. Because as much as Claire's heart said otherwise, she should not be kissing a man she just met.

LIAM PACED the rug by the front door, straightening his tie for the hundredth time as he waited for Melody and Claire to come downstairs.

The last thing he wanted to do right now was spend the

evening with the girls and Dean, sitting through *The Nutcracker*. But he wasn't about to let Claire go alone, even though he had no idea how he was going to survive the entirety of the ballet seated next to her, thinking of how her eyes had fluttered to a close when he'd leaned in to kiss her and how her lips had parted, inviting him to taste of their sweetness.

He scrubbed a hand over his face. He needed to stop this. He and Claire came from two different worlds, had two different futures, two different dreams. Kissing her would have been disastrous because he knew without a doubt in his mind that if he *had* kissed Claire Frost, he would want to do it again and again.

A knock on the door sounded beside him, and he turned to open it, revealing Dean on the front porch.

Liam opened the door wider to allow him in, though he would have rather invited him to wait in the darkness outside.

"You clean up nice," Dean said, adjusting his bow tie. "The birds nearly ready?"

Liam grimaced. It was going to be a long night. "They should be down soon."

They stood in silence in the entryway, Liam pressing his lips shut. The two of them didn't really need to speak, but apparently, Dean thought otherwise.

"So are you dating the friend?" he asked.

The friend? Had he already forgotten Claire's name? "No, I'm not. Claire and I are only friends."

Friends who'd nearly just kissed.

Dean shook his head. "Still as prim as ever. I tell you, if Melody weren't here, there's no way I'd be keeping my hands off Claire."

Liam's jaw twitched, disgust simmering within him. Here was the Dean he knew. No doubt the guy had been on his best behavior around Melody.

"Although," Dean continued, "if you and Claire are just friends, maybe I *don't* have to keep my hands off her."

Dean was just having a laugh, trying to wind Liam up. Liam

knew that. But heaven help him, it was working. He held his hands behind his back, clenching his fingers around his wrist to calm down.

"You're assuming Claire would *want* your hands on her," Liam returned, his stomach roiling.

Dean chuckled. "I find that most women do. You would find them wanting the same from you, if you weren't such a prig."

Liam tipped his head from side to side as if measuring the words. "Prig. Gentleman. They must be one and the same."

Dean sniffed, puffing out his chest as he drew in a deep breath. "Being either is highly overrated."

Liam turned toward him, ready to defend himself again, but when a movement flashed at the top step, they both turned toward the stairs.

Melody appeared first in a dark green dress, flashy diamonds dangling from her ears and peeking through her dark curls. Her grin was wide and confident as she peered down at them, her eyes settling on Dean's.

"Wow," Dean said, pressing a hand to his chest. "You are simply...Wow."

Liam stopped himself from rolling his eyes. Yes, Melody looked great. But Dean was so obviously playing an act. He must have seen that reaction on some movie to know just how to pull it off. What a total...

Liam's words faded from his mind as he glanced back up the stairs, doing a double take as Claire appeared next. He let out a slow breath, all other thoughts vanishing as his heart fluttered at the vision before him.

Unlike Melody's self-assured grin, Claire's smile was subtle, humble, but she held herself with an unmatched air of grace as she moved down the steps in a soft pink, floor-length gown. Shimmering crystals fell down the front of the slender dress like silver raindrops, accentuating her figure. Her hair was piled high in an elegant twist, and dainty pearls dangled from her ears.

Liam was utterly captured. Her blue eyes met his as she

reached the bottom step, but he couldn't look away even if he'd wanted to.

This evening, to put it plainly, was going to be a trial.

"Don't you boys look nice," Melody said, straightening Dean's bowtie that didn't need to be straightened. "Now let's hurry and get some pictures before we leave."

Liam wanted to groan out of sheer agony. First, he took a few of Dean and Melody, who made him snap different angles to "get our best look."

Then she snatched Claire's phone and pushed Claire toward Liam near the front door. Claire's arm slid across his back, his own hand reaching past her waist and curling around her figure.

The first time they'd taken a photo together, their coats had helped to put much-needed distance between the two of them. Now, there was nothing but his suit jacket and her dress, and his racing heart seemed to be well aware of the fact.

"Aw, you guys are so cute," Melody gushed, then she gave Claire back her phone as Liam took a wide step away.

After putting on their coats, the couples—no, not couples— the four *single* adults filed out of the house.

Liam was the last to leave, holding the door open for Claire as he dipped his head like he was one of the footmen in the period dramas his mum had made him watch. Honestly, it wasn't too far from the truth. Claire was leaps and bounds above him, in beauty and class.

She ducked past him. "You look great, by the way."

Why did her simple words buoy him higher than the clouds? "Thank you," he responded, his voice cracking.

He grimaced. That was just great.

She waited for him as he locked the door, Melody and Dean already heading down the sidewalk toward the station. "I'm not overdressed, am I?" she asked.

He checked the lock on the door, then turned to Claire. In hindsight, he probably shouldn't have looked at her again. In the warm light from the porch above, her hair glowed like a halo, and though her white peacoat now covered most of her dress, he'd still never seen anyone so stunning.

A soft breeze blew a few loose tendrils against her cheek, and he fought the overwhelming urge to smooth them aside.

"Liam?"

"Hmm? Oh, no," he stammered. "You will fit in perfectly. There's a wide range of dress there."

Claire sighed with relief. "That's what Melody said, but I just wanted to make sure. You never know with her."

Wasn't that the truth?

"So is this the sort of thing you always pack while on holiday?" he asked, motioning to her gown.

"I wish my life were so glamorous," she joked. "Melody promised me a night at the theater before I left. I wanted to pack a much simpler outfit, but I didn't want to look underdressed with her emerald gown."

He nodded, pulling in his lips as he moved down the pavement. He knew he needed to pay her a compliment, but he didn't want to be over-the-top like Dean had been.

"You look very...nice." Really? That was the best he could come up with?

Claire peered up at him. "Isn't that the word you guys use to describe food over here?"

He fidgeted with his cufflink. "Well, it's the highest form of compliment I could ever offer," he joked.

Claire smiled in return. Her footsteps clicked on the cement as they walked toward Dean and Melody, their arms already around each other as they walked beneath the streetlamps.

But Liam was hardly aware of his cousin any longer. Instead, he couldn't seem to pull his attention away from Claire. As the cars drove by on the road beside them, their lights highlighted her profile and silhouetted her figure time and time again.

It was no wonder he'd almost kissed her. The woman had no equal.

"So are you ready for this?" she asked.

Her words jarred him from his thoughts once again. Ready? Ready for what, to kiss her? Yes. He was ready. But he hardly thought that was what she'd been referring to. "For what?"

She motioned forward with a nod of her head. "To be with them again."

He followed her gaze to where Melody and Dean swung their hands together as they walked a few houses ahead of them. "Oh," he said. "Not really, but I suppose we don't have another option."

"We could always pretend we got food poisoning."

"I think I'd rather have real food poisoning than be with those two all night."

"We'd probably throw up less," she quipped.

They laughed silently, and Liam's anxiousness lessened, if only to a small degree. He needed to remember this was Claire standing next to him, not the angelic being she appeared to be.

She was just the girl who'd suggested getting a tree for his mother. The girl who marveled at Big Ben and the Tower of London. The girl who was following her dreams and trying to get him to do the same.

And yet, the more he dwelled on those things, the more he realized how much he liked those things. How much he *admired* those things. But admiring her would lead to other feelings he couldn't develop.

After a quick ride on the Tube, the four of them reached the Royal Albert Hall, taking their seats in the second tier. Liam shuffled down the aisle first, followed by Claire, Melody, then Dean. Liam helped Claire remove her jacket, careful not to touch her shoulders, then they sat side-by-side. He tried not to be affected by her floral scent that he couldn't help but breathe in and savor.

He pulled out his program, reading the same line over and over again, his brain refusing to focus on anything other than Claire's arm brushing against his or the way her eyes focused on him every so often with a smile on her lips.

He needed to calm down, to acknowledge that everything was fine.

But the truth of the matter was that nothing was fine. *He* wasn't fine. He was tormented, drawn to this woman he could never have.

"Liam?"

He blinked, glancing to the woman occupying his every thought. "Sorry?"

She gave a little smile. "You seem a little...distracted tonight. Are you alright?"

Distracted? Yes, he was distracted. He was distracted by her. Her scent, her smile, her goodness. "Just anxious for the ballet to start."

She eyed him curiously, but he looked away, afraid that she'd be able to read his mind.

Curse his stupid decision making. He never should have agreed to befriend Claire Frost.

TWENTY-FOUR

CLAIRE COULD FEEL THE ANXIOUSNESS OOZING FROM Liam. What was with him tonight? He was usually the picture of calm control, but now, his jaw continually twitched, and he sat rigidly in his seat.

Was it being near Melody and Dean again? Or was it the fact that he and Claire had nearly kissed and were both now pretending it didn't happen?

"So how was your guys' day together?" Melody asked, turning away from Dean for the first time that evening, though their fingers were still intertwined.

Claire's frustration at Melody from earlier that day had already dissipated. She couldn't hold onto that anger when she'd spent the entire day with Liam, instead.

"It was a lot of fun," she responded simply.

"Aw, I'm so glad. Also..." Melody glanced beyond Claire's shoulder, then leaned close in a hushed whisper. "Did you see Liam's face when you came down the stairs tonight? He was totally checking you out."

Panic flapped in Claire's chest, and she shushed her friend in an instant. "Melody, stop. He'll hear you."

Melody just grinned. "He's super into you. Even Dean mentioned it."

Claire shook her head, if only to keep her mind from dwelling on her racing heart. "You guys are both insane."

Did her words sound as weak as they felt?

The lights dimmed, signaling the beginning of the show, and Melody pulled back with a knowing look, leaning closer to Dean once again.

He's super into you.

The words echoed in Claire's mind as the ballerinas tiptoed across the stage, her stomach flipping as she thought of Liam watching her as she'd come down the stairs. She wasn't so blind as to not have seen his admiring eyes. Of course, she'd nearly melted into a puddle at his feet at the sight of his classic black suit and tie combo. She had known no small amount of pride as she'd walked by his side and more than one lady had turned to admire him.

But still, just because Liam might feel some amount of attraction to her didn't mean that he was *into* her. And the same went for her. Just because she thought he was basically the most attractive person she'd ever seen in her life—he rivaled Ross Poldark, for heaven's sake, and that was saying a lot—didn't mean that she felt anything for him. It was more than likely just a minute crush.

A crush that made her want the ballet to end so she could speak with him again. A crush that made heat rush through her body at the mere thought of the kiss that could have been. A crush that made her smile more with him than with any other relationship she'd ever been in.

When the first act finally finished, Claire followed Melody to the bathrooms, anxious for a moment's respite from her thoughts. Even listening to Melody go on and on about how perfect Dean looked was a welcome reprieve.

"I'm just having the best time with him," Melody said as they walked back to their seats. "I already can't wait for next year when we can see each other again."

Claire paused. "How can you even handle that? Being away from him, I mean. Twelve months is a long time."

But Melody merely shrugged. "It's not like I won't have other guys to occupy my time 'til then." She gave a saucy shrug of her shoulders, then led the way down the aisle toward their row.

Claire frowned, unable to understand Melody's logic. But then, they were different people. Claire could never understand the point of falling so hard for a person she couldn't be with—or could only be with for a few days out of the year.

She looked down the row, searching for her seat when she caught Liam's eyes on her, but he swiftly darted his gaze away.

A crush. It was just a crush. It would fade.

And yet, as she sat down beside Liam, her heart refused to pump properly. So much so that she had to ask herself, was it worth falling for someone, enjoying time with someone, even if it was inevitable that it would end?

"Hey," Melody said, leaning forward to address them both, "do you guys want to go out for dessert after this?"

Claire hesitated. She'd much rather be alone with Liam. But then, maybe it would be better for them both to be stuck with Melody and Dean.

"Um, sure," Claire agreed. "We'd love to."

"Don't involve me in this," Liam whispered behind her, and she turned to his smiling eyes.

"If I'm going down, I'm bringing you with me," she whispered in response.

His lips curved, and Claire looked back to Melody, who's curious eyes shifted between Liam and Claire.

Claire sobered, looking straight ahead at the red curtains at the side of the stage. There was no way she was going to let Melody think she liked Liam. Claire would never hear the end of it.

"Claire," Liam said, pulling her attention toward him again. Gosh. How she loved the sound of her name on his lips.

Melody, fortunately, had already turned back to Dean as Liam leaned toward Claire, showing her a message thread on his phone. "From my mum," he explained.

Claire narrowed her eyes, focusing hard on the words to think past their shoulders that now pressed lightly against each other.

Tasha: Oh my goodness. Did you put the tree up? It's gorgeous.

Liam: It was Claire's idea. We can all decorate it tomorrow morning, if you'd like?

Tasha: That would be great. Thank you both so much. It smells amazing. Tell that sweet Claire thank you, as well. Hope you're all enjoying the ballet. xx

Claire pulled back with a smile, joy swelling in her chest. "Makes carting the tree back worth it, doesn't it?"

"Speak for yourself," he said, rolling out his shoulder. "I'll be sore for days."

They smiled at each other, his eyes remaining on her as they softened. "Thank you," he said. "For your suggestion to get the tree for my mum. It was...very sweet."

His words slipped around her heart, causing it to swell with warmth. Before she could respond, the lights dimmed once again, and the ballet resumed.

If Claire thought the first act had been long, the second was sheer torture. Typically, she enjoyed a good show, but each dance that passed by, she grew more and more anxious. First, she bounced her legs up and down, then she took to tapping her fingers against her lower thigh as if that would speed up the tempo of Tchaikovsky's music.

Her tapping continued when Liam leaned toward her. "Are you alright?"

"Yeah, why?"

He focused his gaze on her fidgeting fingers. "You seem a little anxious."

"Sorry," she whispered, stopping her tapping at once as her cheeks warmed.

He gave a little shake of his head, as if to say there was no reason to apologize, but she kept her gaze trained forward. She needed to control herself. Her tapping fingers would only lead to more questions she *really* didn't want to answer.

Another scene passed by, Clara and Prince arriving in the Land of Sweets. Claire drew deep, calming breaths as she focused on the white outfits and shining backdrops behind the ballerinas. She thought she'd stopped her tapping, but when Liam leaned toward her again, his shoulder pressing against hers, she froze.

"You're making *me* anxious now," he whispered, placing his hand over her fingers.

Claire stared down at his hand over hers, her heart ramping up in time with the music, her skin aflame, as if warmed by a fire. She kept waiting for Liam to retract his hand, but when it settled more on top of hers, she looked back up at the dancers.

Liam was holding her hand. *Liam was holding her hand.* Would Melody see and make a big deal out of it later on?

After a quick glance in her direction, however, Claire knew Melody had nothing on her mind but Dean, whom she cuddled up against.

It was a small relief, one that lasted only a moment as Claire's thoughts threatened to spin out of control. Why *was* Liam holding her hand? Was it because he wanted to, or because he just needed to stop her tapping?

She leaned toward him. "I'll stop," she whispered.

He kept his gaze on the performers, leaning slightly toward her with his response. "I'll hold onto you...just in case."

Then he cast her a sidelong glance that sent her heart racing.

Claire bit her lip to keep her smile at bay. Alright, so he was going to keep his hand there, then. That didn't mean he wanted to for any reason other than to keep her from fidgeting. That didn't mean...

He brushed his thumb against her skin so softly, she thought she'd imagined it. But when he did it again, his caress became clearer.

Heaven help her.

The dance ended, applause sounding from the audience. Claire fully expected Liam to keep his hands to himself after clapping, but when he placed his hand on hers once again, this time sliding his fingers around her own, she had to remind herself again and again to breathe.

There was no mistaking his actions. Liam was holding her hand because he *wanted* to. And she couldn't deny the fact that she wanted to hold his right back.

Each time the dances ended, their hands would break apart, and Claire wondered if he would take hers again. Time and time again, however, her spirits soared as he returned his fingers to hers until the final bows were taken, and the lights turned on.

Finally, as those around them stood, Liam slid his hand from hers, the cold instantly accosting her fingers.

"What an incredible performance," Melody exclaimed as she stood next to Dean. "Didn't you guys just love it?"

Claire nodded, though to be honest, she couldn't say for sure. Her mind had been too utterly preoccupied with the perfection seated beside her.

As they made their way from the hall, Claire bumped into Liam so many times, she was beginning to wonder if he was doing it on purpose, his eyes catching hers over and over again until they finally stepped out into the cold air.

Claire breathed in the brisk wind, welcoming the distraction it brought to her mind. She didn't even know what was happening to her right now, having to pull her mind from Liam so often. She couldn't afford to draw closer to him. She didn't want to waste her time falling for a man who didn't have time to date her—or a man who lived halfway across the world.

And yet, as he helped her into her coat, his hands lingering a moment against her arms, she began to care less and less about what her brain argued for, and more and more about what her heart desired.

She turned to face him, smiling with gratitude as he watched her in return. What if, just this once, she allowed her heart to thrive instead of her brain? What if she forgot about the future and focused on the here and now?

Her heart picked up speed at the mere notion of giving in to her desires, but when she turned, catching Melody's watchful gaze, Claire took a clear step away from Liam and focused on the street ahead of them.

Melody would have no way of knowing about Claire's growing feelings for Liam, but it became obvious that Melody was doing her best to find out that very thing as she honed in on Claire and Liam for the rest of the night.

When they went out for gelato, she asked them question after question, paying them more attention than she even did to Dean.

Claire tried her hardest to focus on her friend, but her thoughts were lost as she sat down beside Liam and his knee pressed against hers.

Worried that he'd done so by accident, she swiftly moved her leg away, but a few moments later, she felt him make contact again. She looked to Liam, his eyes already on her.

Common sense told her to pull away, but the warmth spiraling from where he touched her was too captivating to willingly separate herself from it.

By the time they'd finished their dessert and stepped into the cold night air once again, Claire could hardly breathe, leaving her coat unbuttoned to cool her down faster.

Eventually and mercifully, Dean—with more compliments and flattery—captured Melody's attention again, and he wrapped his arm around her shoulder as they broke away from Liam and Claire.

Instinctively, Claire's footing slowed, Liam's doing the same until they were a healthy distance from the others.

Silence marked the air between them, though the rushing sound of buses and taxis hurried by them on the road. Christmas lights decorated the shops they walked past, and streetlamps stamped their golden light onto the pavement in perfect circles.

Though Claire was relieved to have some distance between her and Melody, being alone with Liam now meant that they'd have to speak with one another. But Claire didn't know what to say. Would they discuss the fact that they couldn't keep away from each other? Or would they ignore that fact like they'd ignored their almost-kiss?

Determined to break the ice somehow, Claire settled on the safest topic she could find. "So did you like the ballet?"

"I did." He paused. "Especially the second act."

TWENTY-FIVE

Claire's heart skipped a beat, a single glance at Liam telling her exactly what he was referring to. She drew a deep breath. "I preferred the second act, too."

Just like before, that slight narrowing of his eyes promised of a smile to come, but she looked away, too nervous to hold his gaze any longer.

This was not good. They should not be talking about how much they liked being near each other. Nothing good would come of it. She needed a distraction, something to pull her mind off of him once and for all.

She glanced around her, anxious for anything to capture her attention. Her eyes settled on a red telephone booth tucked in the shadow of a nearby shop, and she smiled.

That should do the trick.

She pointed it out with a tip of her head. "You know, I've seen about a hundred of these, but I have yet to look inside one of them."

Liam watched her, no doubt wondering about her random topic of conversation, but he motioned toward it all the same. "Well, now's as good a time as any."

They stepped to the side of the pavement, Claire opening the door and glancing around the small telephone booth. She could hardly see a thing due to the darkness of the street, but she was going to marvel the heck out of it until she thought of something else to distract herself from Liam.

She held up her dress to step into the booth, Liam holding the door open for her. He stood in the entrance, looking at faded stickers stuck to the top of the structure.

"Not much to write home about," he said behind her.

"I dunno. I think it's cozy."

In reality, it was freezing and smelled of coffee and old paint, but the mere fact that this booth was British made it infinitely more spectacular.

She glanced around her, feeling Liam's eyes on her before she turned to face him. Sure enough, he watched her with an unreadable expression. Was it admiration? Concern? Impatience?

She offered him a small smile as his stare continued, and it seemed to pull him from his musings as he blinked, looking down at the floor of the telephone booth instead of her.

Was he ready to keep going? If he was, he made no move to leave. "I guess we should probably go find Melody before she wonders where we are," she offered, allowing him the chance to break away.

Liam nodded, but still, he remained. "Yeah, you're probably right. Though I wonder if she even realizes we aren't with her."

"Probably not." She paused, considering Melody's watchful gaze throughout dessert. "Although, she did seem more aware of us after the ballet."

"Knowing Melody, she probably thinks there's something between us and is trying to figure out what it is."

Claire's heart rate picked up a notch. "I don't know why she would. There's nothing between us."

He shook his head, his tone as smooth as chocolate. "Nothing."

A moment passed by in silence, Claire biting her tongue before throwing caution to the wind. "Of course, she was probably wondering why you were holding my hand at the ballet tonight."

A small smile reached his eyes. "I wasn't holding your hand. I was merely resting my hand on yours."

"Right." She leaned against the side of the booth's red-pained wall. Liam always seemed perfectly comfortable teasing her. Perhaps it was time for her to do the same to him. "Then what's your excuse for almost kissing me earlier?"

His lips parted. He was clearly surprised she'd had the courage to bring it up. Honestly, she was surprised herself. What was with her tonight? She was supposed to be finding ways to distract herself from Liam's kiss, not bringing it up herself.

"Perhaps I was offering resuscitation," he joked, glancing to her lips.

"To a person who was conscious?"

He shrugged. "You *were* lying on the floor."

He looked again to her lips, and she unconsciously wet them with a touch of her tongue. "Either way, we would have been crazy to follow through with it."

"Just like we'd be crazy to follow through with it now," he returned.

Their eyes connected, and the air hummed between them. They were actually talking about kissing. *Kissing.* What would a kiss from Liam Everhart feel like—dancing to her favorite song by Josh Groban? Being wrapped in a weighted blanket and watching re-runs of *Friends*? Admiring a firework display at New Year's with all the hope of a brighter future?

She glanced through the warped glass of the telephone booth. Melody and Dean must have been farther ahead now. No doubt they were still completely unaware that Claire and Liam hadn't followed them. Or maybe Dean had pulled Melody aside to make out with her down some dark alley.

That meant that Melody wouldn't interrupt them this time. But then...

"We'd be worse than Melody and Dean if we did follow through," she said, her mind spinning. "PDA at its finest."

"Unless we found somewhere more private than a carousel."

A moment passed, his eyes shining with mischief before he took a step forward and joined her in the phonebooth.

Her breath caught in her throat at his close proximity, and she took a step back, bouncing against the wall of the booth. "What are you doing?" she asked, pulling on her best frown, though anticipation burned in her chest.

"I'm giving us a little more privacy."

She tried to take another step back from his commanding figure, but the telephone booth had shrunk considerably with his broad shoulders and towering stance. "You do realize this telephone box is mostly made of *glass*, right?" she asked.

"Inconsequential detail."

She laughed, a giddiness rushing through her limbs. If she drew so much as a single deep breath, her body would be up against his. But then, isn't that what she wanted? To be near to this man, to kiss him, to let go of her inhibitions for one night and just *live*?

"What if someone sees us?" she asked, her voice barely above a whisper as her reserves weakened one by one. "Or what if Melody comes back and finds us?"

"Then we tell her the truth." His eyes delved into hers. "That there is nothing between us." He took a step closer to her. "Of course, even if there is nothing between us, that doesn't mean that I haven't been dying to tell you how absolutely stunning you look this evening."

Her breathing shallowed as his eyes caressed every inch of her face. "Is stunning better than 'nice'?" she whispered.

His alluring half-smile made her head spin. "Far, far better." He slipped his hand beneath her unbuttoned coat, encircling his warm fingers around her waist. "Do you remember at the Christmas Market," he whispered, his eyes moving down to her lips, "you promised me you'd answer a question of my own."

She nodded.

He brought his other hand up, his thumb caressing the skin along the length of her jaw and chin, drawing dangerously close to her lips. "Will you answer my question now?"

She wet her lips again, her mouth dry. "Yes."

He searched her eyes with his dark gaze, the attraction between them buzzing. "Do you want me to kiss you?"

Claire's breath escaped her lips at his question. She knew her longing was written plainly across her face—just as she knew that Liam had asked the question out of respect for her own desires.

So how could she respond? If she lied, he would step away in an instant. But if she told him the truth...

His gaze moved from her lips to her eyes, searching, filled with patience, desire, and something else she hoped she saw but didn't dare to admit.

"Yes," she finally breathed out. "I want you to kiss me."

That was all Liam needed. His lips parted. He pressed his left hand against the small of her back, drawing her closer. His free hand traveled along her jawline to cup the back of her neck, then he finally closed the distance between them.

The moment his lips pressed against hers, Claire knew she'd made the right decision. His kiss was soft, yet firm, commanding every ounce of her attention. Could this be reality? Was she, Claire Frost, truly kissing a Brit in a red telephone box in the middle of London?

His lips pressing tenderly against hers illuminated the truth, but Claire just didn't do this sort of thing. Melody did. And yet, as Liam leaned his head to the side, deepening their kiss, she couldn't help but think that Melody had gotten it right, and Claire had been wrong all along.

Kissing a man she'd just met was sheer euphoria.

His beard, though rough, wasn't scratchy as she'd thought it might be. Instead it tickled her skin and sent pleasant chills up and down her back, pushing her to clasp the arms of his jacket to keep herself steady.

The chill from outside was lost to her as Liam removed his hand from her neck, sliding his fingers along her waist as he encircled his arms around her beneath her coat. He held her tightly, as if he had no intention of ever letting her go.

Claire wrapped her arms around his neck as she stood on her tiptoes, hoping to gain better access to his lips. Their mouths pressed together like the pages of a closed book, holding the promise of a love story in its purest form.

This kiss, it was pure perfection. Just like Liam.

She had known this man for a mere fraction of a week, and already, she was witness to the difference between Liam and every other man she'd ever known. She'd never been held in such a way, so tenderly, so sweetly.

And now she knew that she was in more trouble than she thought.

LIAM COULDN'T BREATHE, so he breathed in Claire instead. His desire to kiss this woman was stronger than anything he'd ever felt in his life. What was it about her that made his mind spin, his heart swirl, and his stomach burn with desire?

He'd stated earlier, and she'd agreed, that there was nothing between them. But that was a lie. There *was* something between them. Something raw and real and beautiful. Something sweet. Something...perfect.

Which was exactly why he should pull away to end the agony before it could worsen.

And yet, he continued to cradle her in his arms, pulling her more tightly against his body. He needed to feel her, to taste her, to connect with her so he could remember all of it forever—how perfectly she fit in his arms, how soft her fingers were in his hair, how flawless her kiss was against his lips.

How he wished they'd met under different circumstances, how he wished they lived closer to each other, how he wished for a lot of things. But life was never simple.

And as that reality settled heavily on Liam's shoulders, he did the impossible and broke off his kiss with Claire.

Slowly, he pulled back, quelling his desire to continue by resting his brow against hers. He didn't want her to think he hadn't heartily enjoyed the kiss, but the right words refused to come. "That was..."

"Yeah, it was," she finished.

They stood that way for a moment, their foreheads pressed lightly together until Liam pulled back, staring into her eyes. "We should probably be heading back."

She nodded in silence, and he led the way out of the telephone booth, holding the door open for her as the night air accosted them once again.

With a sober expression, Claire buttoned her coat as they moved down the pavement. Liam did his best not to become discouraged, but her actions were like an omen. A sign just for him to let him know reality had finally returned.

Knowing the more he put off speaking with her, the worst it would become, Liam drew a deep breath. "We probably shouldn't have done that."

She nodded, her gaze focused ahead, hands tucked in her coat pockets. "Yeah, probably not."

Silence pulsed uncomfortably between them.

"It was nice, though," she said.

A half-smile pulled at his lips. "Very nice."

She returned his smile, though she still didn't meet his gaze. "But...but we've already talked about the different lives we have. Different countries. Different work responsibilities."

Liam nodded. Everything she said was true, but it didn't make it any easier to acknowledge just how often his job interfered with his personal life.

Claire continued, hesitance written all over her pretty face. "I just don't want things to become impossible for me when I have to leave, you know? And kissing you..." She trailed off, shaking her head. "I can't. I'm not like Melody."

Liam nodded, knowing her plight perfectly. "No, you aren't," he replied softly. "And neither am I."

Their eyes met, and an understanding passed between them, though no further word on the subject was shared. Neither of them could continue kissing each other without a relationship growing between them—and neither of them could bear a relationship severed so soon after its beginning.

So they would stop. *He* would stop. Because Claire deserved the world, and that was something he couldn't offer, no matter how much his heart tried to convince him otherwise.

TWENTY-SIX

CLAIRE AND LIAM DIDN'T MEET UP WITH MELODY AND Dean again. After a quick text, Claire discovered from Melody that she and Dean had gone to another Christmas market, so Claire and Liam went home. With Tasha already asleep, they bade each other a simple goodnight, then Claire rushed to bed, hoping to be asleep before Melody returned.

To her disappointment, however, she lay awake for hours, trying to quiet her thoughts by watching *White Christmas* on her phone. But time and time again, her mind strayed to Liam until well after midnight when Melody finally came home.

Claire closed her eyes, feigning sleep to avoid any chance of discussing...well, anything with her friend, but when Melody finally climbed into her own bed and silence filled the room, Claire's thoughts rushed on.

She didn't want to speak with Melody about Liam. But then, she was going to go crazy if she couldn't talk with *someone* about all that had occurred. Tasha was a non-starter, so Melody was her only option.

Claire hesitated still, clicking her teeth together. Maybe her friend *would* help her. She always had before. And now without Dean there, Melody would listen, right?

With a deep breath, she whispered into the darkness. "Melody?"

A moment of silence passed. "Hmm?"

Had Claire woken her? Maybe this was a bad idea. "Um... never mind."

Melody shifted in her bed. "You woke me up for that?" she asked, her words slightly slurred from sleep.

"No. I...I wanted to talk to you."

"Okay. About what?"

Claire stared up at the ceiling, twiddling her fingers against her stomach. "About something stupid I did tonight."

Melody scoffed, sounding more awake. "I highly doubt you're capable of doing anything stupid, Claire. Every decision you make is overcomplicated and overthought."

Normally, Claire would be offended by the words, even if they were true. Instead, she winced. "Not tonight." She dropped her voice to a whisper. "I kissed Liam."

Rustling sounded in Melody's bed as she shot upright, clicking the lamp on as it illuminated the room. "You did *what*?"

Claire spun around from her mattress on the floor to face her, wincing at the sudden brightness. "Shh! You'll wake him up!"

Melody pressed both hands to her forehead, holding her dark hair back from her face. "Are you serious right now?" she asked, her voice barely lowering.

Claire winced again, nodding.

"I knew it! I knew I saw something between you guys tonight!" A grin split across her face. She bounced out of her bed to hop onto Claire's, the mattress jerking Claire upright. "You have to tell me everything. Right now. Like, do you like him? *Like*-like him?"

Claire hesitated. She knew the truth, but how could she admit as much aloud?

"Oh my gosh! You do!" Melody exclaimed. She covered her mouth with her hands as her eyes squinted with barely restrained glee. "If you guys get married, we'll be family for real!"

"Melody—"

"Oh my heck, you guys would make the most gorgeous kids. Oh, and imagine the little accent they'd have! Ah! You better have me as your bridesmaid, or I'll never—"

"Melody!" Claire whispered with vehemence, reaching over to clasp her hand over her friend's mouth. "Stop! If Liam hears you, he's going to think that I'm saying all of this."

Melody swiped Claire's hand away from her mouth, still beaming. "Oh, please. Don't tell me you haven't thought about every one of these things already."

Claire shook her head, then paused. Alright, maybe she had considered a *few* of the things Melody had mentioned. How could she not while kissing a dreamy, dark-eyed, swoopy-haired, British boy?

"We just kissed," she whispered in response. "That's all."

"But you like him," Melody stated matter-of-factly.

Claire hesitated before giving a small nod.

Melody squealed, bouncing up and down on the mattress. "Okay, tell me everything. And I mean *everything*."

Finally, she stopped, leaning forward toward Claire like a seal staring at an offered treat.

Claire just shook her head with amusement. Well, she'd been dumb enough to start the conversation. She may as well finish it.

Over the next half hour, she gave all the details Melody desired, sharing how Claire and Liam had first met at the airport —"My mind is seriously being blown right now, Claire"—and how they had grown close to each other over the last couple of days before ending with their kiss that evening.

"A telephone booth? Are you kidding me?" Melody shook her head with a growing smile. "Not even Dean and I have done that."

"Yeah, it was definitely stupid," Claire agreed.

"Stupid?" Melody guffawed. "Try romantic as heck! But what happened after the kiss? Did you hold hands on your way home? Did he kiss you goodnight?"

Claire's smile faltered. "No. We both agreed it was a mistake and that it would only be a one-time thing."

Melody delivered a deflated sigh. "Seriously?"

"Well, yeah. It would never work between us, so instead of chasing something that wouldn't amount to anything, we're just ending it before it can begin."

"So let me get this straight. You spent the last few days with a guy you're totally attracted to, yeah?"

Claire nodded.

"A guy who's totally into you, too—"

"I don't know that for sure."

Melody scoffed. "Please. My cousin is as disciplined as you are. Trust me. If he kissed you, he likes you. A lot."

Claire stamped out the fire blazing in her heart. It wouldn't do her any good to let it flourish.

"So," Melody continued, "you like him, he likes you, and you *still* won't let yourself be with him? I don't get you, Claire."

Claire looked away, her mood falling. "He doesn't have time for a relationship, Melody." She stopped, careful to sidestep any mention of Liam's employment. "And you know my own hang-up with my parents. I already have a long-distance relationship with *them*. I don't want another one with a guy."

Melody's face fell, and she looked away, deflated. "Yeah. Yeah, that makes sense. Ugh. What a total mood killer."

Claire nodded. "I know."

Melody met her gaze, compassion filling her eyes and reminding Claire why she was friends with her in the first place. "I'm sorry, Claire," she said, wrapping a comforting arm around her shoulder.

They sat in silence, Claire taking a moment to rest in the support from her friend while she could—because there was one thing that still worried her.

How was Claire to live out the next few days—see Liam the next few days—when she was supposed to feel nothing for him, all while she felt *everything* for him?

LIAM TOSSED and turned all night, restless and on edge until he rolled out of bed at six o'clock. He might as well work on editing his photos rather than wasting any more time not sleeping.

However, he only managed a few minutes of edits downstairs before his mum walked into the sitting room in her full-sized, fuzzy robe.

"Morning," she greeted with a sleepy smile. "You're up early."

Liam set his laptop aside. "I couldn't sleep."

"Even after your late night?"

He nodded.

She gave him a searching look, then took out a mug. "Cuppa?"

"No, thanks."

She nodded, then put the kettle on for herself. "So how *was* your night?"

Liam hesitated. Her question was nothing out of the ordinary. But there was something so forced about her disinterest that made him think she was more interested than she was letting on.

"It was great," he responded carefully.

The evening *had* been great, up until the end when his ship had crashed and burned.

"You saw *The Nutcracker*?"

"Yeah."

"Hmm."

Liam narrowed his eyes at her reaction. "What?"

"Nothing. I've just never heard you describe the ballet as *great*. From what I recall, when you were fifteen, you said it was 'the worst way to waste two hours of one's life'."

Liam paused, knowing exactly where his Mum was leading the conversation. "Well, I *was* young, last I saw it. I'd like to think I've matured a bit since then."

"Or you just had better company last night."

She gave him another look, and he smiled. "That could've had something to do with it." He cleared his throat. "So how was working late?"

"Oh, it was fine. Made much better with the surprise of that tree. Was it really Claire's idea?"

Wow. She changed the conversation back to Claire faster than Liam had thought she could. He glanced to the bare tree still standing in the corner of the room. Visions of the pine on its side with Claire lying beside it flashed through his mind. "Yeah, it was all her." No one else was that selfless and thoughtful.

"You've been spending a lot of time with her," Mum said, taking her mug and sitting on the couch opposite him.

Liam stared down at his laptop on the couch cushion beside him, the photo of the deer in the morning light pulled up on his screen—the one Claire liked. "I wasn't given much of a choice in the beginning." He lowered his voice. The girls didn't appear to be awake yet, but he'd hate to be overheard. "Melody's being ridiculous."

"Is that any surprise? She's always been like this around Dean."

Liam shook his head, indignation boiling in his stomach. "It doesn't matter. Claire came all this way to be with her. Melody should at least have the common decency to spend time with her friend, instead of some bloke who's kissed a dozen other women this year alone."

He knew he'd given away too much when his mum's eyes fell on him, but he couldn't help it. The mere thought of any injustice happening to Claire—whether it was by Melody or Claire's parents—riled him up. How had such a pure-hearted woman been dealt such a cruel hand?

"Liam, is there something between..."

Her words faded away as he shook his head, already knowing what she was going to say. "No. No, there's nothing between Claire and me."

Lies.

"She's a wonderful woman," he continued, if only to prove to himself he could be truthful. "We've been having a lot of fun. But we live too far from each other. And you know with my job, a serious relationship just wouldn't work."

"But would you want a serious relationship with her?"

What was this, *Poirot*? He rubbed both hands up and down his beard. "It doesn't matter what I want because I don't have time with my job."

Mum nodded, taking another sip of her drink. "Won't you have more time, now that you didn't get the promotion?"

His eyes snapped to hers. Had Claire told her? No, she wouldn't have broken her promise.

Mum gave him a knowing look. "It was obvious, Liam. You haven't been willing or able to take a day off of work for years. The only reason you would have done so was to get away from the disappointment you felt there."

His shoulders fell. He thought he'd kept up the façade so well. He should've known his mum would see straight through him. "Sorry," he mumbled.

"For what?"

"For not telling you earlier. For not getting the promotion. For being such a disappointment."

To his surprise, she laughed out loud. "Liam, that is the stupidest thing you've ever said."

He pulled back. "Thank you?"

She lowered her mug. "First of all, you don't need to apologize for not being ready to share something with me. Second of all, you could never be a disappointment. And third of all, you should never apologize for the stupidity of that company in not seeing your own value. What you should be apologizing for is staying *with* that company."

Her words sank deep into his chest, joining the conversation he'd had with Claire, as well as the countless words he'd told himself over the last few years.

Why *did* he stay with the company? No, he didn't want to give up all the years he'd put in there. But shouldn't he be putting time now into something he actually *wanted* to be doing, like Claire suggested?

"So," Mum pressed, "are you going to stay with them, then?"

Liam sighed, his mind swimming with confusion. "I don't know. Honestly, I don't know."

It seemed pointless to stay at Peregrine now. Especially after the last few days he'd spent away. He'd felt alive for the first time in years, though he wasn't sure how much of that was time away from work and how much of it was being with Claire. Either way, that had to be some sort of sign, right?

"I just..." He hesitated, his mum still watching him. "It's a big change to jump careers. To give up stability for the unknown. I just don't know if I'm ready for it."

His mum finished off the last of her drink, leaning toward Liam with a soft smile. "If you ask me, even talking about changing careers is a good indication of being ready for it. But it's you who has to decide when to take that first step." She stood, patting him on his cheek in a loving gesture. "Whatever you do, I'm proud of you, Liam. And so is your father."

She smiled again, then placed her mug in the kitchen before excusing herself to get ready for the day.

Liam sat still for a moment, his thoughts rushing about his mind like a four-lane roundabout. His mum was right. He was the only one who could decide to take that first step. But what if it was a half-step in the direction he wanted to end up? That was safer, right?

Before he could talk himself out of it, he pulled up his laptop and typed out a quick email to his boss.

Garrett,

After the disappointing news of not receiving the promotion I'd been promised for years, I have come to realize the

*company does not value my efforts as much as I once
thought. As such, I am requesting part-time employment
beginning at the new year. If that is not possible, I might be
willing to consider freelancing for Peregrine Productions
instead, as it will allow me more time to pursue other venues
where I am more valued.*

Thank you for your time,
Liam Everhart

After a quick read-through with sweaty palms, Liam hit 'send.' Instead of the fear he'd expected to swarm his chest, light filled his heart.

Garrett could either accept his request or sack him. And honestly, at this point, Liam didn't mind either option. He was finished living the way he had for years. He was ready for freedom.

And if he just so happened to have more time to spend with a certain American girl who was staying at his house for the next week, then so be it.

TWENTY-SEVEN

To Claire's relief and utter shock, Melody acted perfectly normal around her and Liam as they decorated the tree with Tasha the following morning. There were no lingering glances from Melody, no winks, smiles, or baited questions—but then, there shouldn't be. Claire had made it clear the night before that she and Liam would never be together.

Even with Melody's distance, Claire found it increasingly more difficult to keep her own spirits up as the day progressed.

After decorating the tree with old tinsel and glass ornaments, she, Melody, and Tasha baked up a storm in the kitchen, fixing mince pies, yule logs, and gingerbread cookies, all of which were to be served the following day for the Christmas Eve party Tasha was holding.

Liam joined in the conversation as they baked, remaining mostly at his computer for the early afternoon. His eyes shifted to Claire every once in a while, though she did her best not to notice.

"What do you think?" Tasha asked, passing around the cookies after taking a bite of her own.

"So good," Claire said, her mouth half-full of the spiced mixture.

"Seriously," Melody agreed.

But Tasha raised an unimpressed shoulder. "They're not as nice as Grasmere's, but they'll do." She faced Claire. "Next time you come to England we'll take you to the Lake District. They make the best gingerbread. Nearly as gorgeous as the scenery."

"That would be amazing," Claire responded, trying to answer flippantly, though her chest ached.

Next time. There wouldn't be a next time.

Claire had made a mistake in coming to England. It had made her realize just how desperately lonely her life back home had become, or perhaps had always been. Even though she loved her job, nothing could compare to how she'd felt walking around London—and nothing could compare to how she'd felt being with Liam, laughing with him, being held by him, kissed by him. Her time with him had been a dream come true.

But just like all dreams, this one was coming to an end whether Claire wanted it to or not.

After the baking had been completed and the late afternoon sun sank low behind the London skyline, Melody managed to convince the others to join her at Harrods for her procrastinated search for Christmas presents, as her parents and younger sister would arrive the following morning.

"You have to come, too, Liam," Melody said before he'd even had the chance to say his preference. "I have to buy something for my dad, and you're the only guy who can help."

He glanced to Claire before reluctantly agreeing. Did he hesitate because he wanted time away from Claire? She couldn't blame him. Neither of them were really being their true selves.

As they rode the Underground toward the department store, Melody spent half her time talking to them about Dean and the other half gushing about a guy she liked back home. All the while, Tasha listened and commented as Claire and Liam sat across from each other in uncomfortable silence.

In those moments, Claire couldn't help but envy Melody. Why could Claire not detach from others, be fine with people coming in and out of her life? If she did, maybe then she'd be able to speak with Liam as they had before, like the friends they'd grown to be.

But of course, she knew why she couldn't. After all, why would she want a fruitless relationship when she already had two with her parents?

Her thoughts continued to sink lower, dragging her spirits down with them as they wandered about the seven floors of Harrods, moving from shop to shop at Melody's request as she spoke of past gifts given to her by her parents.

"My mom and I always get each other some type of perfume," Melody said after she purchased a necklace and soaps for her younger sister, Jen. "I'm thinking maybe something floral this year."

Claire couldn't remember the last Christmas present she'd received from her parents that hadn't been a souvenir they'd originally purchased for themselves. They usually ended up giving her a couple hundred-dollar bills from their wallets before the holidays instead.

"We'd much prefer you buying something you'd actually want, Claire Bear," they'd say.

But Claire knew the truth. They didn't know her well enough to buy her something she'd want, nor did they wish to put in any effort *to* get to know what she'd want. Just like they didn't put in the effort to text her back. Four days had passed, and still, she'd received not a single word from them.

The knowledge pinched at her heart as they moved to a white-lit, marble-floored perfume shop. Melody was in absolute heaven as they walked down the shining center aisle, a crystal chandelier hanging in the center of the shop.

Claire had to admit the store was pristine, but the overwhelming scents, though fine, pressed uncomfortably against her skull. Liam seemed uneasy, as well, for in a matter of minutes, he excused himself from the group to "look at the camera bags they have in stock."

He gave Claire a departing smile, and she watched him walk

away with silent longing. She'd most definitely rather look at camera bags than listen to Melody going on about the perfect fragrance for her mom.

But Liam would never invite her to go along with him. Not when they were supposed to be growing apart.

Instead of following after Liam uninvited, Claire held back from Tasha and Melody, pretending to be very interested in a crab apple blossom scent.

Had her mom and dad thought of Claire even once on their trip? Or were they so taken with everything to do on board the cruise they had no time to think of anyone but themselves?

Claire wanted to deny it, but she missed her mom and dad. Not the ones who ditched her over and over again, but the ones who showed up just enough to make her have the hope that maybe, one day, they'd be there for her always.

Could they be tonight? Could they speak with her and give her the boost she needed to see her through the garbage she held onto so tightly this time of year? Or would they rattle off some other excuse she couldn't believe?

The only way to know for sure is to call them yourself.

She far preferred a less risky solution, but Claire pulled out her phone all the same.

Trying not to get her hopes too high, she waved lightly to Melody and Tasha, signaling that she was going to make a call. They smiled at her with understanding, then Claire slipped out of the fragrance shop, drawing in a deep breath of the air that still stunk, but luckily, she could no longer taste.

Alright, so she'd call them. If they picked up, great. If not, she'd leave a message and hope for a call back. If they didn't call back, that was fine, too. She was easy breezy. Chill. As cool as a cucumber.

And yet, as the other end continued to ring, that cucumber was cut shorter slice by slice.

Maybe they were just out of cell service. Or maybe they were just too busy. They were five or six hours behind in the Caribbean, so they might be—

"Claire Bear?"

Her heart raised, and Claire beamed, her mom's voice bringing tears to her eyes in an instant. She turned toward the glass display of the shop so no one else could see her emotion.

"Hey, Mom," she responded with a steady voice she could be proud of.

"Oh, honey! It's so good to hear from you! Jeremy, it's Claire Bear! Oh, baby, how are you? How is London?"

Warmth spread in her heart like blazing fire. "I'm good. And London is amazing."

"Oh, isn't it? I'm so glad you finally get to see what we saw. There really is no other place like it on earth."

"Claire Bear! How you doing?" Her Dad's voice boomed into the phone next, and Claire grinned.

"Hey, Dad. I'm really good."

"Aw, that's great, honey. Who would've thought you'd be a little world traveler, just like us?"

"Isn't it amazing?" Mom said.

"So amazing. I never thought—"

"Oh, just a minute, Claire Bear. Jeremy, is that them?" Her mom's voice sounded as if she'd moved the phone away from her ear. "Oh, it is. Can you get it?"

Claire listened to the one-sided conversation, trying to keep the waning fire alight in her chest. "Mom?"

"Sorry, baby," her mom said, coming back on the phone. "You actually caught us at a bad time. We were just on our way to brunch with some friends we met on the cruise."

"Oh, okay," she said, her hope deflating. "We can talk later then."

"Would you mind? We'll call you right after, okay? We can't wait to hear all about your trip!"

"Yeah, that's fine."

"You're the best, Claire Bear!" Dad piped in. "Talk to you soon!"

"Okay. Sounds—"

The phone fell silent on the other end, her words ending prematurely.

That was alright. She probably needed to get back to Melody and Tasha anyway, give her perspective on which fragrance to buy. But Claire's feet refused to move. Instead of entering the shop shrouded in perfume and pleasant memories that would never belong to her, she remained near the escalators, pulling up Facebook to numb the feelings burgeoning in her chest.

When she was met with the sight of at least fifty new photos from her parents, however, posted only minutes ago, a crushing weight pressed against Claire's chest.

So they'd had time enough to go through all their photos, upload all their photos, and post all their photos...but not enough time to carry on a two-minute conversation with their own daughter?

She tried to spin her thoughts into something more positive, but the truth was as clear as the pictures they'd posted. If they'd wanted to talk to her, they would've made time.

Tears flooded her eyes. Why wasn't she good enough for them? Was she so great a burden to them that they couldn't even bear a few minutes of speaking with her? She'd been an idiot to think that things could change. This is how it had always been and how it always would be. She was always going to be alone. She was always going to be second choice.

Despite her best efforts, her tears spilled down her cheeks. If Tasha and Melody saw her this way, there would be no end to the attention and questions and extra efforts they'd make to help her feel more welcome and included.

Claire didn't need any of that. She just needed a minute and some fresh air. She could compose herself. She *would*.

But as she turned toward the escalators, her vision blurred by her tears, she collided with a solid chest.

She gasped, teetering backwards before strong hands encircled her upper arms, steadying her stance.

"Claire?"

Liam. Of course it would be him.

"Are you alright?"

She nodded, unable to meet his gaze.

"What's the matter?"

She shook her head, biting her tongue more fiercely than she ever had to keep her emotion at bay. But when he smoothed his thumbs along her arm, and she looked up at the concern etched across his brow, she was undone.

TWENTY-EIGHT

LIAM HAD NO IDEA WHAT HAD HAPPENED TO CLAIRE after he'd left the perfumery, but as he watched the tears rolling down her cheeks in unstoppable waves, he had no other thought or desire other than to ease whatever burden she was carrying.

A few people walked by them outside the shop, their curious eyes focused on Claire as she attempted to hide her face. Without hesitation, Liam shifted his body to shield her from the others.

"Come on," he said softly. "Let's get some fresh air."

Claire didn't protest when he took her hand, her fingers tightening around his.

Together, the two of them traveled down escalator after escalator, walking through the maze of customers, Christmas trees, and shops, neither of them stopping until they reached outside. Liam directed her toward the less-popular window displays at the far end of the department store, turning her gently to face the window so passersby couldn't witness her continued emotion even in the darkness.

"Is this alright?" he asked, still holding on to her hand.

She nodded, sliding the tips of her fingers beneath her eyes to wipe away her tears. "Sorry. You can go back inside with the others if you want."

Liam shook his head. "I'd rather be out here with you than listen to Melody prattle on about perfume."

He'd hoped to make her smile, but she just stared harder at the window display—a stuffed mountain goat perched beside mannequins boasting white winter coats and blue scarves.

Instead of looking at the display himself, Liam studied Claire, wanting to help her but not sure how when he didn't even know what the problem was. Had Melody hurt her by ignoring her again? Or had Liam done something to offend her—other than kissing her when he shouldn't have?

Knowing he wasn't going to get anywhere by asking the questions to himself, he faced her more directly.

"Do you want to talk?" he asked. "If you don't, that's fine. Or if you'd rather be alone..."

His words faded when she shook her head. "No, it's fine. I can talk about it. I'm just embarrassed about being an emotional wreck around you."

As if on cue, her eyes filled with tears again. The white Christmas lights around the display reflected in her eyes like diamonds.

"You don't need to be embarrassed around me, remember?" he said gently.

She nodded, ducking her head as she pulled out her phone. He thought for a minute she was trying to distract herself, but when she held up her phone toward him, he examined a photo of an older couple standing against a blue railing with the sea behind them.

He narrowed his eyes, struggling for context before realizing the couple were on a ship at sea. "Your parents?"

She lowered her phone with a small nod. "I called them tonight. They could only talk for a few seconds before leaving, which was fine. But then I saw all these pictures on Facebook and..." She trailed off with a shrug. "It's just hard to see how they prioritize their time."

She swiped at another tear, and Liam's heart constricted. Of course her parents would be the culprits of her state. No wonder she'd avoided talking about them every time they'd come up in the last few days. She might wish to show that she was fine with their negligence, but clearly, she was left with understandably gaping wounds.

"I'm sorry," he said softly, not knowing what else to say. He had a slew of other comments he'd like to make about her parents, but that would hardly be helpful in this situation.

"I just don't get it," she whispered, her breath coming out in cold wisps of air. She focused her gaze on the window display, though her eyes looked a million miles away. "I must be just a giant pain to have them not even want to talk on the phone with me. Either that, or I'm just...forgettable."

He instantly shook his head. "You are neither of those things, Claire."

She turned to face him, the look of pleading in her broken eyes cutting him to his core. "Then why do people keep treating me like this? I've dealt with it my entire life, whether it was my parents, aunts, uncles, friends in school. Even Melody drops me the second she has a better offer. So what is it? What is so fundamentally wrong about me that makes everyone choose me last?"

Her rush of words stopped, her chin quivering before she looked away, as if only just then realizing how much she'd revealed.

A couple walked by, and Claire averted her gaze until they passed.

"Sorry," she whispered up to him. "I didn't mean to unload all of this on you. I just..." She stopped, swiping another tear away. "I don't know what's wrong with me."

Her voice broke at her last word, and so did Liam's heart. He knew they'd promised to keep their distance from each other, but he couldn't stop himself from comforting her any longer.

With slow movements, he released her hand and pulled her toward him, encircling his arms around her in a tight embrace.

She melted into him, her arms wrapping around his waist and trembling as she released silent sobs into his chest.

How long her cries must have been pent up, Liam didn't know. What he did know was that he would do whatever was in his power to ensure she never felt the need to cry so bitterly again.

CLAIRE HAD NEVER ALLOWED herself to release such emotion in front of anyone—let alone a man she'd just met. But as Liam's arms held fast around her, she lost complete control, allowing him to take away her burdens as she cried into his chest.

"There's nothing wrong with you," he whispered down to her, resting his cheek on the top of her head. "You've been wronged by people who should be there for you. But that is never, *could* never be, your fault."

She wanted to believe his words, but years of evidence stacked up against them, making them nearly impossible to see beyond her grief.

And yet, as her tears eventually slowed, Liam's mere presence soothing the sorrow in her soul, a calm wave unfolded over her heart.

Liam's words, whether she believed them or not, had spoken peace to her suffering. But now that the storm had passed, she became keenly aware that she stood in the middle of a sidewalk in London, crying in the arms of an Englishman—whose culture was not typically known for appreciating public displays of emotion.

Gently, she pulled out of his embrace, the cold air circling around her instead of Liam's warm, comforting arms.

"You alright?" he asked, concern still clouding his eyes.

She nodded, unable to meet his gaze for long. "I'm sorry for all of this. I usually can handle it, but today...I don't know. It just got to me, I guess."

She tucked her hair behind her ear, growing more anxious as his eyes focused all the more intently on her.

"We should find your mom and Melody," she said, unable to handle the attention any longer. "They're probably wondering where we are."

She backed away, but Liam remained where he stood, merely shifting his footing to face her again. "Wait, I'd like to say something, if I may."

She swallowed with a wary nod. Would he now tell her the real reason why no one wanted to be with her? Or would he beg of her to never lose control of her emotions like that again?

"I requested a part-time position for work today."

Her brow rose. That was the last thing she'd expected him to say. "You did?"

He nodded. "I don't know if they'll honor the request, but if they do, I'll finally have time to pursue my photography. Perhaps even make a living off of it."

Her heart picked up at the mere notion of Liam's happiness becoming a permanent fixture in his life. "I'm so happy for you," she said with an earnest smile. "After so long, you deserve to do something you love."

His gaze softened, taking on that nearly invisible smile as he stared down at her. "Do you know how I found the courage to finally send that email?"

She had an inkling, but she'd never be so prideful as to actually think she'd helped the man. "Asked the Wizard of Oz?"

His lip curved. "No. I sent that email because of you." He drew closer to her, his eyes flicking between her own. "You inspire me, Claire. I've known you for only a handful of days, but that was all it took for me to realize just how special you are. You have encouraged me, corrected me, made me laugh when no one else could. You brightened my day, even my life."

She stared up at him, wondering if she was in some too-good-to-be-true dream as he reached forth to cup her face in his palm.

"You, Claire Frost, are second to none."

His words penetrated the defenses around her heart, and the barricades crumbled like sand to the pavement at her feet. She reminded herself to take the words lightly, to tread carefully toward her future, but the truth was in Liam's eyes, and her heart swelled because of it.

"You know," he continued, "if I'm working less, I'll have more time for other things, too."

He swallowed, and desire swirled in her lower stomach as his eyes dropped to her lips.

He was referring to her, a *relationship* with her. He had to be. But then, what would that even look like? Flights from Colorado to the UK every other month, getting to know each other over chats and FaceTimes? Could a relationship even cope with that?

But as he smoothed his thumb over her cheek, she found herself caring less and less about *how* they would make it work—and more and more on *wanting* to make it work.

"I don't know if you..." He stopped, glancing over her shoulder as his face fell.

She turned her gaze, his hand slipping from her face in the process as she caught sight of Tasha and Melody striding toward them as they left Harrods.

"Of course," Liam muttered, looking away in clear frustration. "I'd really like to finish this conversation, preferably in private."

Claire stared up at him, still reeling from his touch. "So would I."

Their eyes met, and that same desire from before shifted to her heart before Melody's calling finally broke their concentration.

"There you guys are! Claire, we tried calling you, but you didn't pick up."

Claire checked her phone, relieved at having something else to focus on as Tasha's heavy gaze shifted from Liam to Claire. Sure enough, Melody's missed call lit up on the screen.

"Oh, sorry," she said. "I didn't feel it buzz."

She had been too distracted by Liam's comforting embrace to pay attention to anything else.

"We figured you both needed a breather after the perfumery," Tasha said. She focused on Claire's no-doubt red eyes. "Are you alright?"

Claire glanced up at Liam, who watched her closely. "Yeah," she stated, averting her gaze. "I'm getting kinda hungry, though."

"Ugh, yes," Melody said. "I'm thinking a big ole juicy steak will hit the spot. Oh, you know who likes steak? Dean."

And then she launched into another monologue of the many delicious qualities of her part-time boyfriend as the four of them set off down the sidewalk.

"Honestly, guys, I just think I'm in love," Melody said with an airy sigh.

Instead of rolling her eyes, Claire could only smile in amusement. Because although her mind was occupied with Liam and what he'd been about to say to her before they'd been interrupted, all she wanted to do was respond back to her friend by saying, "Melody, I think I am, too."

TWENTY-NINE

To Claire's dismay, the opportunity to speak with Liam never came up. The four of them spent the entire evening together instead, wrapping presents and watching *Home Alone* and *Home Alone 2* as Melody chatted everyone's ears off before they all headed to bed.

Claire then spent a restless night tossing and turning, deciding to wake up first thing the following morning to attempt to catch Liam on his own once again.

To her dismay, however, Tasha was already with her son, the two of them sitting across from one another at the kitchen table. Two pieces of toast were situated before each of them, and Liam's camera and tattered neck strap was situated next to his arms that rested on the table.

Liam's eyes met hers in an instant, and her heart warmed to see their dark depths smiling at her.

"Morning, Claire," Tasha said. "Would you like some toast?"

"Yeah, thank you. I can get it, though."

She made her way to the bread on the kitchen counter, her heart skittering as Liam stood to join her.

"Hey," he said softly, glancing over his shoulder at his mom.

She still sat at the table, her eyes trained on her phone. "We still need to finish our conversation from last night."

Claire placed the bread in the toaster. "Yeah, we do."

"Maybe we could go on a walk later today?"

Excitement flourished in her chest. "That sounds great."

"Perfect. Then—"

"Liam," Tasha interrupted, "is that your phone going off?"

Liam and Claire turned to the table, his phone lighting up with an incoming call. He narrowed his eyes at the screen before a frown marked his brow.

"Anything wrong?" Tasha asked, having caught his scowl, too.

He shook his head, walking to the table and reaching for the phone. "No. I just need to take this."

He clicked the green button on the screen, then held the phone to his ear and walked down the hallway.

As he disappeared from her view, an uneasiness crept over Claire. She hadn't seen his frown that intense since the airport.

She didn't know who was behind the call, but based on Liam's reaction, she didn't think it was someone he wanted to speak with.

SEEING his boss's name emblazoned across the phone's screen had sent dread straight through Liam's limbs. For a split second, he'd considered not answering, knowing this was going to be the phone call that ended his job. Then he'd reminded himself that he had every right to find happiness in his career, so he picked up the phone anyway.

Still, hearing Garrett's voice on the other end did nothing but rattle Liam's nerves.

"So," Garrett said. "I'm sure you know why I'm calling you, Liam."

"I've an idea."

"I have to say, your email came as quite a shock. I still can't understand why you'd wish to change to part-time."

"I explained my reasoning." Liam knew he was being short with his boss, the man who held his future in his hands. But honestly, the worst he could do was sack Liam from Peregrine Productions, and right about now, that didn't sound too bad.

"Mmm, yes. I was also surprised to learn that you were interested in becoming an executive producer."

Liam's jaw shifted as he shook his head in disbelief. "Garrett, you know full-well I'd been promised that position by you for years."

Silence met him. Would the dismissal occur now?

Garrett cleared his throat. "Either way, I'm concerned, Liam. I would never wish to think that any of our employees, you especially, would accuse Peregrine Productions of not valuing those who work for us."

Liam grimaced. Garrett sounded just like he was pitching to a potential client. "I used to think I was valued, but things change."

"Indeed."

When he said nothing further, Liam sighed. He couldn't take it any longer. For years, he'd dealt with this sort of rubbish. He was over it. "Look, Garrett. I'll be frank with you. You either offer me the part-time position, or I'll be handing in my weeks' notice."

Liam nearly fell over at his own words, but the moment they left his tongue, a weight lifted from his shoulders. He drew a deep breath, as if for the first time in years.

This. This was what he wanted. To be free of the company that had been holding him back for far too long. To be free of—

"What would you say to becoming an executive producer instead?"

Instantly, the weight returned, and Liam's jaw went slack. Garrett was stringing him along again. It's what he'd done since the beginning.

"Liam?"

"I'm here." He hesitated, his thoughts spinning so greatly, he had to sit on the third step of the stairs.

"What do you say?"

So Garrett was serious? "What about the person you already hired?"

Garrett cleared his throat. "Unfortunately, Miss Davies and the company have parted ways."

Already? Liam frowned. This didn't make any sense. The woman had been hired days ago. How could she already be leaving the company?

"I know you must be in shock, Liam, but I'm afraid we're going to have to receive an answer from you soon."

"How soon?"

"We would need you to come in this morning."

Liam frowned. "It's Christmas Eve."

"Yes, I am well aware. You won't be required to work Christmas day, of course, but if you can't come in today, I'm afraid we'll have to look for someone else to fill the position. We've a few others in mind and quite a deal of work to accomplish, which is why we need an answer now."

It was true, then. Liam was finally being offered the position of executive producer. This had been his dream for years. It was finally coming to fruition. So why were his insides tied in knots?

"So, what do you say, Liam?"

His heart raced, and his stomach turned. He couldn't give up eight years of his life. Not with the promotion finally within reach. No, not within reach. Within his very hands. Working as an executive producer should also allow him more flexibility over his traveling schedule, so he'd have more time to photograph. He'd be crazy to say no. Right?

"Yes," he said, his voice low. "I accept the offer."

The words felt as hard as treacle toffee on his tongue.

"Excellent. We'll see you within the hour. Congratulations, Liam. We look forward to working with you for many years to come."

The line clicked before Liam could respond. Slowly, he lowered his hand in a daze, staring down at the phone until the screen went black.

Well, he'd received his promotion. After eight long years, he'd finally been rewarded. He should be happy. Thrilled. Ecstatic.

But he wasn't.

CLAIRE DID her best not to overhear Liam as he took his call, but the suspense was killing her. She had an idea as to who had called him, but she wouldn't allow herself to focus on the negative until she learned the truth.

That came sooner than later, however, as Liam moved into the kitchen, his gaze focused on the floor.

"Who was that?" Tasha asked flippantly, though Claire could hear the curiosity in her voice.

"Garrett," Liam responded.

Garrett. Wasn't that the name of Liam's boss? Claire's stomach clenched.

"What did he want?" Tasha pressed, her eyes flitting to Claire's.

"He offered me the position of executive producer. And I accepted."

A rush of emotions clawed their way around Claire's heart. Of course she was thrilled for Liam to receive his sought-after promotion. But then, hadn't he wanted to do his photography instead?

"Oh my goodness," Tasha said, surprise registering across her features before she moved to embrace her son. "Congratulations, darling. That is wonderful."

Liam's dark eyes met Claire's as he hugged his mom. She

forced a smile on her lips, waiting for Tasha to pull back before speaking.

"That's..." The word caught in Claire's throat, so she tried again. "That's awesome, Liam. Congratulations."

He nodded his gratitude, though any semblance of a smile had yet to stretch across his lips or even hint in his eyes.

More than anything, Claire wanted him to be happy. Never mind that she'd thought that the two of them might have...That they...

But that didn't matter. Nothing else mattered so long as he was happy.

So if this promotion was what he really wanted, why was he *not* happy?

"Are you excited?" Tasha asked, seemingly aware of Liam's hesitance, as well.

"Yes," he stated a little too forcefully. "I'm just...surprised. He asked me to come in today."

Claire's spirits spiraled even lower, her chest tightening, squeezing every last ounce of happiness from her heart until it felt like a wrung rag.

Tasha's face fell before she quickly righted her expression with a smile. "That's alright. We'll have tomorrow together at least. And you can make it back for the party tonight, I'm sure."

He nodded, then looked to Claire.

As if reading her son's mind, Tasha glanced between them both. "I wonder if Melody's awake yet. I'll go see."

She walked away, then disappeared down the hallway and up the stairs.

Claire and Liam stood in silence for a minute, their eyes lingering on each other before he finally spoke.

"Listen, about that walk. I'm sorry, but..."

Claire was already shaking her head. She couldn't learn anything about what he'd planned to say or what she'd hoped to hear.

Instead, she pulled on her best smile and spoke with a light shrug. "There's no need to apologize. It's alright. I understand with your new job, you'll be even busier than before, so it's totally fine. Just so long as you're happy." She paused. "You *are* happy, right?"

He took far too long to respond. "Yeah, I am. I mean, I've been working towards this goal for so long, why wouldn't I be?"

She searched his eyes, seeing the lie behind them in an instant. But it wasn't her place to judge. It was her place to support her friend.

"I'm glad," she said. "Because you *should* be happy. You've just received something you've worked really hard for, so celebrate it."

He nodded, though his shoulders still hunched slightly forward, as if the weight of the world bore down on him.

Seconds ticked by in silence, but Claire couldn't handle it any longer. "Hey, don't you have to get ready? You wouldn't want to be late."

He shook his head, backing away as he averted his gaze. "I'll see you tonight, then?"

"For sure. See you tonight."

When he walked away from her, Claire instructed her tears to remain behind her eyes where they belonged. This time, they obeyed.

THIRTY

LIAM LEFT FOR WORK A MERE HALF HOUR LATER, AND the house fell silent until another distraction arrived in the form of Melody's family. Claire had always liked her friend's parents. They were a bit eccentric, like their daughters, but they were also loving and kind, greeting Claire with smiles and hugs alongside Melody and Tasha.

Together, the families and Claire spent hours visiting, eating, and readying the house for the party that night. Claire did her best to stay distracted, but it was difficult when everywhere she looked and everything she heard reminded her of Liam.

She'd made the decision before coming to England to make this the best Christmas she'd ever had. Aside from Liam leaving that morning, it *had* been. Unfortunately, that was all because of the time she'd spent with him.

The fact that she couldn't see him any longer could absolutely put a damper on her time there, but their limited interactions should make it easier to leave when the time came.

So, after giving herself a stern talking to, Claire picked her spirits up and made herself busy by helping Tasha religiously until six o'clock rolled around and the guests began to arrive.

With over twenty people in attendance, the house was filled to its capacity, but Claire didn't mind as everyone made her feel warm and welcome. She had never been to such a wonderful, home-feeling party. Christmas music played out from a speaker in the kitchen, the tree glowed magically in the dim light of the front room, and laughter and happy conversation abounded throughout the house.

The only thing to make the evening better would have been for Liam to arrive. That had to be any minute now, right?

And yet, an hour later, he still hadn't shown up. Claire did her best to stay positive, but when Tasha came up to her with a sober expression, Claire's hope scattered.

"Liam texted," Tasha said. "He's not going to be able to make it back in time for the party."

Claire attempted to hide her disappointment, though she knew her crestfallen features were a dead giveaway. "I'm sorry to hear that."

Tasha nodded. "I suppose we should've expected this. They really do take advantage of him there. They always have."

Her deflated tone made Claire instantly chastise herself. Here she was, thinking all about her own disappointments without even considering how Tasha would feel missing her son.

"I'm sorry," Claire said.

Tasha took Claire's hand in hers. "So am I."

JUST AFTER MIDNIGHT, Liam arrived home. He closed the door softly behind him as he yawned, dropping his wallet and keys onto the table and hanging his coat on the hook near the door. It had been a long day—a foreshadowing of the next few years of his life as he took on his new responsibilities of the promotion. How was he ever going to last?

"Liam?"

He looked down the hallway, Mum's voice coming from the sitting room. "What are you still doing up?" he asked.

"Wrapping a few presents. You can come chat, if you'd like."

He made his way to the sitting room, finding Mum seated on the floor, wrapping paper, scissors, tape, and boxes all around her.

She looked up at him with a warm smile. "So?"

He paused. "So, what?"

"How was the new job?"

Realization dawned, and Liam flopped down on the couch. "It was..." Exhausting. Grueling. "Fine."

"Just 'fine,'" she repeated, her eyes narrowing.

He nodded, though describing his new job as 'fine' was even a stretch. What made matters worse was that he'd discovered that he actually hadn't been given the promotion based on his own merit, but by the company desperately scrambling. Apparently, the woman they'd hired before had left them high and dry in a matter of hours, using her new position at Peregrine to obtain a better job somewhere else.

Liam wouldn't be surprised if they ended up demoting him at some point or hiring someone else to replace him. Because that was just the way they worked.

Realizing his mum was still waiting for more of an explanation, he leaned farther into the couch. He didn't want to worry her unnecessarily. It would be better to just let her think he enjoyed it. "No, it was great. I'm just going to be...busy."

"Even more than you already were?"

Liam nodded, focusing instead on the lights still twinkling away in the Christmas tree, presents pouring out beneath the branches. He still hadn't wrapped the gifts he'd purchased for everyone. He had been planning on doing that after his walk with Claire that never happened.

His chest tightened. He'd tried so hard not to think about her, and still, her blue eyes occupied the majority of his thoughts all day long. He'd been furious when Garrett asked him to stay longer, forcing him to miss his mum's party and, of course, more time with Claire.

"*We need to land this new client, Liam,*" Garrett had said. "*Armstrong Glass doesn't celebrate Christmas, so this year, we aren't either.*"

Obviously, Liam had protested, taking a silent stance by staying late Christmas Eve so he wouldn't have to come in Christmas day—despite his boss's earlier promise. Only time would tell if Garrett would honor the effort.

"I'm sorry I missed the party," he said, watching his mum wrap another present. "How was it?"

"It was really nice," she replied with a smile, her eyes focusing on the red reindeer wrapping. "I think everyone had a great time. They all asked where you were and said they were sad to miss you." She gave him a sidelong glance. "Claire, too."

Liam's heart twinged. So much for avoiding any mention of her. "How was she?"

Mum taped up one side of the wrapping. "She was missing you, I think."

Liam didn't know what to say. He'd missed Claire, too.

Taping up another side, his mum continued. "Liam, can I ask what's going on between you two?"

He shrugged, attempting to play it off coolly. "Nothing. I mean, we like each other, but there are too many obstacles between us, so we both decided just to...not."

She didn't look up at him, turning the final wrapped present over and sliding it beneath the tree. "Would you have wanted to date her if you hadn't gotten the promotion?"

Liam hesitated. He'd been avoiding that same question in his mind all day. "I don't know," he lied.

He had wanted to date her. He still wanted to date her. But he couldn't very well string her along when this new job would make him busier than the last, despite his hopes that it would not.

"But...you're happy with your new job?" Mum asked.

"I—"

"Be honest, Liam," she said softly.

Liam let out a heavy sigh. "Honestly, I don't know. I *should* be happy. Isn't that enough?"

Mum stood, straightening a few presents beneath the tree. "If you ask me, no. That's not enough. You deserve happiness, whether that's with Claire or not. Ultimately, that's for you to decide." She gathered the wrapping materials from the floor and tucked them beneath her arms before giving him a soft smile. "Now get some rest. We've an early morning ahead of us." She walked away from him before pausing. "You'll get the lights?"

He nodded in silence, his thoughts churning.

"Happy Christmas, son," she said with a warm smile, then she turned away and headed upstairs.

Liam remained on the couch, staring at the tree as his mind churned through the days he'd just spent with Claire. Apart from taking photos and key moments from his childhood, Liam couldn't remember ever being so happy as he'd been with the woman.

So what did that tell him about his decision making, that he was giving up photography *and* his time with Claire for a promotion that hadn't brought him any happiness at all?

He had to give the job a chance, though, right? He would feel better about it in time. Or...would he always regret not giving his relationship with Claire a chance—not giving his photography a chance?

He sighed, scrubbing his hands over his eyes. Mum was right. He needed to get to bed. Tomorrow would be another long, taxing day. Not because of his work, but because of his own stupid mind and his inability to make a logical decision.

Happy Christmas, indeed.

THIRTY-ONE

CLAIRE HAD ALWAYS BEEN A SUCKER FOR SNOW ON Christmas, but as she looked outside that morning, mist cloaking the world in a cozy gray darkness, she knew one thing was for certain—she could get behind a gray Christmas just as much as a white one.

"Alright, are we ready?"

She looked over her shoulder as Tasha spoke, the families congregating in the front room. Claire's eyes met with Liam's at once, but she looked away after a quick smile, moving to sit next to Melody on the kitchen chairs brought in and situated by the tree.

She hadn't spoken with Liam beyond a few words that morning. She'd asked after his new job—which he'd described as "fine"—before he swiftly changed the subject to her Mando pajamas.

"Melody made me wear them," Claire had said with a blush.

Liam hadn't had the chance to respond as Melody's family arrived in that moment from the Airbnb they were staying at.

Claire tried to tell herself she was better off without talking to Liam at all. She knew his job would usurp a lot of his time, so she may as well get used to being without him as soon as possible.

Of course, that was easier said than done when she couldn't even keep her eyes off the guy. Honestly, how could someone look so good with tousled hair, a black t-shirt, and gray sweats?

With Nat King Cole's *The Christmas Song* playing in the background, the gift opening began, and as Claire was delivered present after present, her mind was finally occupied with something other than Liam.

She wasn't surprised to receive a few gifts from Melody, but when more were sent her way from Tasha and Melody's family— matching t-shirts for her and Melody, a Jane Austen series set, floral notebooks with pens to match and more—her heart overflowed with gratitude. She had no idea how she was going to cart all of this home in her suitcase, but she had to blink back tears on more than one occasion at the family's thoughtfulness, especially when she compared them to her own parents' actions.

They still had yet to call her back, but they had managed to send a "Merry Christmas" text the night before with the promise of delivering her money as soon as they arrived home from their cruise.

Their behavior had been expected, and though Claire was once again disappointed, she refused to let them cast a pall on how incredible Christmas morning was with the Bancrofts and Everharts.

As the pile beneath the tree thinned, and everyone was occupied with opening their own presents, Melody pointed to one of the final gifts. "There's another for you, Claire."

"From you?" Claire asked, reaching for the neatly wrapped box.

Melody shrugged. "No. I don't know who it's from." Then she turned to her sister, Jen, who opened Melody's gifted earrings with a gasp.

Claire could focus on nothing else but the gift on her lap, ignoring the suggestion her heart gave when there was no note on the box.

It wasn't from Liam. It couldn't be.

And yet, when she unwrapped the packaging and peered inside the box, a smile split across her lips. She reached down and pulled out the Grogu beanie Liam had found at the Christmas Market.

There was only one person who could have given this to her.

As if on cue, Melody stood from her seat, moving to point out the quality of her sister's earrings, and Claire's view of Liam opened up from where he'd been seated on Melody's opposite side.

He was already looking at her, his eyes shining. "I couldn't resist," he said, motioning to the beanie.

She grinned. "You're lucky I wore these pajamas this morning. Now you can see the whole outfit complete." She slipped the beanie on and turned to face him. "Still just as awful as before?"

"Oh my goodness," Tasha laughed from across the room, preventing Liam's response. "I love it. It matches your pajamas perfectly."

A few more compliments sounded, and Claire looked down to hide her blush, only to discover more items in the box. When the attention had once again returned to Melody and Jen, Claire pulled out a luggage tag in the shape of a flower.

"Couldn't help but be a bit cheeky with that one, as well," Liam said, giving the weakest attempt at an apologetic grin Claire had ever seen.

She laughed. "I just hate that I'm actually going to find use for this."

Finally, she pulled out the last gift, an ornament of a red telephone box hanging from a gold string. Her smile faded, all of her energy expended on her racing heart.

Hesitant, she glanced toward Liam, his own smile softening. "To remember your time here," he said softly, a hint of sadness in his dark eyes.

Claire couldn't meet his gaze for long, turning away to avoid feeling that same sorrow. "Thank you."

She wanted to add more. She wanted to tell him that she

would cherish these gifts forever, that she would never forget Liam even without the tokens.

But what good would it do? He had made his decision, and so had she. Separately, they would have to stick to them, no matter how painful the repercussions.

LIAM HAD WONDERED if the gifts would be too much for Claire, but she seemed to genuinely appreciate each one, which wasn't surprising. She had always expressed her gratitude to him —whether he'd deserved it or not.

After the present opening had concluded, the rest of the day crawled by slowly for Liam. He didn't have much chance to speak with Claire, but it was for the best. Even still, after a full day of games, snacking, and chatting—all while reminding himself he should not be looking at Claire so often, he was exhausted.

Just after dinner, he snuck away to his room for a respite from trying not to stare at how gorgeous she looked in her white, fuzzy Christmas jumper. Honestly, the woman would look amazing in anything she wore. Which was precisely his problem. He needed to stop thinking about her altogether.

That became much harder, however, when he found a small, red-wrapped present at the foot of his bed. Narrowing his eyes, he approached the package, unwrapping it to find a fine, leather camera strap.

He glanced back down to the box, discovering a folded note within. Pulling it out, he read it with a thrumming heart.

Liam,

Sorry I didn't give this to you earlier. I wasn't sure if you wanted to open it in front of everyone, so I figured this would be the safer bet. I hope you like it and that you'll still be able to make good use of it.

I want to tell you how grateful I am to you for the last few days. They were some of the best of my life, though they wouldn't have been without you. So, thank you.

I really wish you all the best at your new job. You worked so hard for it. I hope you'll be happy there and that they treat you right.

If you're ever in the States, I hear Colorado has some pretty special scenery and wildlife. (Just one native Coloradan's opinion.)

Thank you again,
Claire

Liam smiled as he finished the letter, looking back to the camera strap in his other hand and admiring the sturdy stitching and dark leather. She must have noticed how scratty his orange strap had become and purchased this to replace it.

His shoulders sank, a defeated sigh escaping his lips. He needed to thank her for her generosity. His self-pitying nap could wait.

Placing the strap carefully back in the box on his bed, Liam headed downstairs, finding Claire next to Melody and Jen, unwrapping a new board game of *Harry Potter Cluedo* they'd received for Christmas.

Not wanting to interrupt their game, he paused, but Claire turned to face him with a curious expression.

"Do you want to play?" Melody asked, facing him, too.

"Maybe later. I was just..." He faced Claire, lowering his voice, though he noted Melody leaning in further as he did so. "Claire, would you like to take a quick walk with me?" She hesitated, looking to the game, so he rushed on. "It will only take a minute."

"Go on," Melody said, "we'll get the game set up and wait for you."

Claire then faced Liam, her expression filled with nothing but hesitance. "Sure."

He didn't blame her for not wanting to join him. Honestly, a walk wasn't warranted for the simple "thank you" he needed to express. But he still felt terrible for what he'd done to her. He could only hope an explanation would alleviate his guilt—or at least a fraction of it.

Together, the two of them put on their coats and stepped outside into the frigid air. The rain had finally relented that evening, though the pavement still glistened with moisture, reflecting the lights of the cars and streetlamps.

They moved in silence until they crossed the street to where a small park stretched the length of the nearly silent road.

"Have you had a good Christmas?" he asked, their footsteps soft against the pavement.

She nodded. "Yeah. How about you?"

"Yes, thanks."

These questions and answers were not befitting the relationship and connection they had. And yet, the awkwardness between them was there for a reason.

"Sorry for bringing you out here. I won't take you away from the others for very long."

Claire shook her head. "It's alright."

Again, their discomfort continued.

Liam cleared his throat. "I just wanted to tell you thank you for the gift you gave me. That was really sweet of you."

She averted her gaze. Was that due to her embarrassment over the attention she received or the regret she may feel for giving him a gift in the first place?

"Oh, no problem." She chewed on her lower lip. "I bought it

before you got the promotion at your job. If you can't use it now, you can always return it. Sorry."

A stabbing pain cut through his heart. She should not be apologizing right now. "I'll still be able to use it," he reassured her, although he really didn't have the right. If yesterday's day of work was telling, he wouldn't have much time to take photos at all.

Silence grew heavy around them, and Liam grimaced. This was all his fault. He never should have kissed her. He never should have fallen for her so hard. He'd always known his allegiance lay with Peregrine Productions. Why had he ever thought he could escape their talons?

Overcome with regret, he stopped, turning to face Claire. "I know we never got the chance to speak earlier, but I just...I need to apologize again for how..."

He paused as she waved a hand in a gesture for him to stop. "Look, we don't have to do this," she said softly, darkness shrouding half of her face as she looked up at him. "We've already agreed that a relationship wouldn't work between us. Talking about it again would just be too painful, you know?" She looked away, her shoulders falling forward as she continued in a voice barely above a whisper. "Honestly, being *around* you is painful. I just can't do it anymore."

His chest tightened. "What do you mean?"

She looked up at him, her features downcast. "I think I'm gonna catch an earlier flight home."

Panic gripped his chest. He knew he'd be busy with work, but a small part of him had clung to the hope that he'd still have the chance to speak with Claire in the late evenings. Now, with her leaving, that one light in his dark life was being taken away too early.

"You-you can't leave," he said, shaking his head, feeling the threads of his life snapping one by one. "You came all this way. I'll just stay at my own apartment after Christmas. That way you won't have to see me."

Would it be enough for him to simply know that Claire was

still in England, even though he couldn't see her? Or was he simply stringing out the painful inevitable?

She gave a half-smile, her brows turned upright. "It's not being with you that's painful, Liam. It's knowing that I *can't* be with you. And I don't want that constant reminder anymore." She took a step away from him. "Please don't make this harder than it needs to be."

She turned around and walked away. He watched her retreat in a sort of daze. She was leaving England, cutting her holiday short, flying all the way back to Colorado...just because she wanted to be with him but couldn't?

His heart tapped against his chest, as if learning to beat for the first time. Did she really like him that much? Did she feel as deeply for him as he felt for her?

Needing to know the truth, though he didn't know what he'd do with it, Liam jogged toward her. "Claire, wait."

But she shook her head, still walking away. "No, Liam. We need to make a clean break."

"We can't." He ran in front of her so she had to stop, but she wouldn't meet his gaze. "I need to know first how...how exactly you feel about me."

She wouldn't respond. He reached forward, but she pulled back.

He didn't blame her, nor would he push it, but his heart ached at that need for connection, to experience her warmth, to physically feel what her heart felt.

"Please," he said softly, "just tell me—"

He stopped, his phone pulling him from their conversation as it rang. Claire dropped her eyes to his pockets, but he merely reached back and pressed the side button to silence the generic ringtone. Pulling his mind back to the conversation, Liam drew a deep breath and gathered his thoughts. Claire remained silently watchful.

"Claire, too much has gone on between us for us to—"

Again, his phone went off. He sighed, pulling it out to silence it indefinitely before pausing as he read the name emblazoned across the screen.

Garrett. What the devil was he doing calling right now?

"Is that your boss?"

Liam looked up, Claire's eyes on him. "Yeah."

She looked away. "Go ahead. I'll wait."

Frustration filtered into his heart at Garrett's interruption. "I'll just be one minute."

She nodded, turning away to allow him to take his call in private. Liam accepted the call, facing the other direction. "Hey, Garrett." He hoped his voice revealed just how annoyed he was.

"Liam, I need you to come in."

Liam paused, scoffing. "Can you tell me why?"

"Armstrong Glass is losing interest. We're putting together a presentation for them, and we need you to head it up."

Liam lowered his voice as he responded, though he knew Claire would hear no matter what. "I was under the impression that, since I worked through the night yesterday, I wouldn't be asked to come in on Christmas. I missed my mum's party, visiting with my family—"

"We're all making sacrifices here, Liam. I'm also away from my family tonight."

Liam clenched his jaw. Garrett had never revealed any hesitation about leaving his family during any holiday or celebration. The man was a workhorse.

But Liam...he wasn't.

Turning to Claire, he held up a finger to signify that he wouldn't be much longer, but she wasn't there. He frowned, looking down the park as her pink coat retreated into the darkness.

He winced. Had she simply lost patience? Or was she walking away because she'd lost the heart to fight for a relationship?

Without caring if his boss overheard, Liam moved his phone away from his lips and sped toward her. "Claire, wait!"

She turned to face him, though she continued her retreat backwards with a shake of her head.

"Please," he said, "I just need one minute."

"Liam?" Garrett questioned.

Claire gave him a wary look, but she remained where she stood.

"Liam!"

"I'm here," he finally responded.

"Well you shouldn't be there. You should be on your way already."

Liam stared down at Claire, the light from the nearby street-lamp cascading down her blonde waves, her blue eyes averted from his once again.

He couldn't leave her right now. They needed to finish this conversation. *He* needed to finish the conversation.

"I can make it in a few hours," he responded.

Garrett scoffed across the line. "No, you need to be here now."

Liam gritted his teeth. If the choice was between going to work that evening and putting Claire first—apparently the only person in her life to do so—he already knew what he was going to do. "I'm sorry. But I can't do that tonight, Garrett."

Claire's eyes whipped toward Liam, wide with shock, pouring fuel on his courage.

"You can't?" Garrett stated incredulously.

"Yes, that's correct."

Liam's heart raced, heat flushing through his body despite the cold, winter air.

"Well I'm sorry to hear that," Garrett said, though not an ounce of sorrow painted his tone. "Because either you make it in the next half hour, or we will find someone else to fill your position."

Shock jolted through Liam's body, an icy chill replacing the heat and sliding down his spine. Garrett had threatened him in this way before, and Liam had always buckled under the pressure for fear of losing his job.

But now, as he stared down at Claire, her eyes connecting with his, his fear melted away and a clarity he'd never before known settled in his mind. If he went into work that night, he would be allowing his life to be run by someone who didn't value him—who didn't want him to be happy.

On the other hand, if he remained home, yes, he would lose that job, but how much more would he be gaining in return? A life? A chance at freedom? An opportunity to pursue photography professionally?

Claire?

"Liam, I need your answer now," Garrett barked across the line.

With a stalwart gaze, Liam stared down at Claire. "I'm sorry, Garrett. But I will not be coming in today."

Claire stared up at him, unmoving as shock flashed across her features.

"You're telling me that you're seriously going to consider throwing away the last eight years of your life?" Garrett asked.

"Yes, that's right," Liam stated calmly. "Garrett, I quit."

Claire shook her head. "Are you crazy?" she whispered, but Liam had never felt sounder.

Garrett's frustration was obvious as he growled out his words. "If I find out that you are leveraging this position for another at a different company, I will—"

"I'm not," Liam interrupted, still looking down at Claire, caressing every curve of her face with his eyes. "I don't want another position. I want another life."

"How unbelievably unprofessional to drop the company that made you into who you are today," Garrett snapped. "You are finished with this line of work. I'll make sure you never step foot in another—"

But Liam was done. He ended the call, silenced the ring, then slid the phone into his pocket. A strange sensation filled his chest, one he didn't recognize at first. An emptiness? No. It was more a calmness. A feeling of peace.

Peace. Is that what it felt like? It had been so long since he'd experienced it. And yet, he knew at once that was what he was feeling. Peace and an overwhelming sense of joy.

Claire, however, still stood in front of him with a pursed brow. "Liam, what are you doing?"

"I'm doing what you said."

She swallowed. "I said a lot of things..."

He gave a soft laugh. "I'm no longer waiting for the stars to align."

Her lips parted. "But what about your job? You worked so hard for that promotion."

"It is not for me. It might bring me more money and accomplishments, but in reality, all it was doing was keeping me away from the things I actually wish to do with my life."

"And what is it you want to do?" she asked, the innocence in her expression wrapping around his heart.

He gave a half-smile. "I want to take photographs. I want to be free to control my own narrative." He reached for her hand. This time, she didn't pull back. "And I want to be with you."

Hope sparkled in her blue eyes, but still, she shook her head. "I have to go back to Colorado next week. And I have a job of my own. Wouldn't we just be setting ourselves up for failure by starting a long-distance relationship when we've only known each other for, what, five days?"

Feeling lighter and more carefree by the minute, Liam gave a flippant shrug. "I hear there's some fascinating wildlife in Colorado."

"What?" she breathed.

He moved forward, the words falling from his lips as the ideas came to him. "I could come for a month or two. Then after that, you could visit England for a week, whatever your job permits."

Her smile had grown as he'd spoken, even though she shook her head. "But...that'd be crazy."

He laughed, smoothing a lock of hair behind her ear. "That is most definitely true. But then, I don't feel like it *would* be crazy. I know we haven't known each other for long. But you've seen me at my worst and my best. You've heard more about my dreams and wishes than any other person on the planet, and you know what I really want in life. Honestly, I think we'd be mad *not* to see what happens." He sobered, staring down at her with an intensity he hoped spoke to her of his devotion. "I want to make this work, Claire. I want to see if what we have between us is real. Because I already know, I've fallen in love with you."

The moment he spoke the words, a rush of warmth overcame him stronger than any feeling he had ever experienced. He'd spoken the truth, and blast, did it feel good to own it.

CLAIRE LISTENED to Liam's admission of love, her head spinning as her heart overflowed. Love? This man—this charming, thoughtful, gorgeous man—loved *her*?

Tears filled her eyes as the truth rushed toward her. He had quit his job, lost his career, and given up the last eight years of his life, not only to seek his photography, but to give their relationship a fighting chance, even offering to follow her to Colorado.

This was something Claire had never experienced in her life—this was someone putting her first. *Choosing* her first.

And yet, deep down, she wasn't surprised. She was at peace. Liam had already put her first so many times over the last few days. Showing her around London on his day off, joining her at Winter Wonderland to save her from Dean and Melody, rescuing her from each embarrassing situation instead of saving face for himself.

And now this.

She looked up at him, staring into his dark eyes as he waited patiently for her to either respond to or reject his declaration of love.

Slowly, she took a step toward him, bringing her hands to rest against his chest. "I love you, too, Liam," she said softly. "And I want to make this work."

His chest moved up and down against her fingers, his expression sobering, then he leaned toward her and pressed his lips against hers. She didn't hesitate to kiss him right back, wrapping her arms around his neck as he encircled her in his embrace.

After a moment, she pulled back, staring deep into his eyes. "Melody's going to be unbearable with us now, you know that, right?"

"Hopefully I'm worth it," he said with a wink.

She ran her fingers through his hair just above his ear—the strands as soft as she'd imagined. "Liam, you'll always be worth everything to me."

Then she reached up and pressed her lips to his again.

Their first kiss, Claire had been so preoccupied with what was going to happen afterward that she couldn't focus on the present. But she wasn't going to worry about the future anymore.

Because right now, she had Liam standing in her corner, fighting to be with her, and loving her for who she was.

And *nothing* was better than that.

EPILOGUE

One Year Later

Liam walked with Claire beneath the row of arbors that lined the pathway toward the garden folly at Kew Gardens. Brown branches of dormant ivy crawled across the wooden eaves. Only a few green leaves still hung on, despite the thick, December snowflakes falling down around them.

Liam hadn't seen a snowfall like this in years, the grass fully covered with sheets of crystal white snow. It really couldn't have come at a more perfect time.

"It's so pretty," Claire breathed next to him, her arms wrapped around his like a koala bear as they walked. "It reminds me of the snow we got up at Yellowstone."

"That was an adventure," he said, recalling the holiday they'd taken together last summer. Who would have thought it would snow in June?

Despite sliding from the road a few times, Liam had managed to capture some pretty spectacular photos—photos he was still benefiting from today. Apparently, people loved to purchase images of bison in the snow.

He and Claire continued together down the empty pathway.

Kew Gardens would be closing in less than an hour, but Liam had one more stop to make before they could leave.

Claire had only arrived that morning from the States, and already, it was a relief to be reunited with his girlfriend. The past year had been the fastest and slowest of his life. His time with Claire always flew by, despite his living out of a suitcase at various Airbnb properties for weeks at a time.

But when they were apart—the eternal flights, the hour-long phone calls just to connect, the ache that always came from being away from each other—he certainly wasn't going to miss it when things changed.

And things would be changing soon. All he needed to do was reach that folly.

He focused on the stone structure perched on top of a small hill covered in snow. Five pillars held the domed roof high above the flat, open platform, providing just enough shelter from the snow, while still allowing a view of the fluffy flakes drifting down on the gardens.

Thank goodness the folly was empty.

He grasped the small, velvet box in his coat pocket for the hundredth time, his heart pounding as he contemplated what he was about to do.

They'd spoken of marriage before, and of having children, where they wanted to live, and all the other things pertaining to their futures. They knew they were on the same page with things. But when he glanced down to Claire, snowflakes caught in her blonde locks, her blue eyes peering up at the world around her, his heart twinged.

"Are you going to miss it? The snow, I mean. I know you get a lot of it in Colorado."

She seemed to think for a minute. "Yeah, I'll miss it. But not more than I would miss you."

He pulled in his lips, not yet satisfied with her response. "But what about the sun? You'll miss that, right? You do remember how much it rains here."

She gave him an odd look. "Yeah, I'm well aware of the rain. I've been here, like, four times now."

He bit his tongue, not wanting to bring up the next sore topic. But then, how could he propose without giving her the chance to back out now? Yes, moving to London had been her idea in the first place, but Liam would never forgive himself if he tore her away from where she actually wanted to be.

"And you'll be fine away from Colorado, your job, and Melody? And...your parents?"

Claire peered up at him, her features dropping only the slightest fraction before she nodded. "I'll miss them all, of course." She looked away. "Even my parents."

Liam regarded her carefully. He'd finally met her mom and dad back in the spring, and while they were kind and respectful, Liam had seen, clear as day, the strained relationship they had with their daughter. Of course, that only deepened his desire to provide a stable home for Claire and their future children—a home and a family they could both be proud of.

"Like I said before," Claire said, her words drawing him back to the present, "I'm ready for my next adventure. And that's here. With you."

She reached up, placing a sound kiss to his cheek before they walked on.

Liam's anxiousness was settled once again. How had he ever been so lucky as to win the heart of this amazing woman? His own mum could hardly believe it.

"She's truly one-of-a-kind, Liam," Mum had said on more than one occasion, having taken to Claire as if she was her own daughter. "Your father would have loved her."

Liam knew that to be true, as well.

He squeezed the box tighter in his pocket, hoping to ease out some of his stress. He didn't know why he was so nervous. He knew she'd say yes. Well, he hoped she would. Just as he hoped he'd say the right words and kneel without toppling and not drop the ring and—

"So what are we doing tonight?" Claire asked, unknowingly pulling his attention to the present again.

"I thought it would be good to just relax. Give you a chance to get to bed early to recover from jetlag...and to rest up for tomorrow."

She paused. "Wait, what's tomorrow?"

He glanced at her sidelong. "Melody's booked us tickets to see *The Nutcracker* again this year, this time with the whole family... and Dean."

She released a sigh. "I guess we should've expected this. Oh, well. If we end the night how we did the last time we saw the ballet, I'm all for watching it again."

She gave him a saucy wink, and he laughed. "You can count on it."

A few minutes later, the two of them reached the stone structure. Liam stood behind Claire, wrapping his arms around her as they admired the view together. Large snowflakes still filled the air around them, falling down on the green bushes and red boxwoods to give them the appearance of having been decorated with royal icing.

"It's stunning," Claire breathed.

She was right. It *was* stunning. But she was even more so.

"Maybe I'll work here instead of getting another job at a floral shop," she said, nuzzling closer against his chest.

"Whatever you fancy, my darling."

And he meant it. After spending the last year working remotely on his own passions, all of which Claire had fully supported and encouraged, he would do anything for the woman. Not only had he gained more followers, started up a website and shop, and sold prints to individual buyers, magazines, and private collectors, he'd also started up a funded YouTube channel to teach the basics of photography. And none of it would have been possible without Claire and her never-ending devotion.

"Whatever I fancy, huh?" she said. "Then maybe we could move to Cornwall so I could open up a shop there?"

He smiled, thinking back on their time spent there last September. "Just so long as you don't have me repeating Ross Poldark's lines at the cliffside again, we can live wherever you like."

She laughed. "You enjoyed that, admit it."

But he shook his head. "Never."

With an exaggerated look of disappointment, she turned around to face him, her hands linked at the back of his neck. "Does that mean you won't quote Mr. Thornton for me in the north either? Or Mr. Darcy in Derbyshire?"

He shook his head. "How about I come up with my own lines instead?"

She narrowed her eyes. "You think you can beat what Mando says to Grogu?"

He grinned. "At least allow me to try."

She nodded, and instantly, Liam's heart raced.

It was time.

THE MOMENT LIAM looked down at her, Claire knew what was about to happen. They'd discussed marriage before, of course, but for some reason, her insides were a jumbled mess.

Liam's eyes caressed her face, their dark depths taking on that squinting smile she now cherished more than anything on earth. "Claire Frost, you are, without a doubt, the most incredible person I've ever known."

His features softened as he continued, and Claire felt as if she was melting into a warm puddle at his feet. She still could listen to that accent for ages.

"You captured me from the moment I saw you," he continued. "And I will never grow tired of being with you, my darling, my best friend, my love."

He got down on one knee before her, and she drew in a shaking breath. This had to be a dream. The man kneeling before her, the perfect moment, the snow. There was no way this was her life, there was no way this was reality.

"Will you marry me?"

Claire's lips trembled, her tears falling past her smile. "Yes, Liam. Of course I will."

Unable to keep from him any longer, she reached forward, wrapping her arms around his neck where he still knelt on the ground. He embraced her in return before pulling back, removing the glove from her hand and sliding a diamond ring with a rose gold band onto her finger.

"It fits," he said with relief, and she laughed as he stood, wrapping her in his arms and delivering a kiss she would never forget.

After a moment, he pulled back, resting his brow against hers as he shook his head. "That was terrifying."

She laughed. "Well, you did an amazing job. And you didn't even use any lines from a movie."

"Well, I was tempted." He glanced around at the snow swirling around them. "I wanted to propose in the first place we met, but the airport is probably the least romantic place on earth."

She laughed, hardly able to contain her joy.

"Then I thought of the next place we met," he said, squinting. "But I hardly thought my bed would be the right place to propose...for obvious reasons."

She rolled her eyes with a playful swat to his chest. "So why did you settle on Kew Gardens? Because it was the first place I shouted at you?"

"I do enjoy a good telling-off." He winked. "But I chose the gardens because it was here I started to fall for you—seeing your passion for flowers, how you were living your best life in a way I could only imagine." He sobered, looking down at her. "Thanks to you, I was able to make that my reality, too."

After that, she was powerless to keep from kissing him again.

Before long, the two of them made their way out of the

gardens, their hands intertwined as they discussed how excited they were to tell Melody and Tasha the news.

"They're both chomping at the bit to get this wedding planned," Liam said.

Claire grinned. Both women had been her and Liam's number one advocates over the last year—providing them both with support, living arrangements, space, and joy. Claire couldn't wait to have Tasha as a mother-in-law, and she couldn't wait to ask Melody to be her maid-of-honor.

But for now, she was going to focus on Liam—the very man of her dreams.

"So," she began, "how attached are you to top hat and tails for the wedding?"

"Why? What else did you have in mind?"

"I was thinking—now hear me out...Mando's armor. I mean, those pauldrons on your shoulders? Mmm. I could definitely get behind that."

"Alright. But only if you have your hair fashioned after Leia's cinnamon buns."

Claire pulled a face, and Liam laughed, wrapping his arms around her and swinging her round in the air until they kissed again.

She could hardly breathe, she was so happy. How much better was her life, now that Liam was in it?

Yes, she would be leaving her old job behind, but she was looking forward to newer and bigger opportunities. Yes, she would be leaving Colorado, but she'd fallen in love with London and would never look back.

Her parents were still gallivanting around the globe, promising to attend whatever wedding occurred, but Claire knew, no matter what happened, she would have Tasha and Melody to rely on—a new family who would always show up.

And Liam...Liam was her one constant. He was her joy, and he was her life. He'd helped her to finally leave behind the Christmas baggage she'd collected for years. He'd chosen her above all else, and together, they'd brought the joy back into each other's holiday seasons.

What happy Christmases they would share together for many years to come. Because this one was turning out to be a happy Christmas, indeed.

THE END

AUTHOR'S NOTE

I went back and forth on whether or not I should write this book. Just ask Kasey Stockton, Martha Keyes, and Jess Heileman. I kept asking the same questions over and over again.

Should I write contemporary? Is it a waste of time? Would I not be better off putting all of my energy into writing Regency? After all, it is what I love the most. Or do I need a break to write something just for fun?

So. Many. Times. So. Much. Back. And. Forth.

Can I just say how glad I am that I ended up writing this story?? I had so much fun—probably the most fun I've *ever* had—brainstorming all of the scrapes Claire could get into, all the while embarrassing herself in front of this perfect, British gentleman. Writing the book wasn't easy by any means, but it was freeing. I was finally allowed to let go of all the restrictions that writing historical places on an author and wrote what I wanted to, all without worrying if it was historically accurate.

That's not to say I didn't do my fair share of research for this book, though. I spent way too long watching videos of the Underground on YouTube, exploring the entirety of London via Google Maps, and looking up images of Greggs during the holidays and nearly extinct flowers housed at Kew Gardens.

It's a good thing research is one of my favorite parts of the writing process, eh?

One of the biggest scenes I had to research for was Kew Gardens. I spent hours virtually touring the property and taking notes about all the flowers they have there before finally—and fortunately—I was able to explore the gardens myself during my recent trip to England in September. It was as gorgeous as I had hoped it would be, especially the Temperate House. It was so fun walking up the spiral stairs and seeing all of the plants Claire saw. It was marvelous!

To add further detail to my story, I was also able to visit Big Ben and Westminster Abbey, shop at Harrods, ride the Underground, eat at Greggs, and explore the beauties of London. It was fantastic!

After my research, I usually like to add in a few things to my story that I already know more about, just to make my life easier.

My husband actually was an executive producer for a company, so I had no shortage of knowledge in that department for Liam's job. For Claire's career, however, I have the opposite of a green thumb, so I had to do quite a bit of reading to see how one runs a flower shop.

As for everything else, Claire and I have quite a lot in common. We both took a soils class in college (though, admittedly, it bored me to tears). We both obsess over movies—all the period dramas,

Harry Potter films, and Star Wars movies I can get my hands on. And I, too, find Mando's armor oh-so-tasty. And one last thing? I've tasted Branston pickle, and I will not, nay, *cannot* get behind it. Seriously...one of the worst things I've ever tasted.

Along with similarities between myself and my characters, I like to add in little Easter eggs in each of my books. Of course I have the quintessential mention of Cornwall, but in this book, my favorite Easter egg has to be "Honeysett's Fish and Chips." In my Cornish Romance series, I've named a fisherman and his family the Honeysetts, so it was fun to be able to add their name as a chippy in London.

One of my favorite things about this book was being able to write in Liam's perspective, as I was finally able to use all of these fun British words my husband says, as he was born and raised in England himself. Here's a list of my favorite words he uses often, as well as a simplified definition with each.

Whingeing (or whinging): whining
Stroppy: bad-tempered
Shirty: annoyed
Kip: nap
Tenner: a ten-pound note
Cuppa: a cup of something, usually tea
Scratty: unkempt
It's a good job: just another way to say, "it's a good thing"

Are they not the most delightful of words??

Well, that's it from me for now. Thank you all so much for reading through to the end! Author's Notes are always so much fun for me to write, as I feel like I really get to connect with my readers one-on-one.

Another way I love to connect is by sharing photos on Instagram and Facebook, so if you aren't following me yet, I'd love to have you do so! I hold giveaways often and share the latest news about my books there, so we're sure to have some fun together!

If you're interested in learning more about the behind-the-scenes facts for this book, I also post photos on my accounts, so be sure to follow me so you don't miss them!

Also, if you enjoyed this book, please consider leaving a review here. I read every single one of my reviews wherever I can find them, as it helps me feel connected to those who love my books. Never hesitate to write reviews for authors, even if it's just a simple word or two. We love hearing your kind thoughts!

See you around!

Deborah

ACKNOWLEDGMENTS

Ah, the acknowledgements, where I finally get to thank all of my peeps for helping me with my book. Let's dive in straightaway, shall we?

First, thank you, Christmas Escape ladies, for making these books come to fruition. Cindy Steel, Kasey Stockton, Kortney Keisel, Jess Heileman, Gracie Ruth Mitchell, and Martha Keyes, you girls made this a blast. Although, I really could have done without the constant reels you forced me into doing. Thanks for that.

Thank you to my editor, Emily Poole, for fitting me in at the last minute! Your eagle eye is much appreciated!

Thank you to our cover designer, Melody Jeffries Designs. I was thrilled to see what you created and could not be happier with the end result. You are incredible!

Next, I have to thank my sister Joanna and my mom for always supporting my writing, for being patient with me when I have to meet a deadline, and for reading everything I've ever written. You guys mean the world to me.

Thank you to Desiree C. for giving me the inspiration for the last name for Melody, "Bancroft." Although I really did love the other suggestions from your family, including Crumblbottomz and Wiggliwiggens.

Thank you to Tasha for allowing me the use of your name in the story. Every time I typed it out, it just made me happy thinking of you!

Next, my ARC team is always instrumental in spreading the word about my books, and this one was no different. Since I can't thank a hundred of you individually, I hope you all know how much I love having you on my team!!

Next, I want to properly thank my amazing friend, Ali, AKA, Ale, whom this book is dedicated to. Ale, you're the reason I had the courage to pursue my British boy in college, and for that, you're the only person I'll ever allow to call me Li'l Debbie. You lucky duck. Seriously, though, I'm so grateful for our friendship and the influence you are in my life. Love you!

I seriously have to thank Ben Barnes for his *sigh* perfect looks. I used him as inspiration for Liam Everhart, and let me just tell you, it was an utter delight having Ben Barnes's picture pulled up every day on my laptop for months. If anyone knows him, hook a girl up. (Just for a picture, mind you. That's all I'm looking for.)

A huge shoutout must go to my four children. You guys really try hard to not make me meet my deadlines...But I wouldn't have it any other way. Thank you for being patient with me and the best children a mom could ever ask for.

Lastly, my sweet, patient, encouraging, wonderful husband. You, Christian, deserve a medal for all you did to help me get this book out. (I'll just let the rest of you know that he's the one who came up with the idea for the kiss scene taking place in a telephone booth. I mean, come on. How perfect was that? Also, he came up with the title, too!) Thank you for helping me feel the romance when I definitely *wasn't* feeling the romance. Also, thanks for not being weirded out about Ben Barnes's picture being on my screen for so long. Love you, BABE.*

*as said in Bingo's voice from Bluey, *the greatest show on earth.*

ABOUT THE AUTHOR

Deborah M. Hathaway graduated from Utah State University with a BA in Creative Writing. As a young girl, she devoured Jane Austen's novels while watching and re-watching every adaptation of Pride & Prejudice she could, entirely captured by all things Regency and romance.

Throughout her early life, she wrote many short stories, poems, and essays, but it was not until after her marriage that she was finally able to complete her first romance novel, attributing the completion to her courtship with, and love of, her charming, English husband. Deborah finds her inspiration for her novels in her everyday experiences with her husband and children and during her travels to the United Kingdom, where she draws on the beauty of the country in such places as England, Scotland, and her beloved Cornwall.

Made in the USA
Middletown, DE
24 October 2023

41345723R00179